A FASCINATING AND MULTIFACETED LOOK INTO THE MACABRE GENIUS OF STEPHEN KIN

* STEPHEN ... gs that frighten him
* WHITLEY ... *Wolfen* and co-autho ... explains why King's writing so greatly inspires him.
* CLIVE BARKER, the brilliant new British horror writer, enumerates the special skills that make King unique in the horror genre.
* HARLAN ELLISON, winner of eight Hugos and Nebula Awards, reveals why to his mind the quality of King's films does not match that of his books.

These and many other writers examine why a devoted and growing audience loves being frightened by the horrific genius of Stephen King.

KINGDOM OF FEAR

TIM UNDERWOOD and CHUCK MILLER are publishers of Underwood-Miller, a small press specializing in hardcover fantasy and science fiction.

KINGDOM OF FEAR

THE WORLD OF STEPHEN KING

Edited by
Tim Underwood and Chuck Miller

A SIGNET BOOK

NEW AMERICAN LIBRARY

PUBLISHED BY
THE NEW AMERICAN LIBRARY
OF CANADA LIMITED

NAL BOOKS ARE AVAILABLE AT QUANTITY DISCOUNTS WHEN USED TO PROMOTE PRODUCTS OR SERVICES. FOR INFORMATION PLEASE WRITE TO PREMIUM MARKETING DIVISION, NEW AMERICAN LIBRARY, 1633 BROADWAY, NEW YORK, NEW YORK 10019.

Acknowledgments

"The Horror Writer and the Ten Bears" by Stephen King was originally published in *Writer's Digest* as "The Horror Market Writer and the Ten Bears" and is reprinted with permission from the author.

"Stephen King's Horror Has a Healing Power" by Andrew M. Greeley is reprinted with permission from the author and from Doubleday Publishing Co.

"Two Selections from the Column 'Harlan Ellison's Watching' " originally appeared in *The Magazine of Fantasy and Science Fiction*; copyright © 1984 by The Kilimanjaro Corporation. Reprinted with permission of, and by arrangement with, the Author and the Author's agent, Richard Curtis Associates, Inc., New York. All rights reserved.

Some of the excerpts appearing between chapters of this book are from interviews with Stephen King conducted by critic and columnist Stanley Wiater.

Published by arrangement with Underwood-Miller

Kingdom of Fear was previously published in a Plume edition by New American Library and simultaneously in Canada by The New American Library of Canada Limited.

First Signet Printing, October, 1987

2 3 4 5 6 7 8 9

SIGNET TRADEMARK REG U S PAT OFF AND FOREIGN COUNTRIES
REGISTERED TRADEMARK – MARCA REGISTRADA
HECHO EN WINNIPEG, CANADA

SIGNET, SIGNET CLASSIC, MENTOR, ONYX, PLUME, MERIDIAN AND NAL BOOKS are published in Canada by The New American Library of Canada, Limited, 81 Mack Avenue, Scarborough, Ontario, Canada M1L 1M8

PRINTED IN CANADA
COVER PRINTED IN U.S.A.

Contents

People in general scare me. That's why I live in isolation in a remote area of Maine. I'm afraid of choking to death. I'm afraid of the San Andreas Fault. I don't sleep on my left side because that's where my heart is. I'm afraid it will wear out too quickly. I also have a recurring dream about the lake next to my house boiling and blowing up.

—*Stephen King*

The Horror Writer and the Ten Bears

Foreword by Stephen King

At parties, people usually approach the writer of horror fiction with a mixture of wonder and trepidation. They look carefully into your eyes to make sure there's no overt bloodlust in them, and then ask the inevitable question: "I really liked your last story . . . where do you get your ideas?"

That question is common to any writer who works in a specialized genre, whether it's mystery, crime, western or science fiction. But it's delivered in different tones for different fields. It's directed to the mystery writer with real admiration, the way you'd ask a magician how he sawed the lady in half. It's directed to the science fiction writer with honest respect for a fellow who is so farseeing and visionary. But it's addressed to the horror writer with a sense of fascinated puzzlement—the way a lady reporter might ask mild-mannered Henri Landru how it feels to do away with all those wives. Most of us, you see, look and seem (and *are*) perfectly ordinary. We don't drown house-guests in the bathtub, torture the children, or sacrifice the cat at midnight inside of a pentagram. There are no locked closets or screams from the cellar. Robert Bloch, author of *PSYCHO,* looks like a moderately successful used car salesman. Ray Bradbury bears an uncomfortable resemblance to Charles M. Schulz, creator of *Peanuts.* And the writer generally acknowledged to be the greatest master of the horror tale in the twentieth century, H. P. Lovecraft, looked like nothing so much as a slightly overworked accountant.

So where do the ideas—the *salable* ideas—come from? For myself, the answer is simple enough. They come from my nightmares. Not the nighttime variety, as a rule, but the ones that hide just beyond the doorway that separates the conscious from the unconscious. A good assumption to begin with is that what scares you will scare someone else. A psychologist would call these nightmares phobias, but I think there's a better word for our purposes.

Joseph Stefano, who wrote the screenplay for *Psycho* and who produced a mid-sixties television series called *The Outer Limits,* called these fears "bears." It's a good term for the aspiring writer of horror fiction to use, because it gets across the idea that general phobias have to be focused on concrete plot ideas before you can hope to scare the reader—and that's the name of the game. So before we go any further, let's take a few bears—ones we're all familiar with. You may want to rearrange some of the items on my list, or throw out a few and add some of the skeletons in your own closet. But for purposes of discussion, here is my own top ten:

1. Fear of the dark
2. Fear of squishy things

3. Fear of deformity
4. Fear of snakes
5. Fear of rats
6. Fear of closed-in places
7. Fear of insects (especially spiders, flies, beetles)
8. Fear of death
9. Fear of others (paranoia)
10. Fear *for* someone else

The bears can be combined, too. I took a #1 and #10 and wrote a story called *The Boogeyman,* which sold to *Cavalier* magazine. For me, the fear of the dark has always focused on a childhood fear: the awful Thing which hides in the closet when you're small, or sometimes curls up under the bed, waiting for you to stick a foot out from under the covers. As an adult looking back on those feelings (not that we ever conquer them completely—all those of you out there who don't have a bedroom lamp within reach of you please stand up), it seemed to me that the most frightening thing about them was the fact that grown-ups don't understand it very well—they forget how it is. Mother comes in, turns on the light, smiles, opens the closet (the Thing is hiding behind your clothes, well out of sight—it's sly) and says, "See, dear? There's nothing to be afraid of." And as soon as she's gone, the Thing crawls back out of the closet and begins to leap and gibber in the shadows again. I wrote a story about a man who finds out that his three children, who have all died of seemingly natural causes, have been frightened to death by the boogeyman—who is a very real, very frightening monster. The story takes a childhood fear and saddles an adult with it; puts him back into that dreamlike world of childhood where the monsters *don't* go away when you change the channel, but crawl out and hide under the bed.

About two years ago I decided that the scariest things going would be rats—great big #5's, breeding in the darkness under a deserted textile mill. In this case, I began with the fear and built the plot (including the deserted mill) to fit it. The story climaxed with the main character being overwhelmed by these giant rats in the dark and enclosed subcellar of the mill (slyly hedging my main bet by working in a generous dose of #1 and #6). I felt sorry for the poor guy—the thought of being overrun by giant rats frankly made my blood run cold—but I made $250 on the sale and managed to take one of my own pet fears for a walk in the sun at the same time. One of the nice things about working in this field is that, instead of paying a shrink to help you get rid of your fears, a magazine will pay you for doing the same thing.

George Langlahan, a Canadian author, wrote a novelette called *The Fly,* using a #7 bear, made a sale to *Playboy,* and has since seen his bear made into three movies—*The Fly, The Return of the Fly,* and *The Curse of the Fly.* The late John W. Campbell wrote a cracking good horror story in the early 50's called *Who Goes There?* using a #2 bear which turns out to be a sort of walking vegetable from another planet. The story was turned into a classic horror movie called *The Thing.* Hollywood has always understood the principle of working from the bear out—surrounding a basic fear with a plot, rather than the other way around. Edgar Allan Poe wrote the same way, and suggested again and again in his literary essays that the only way to write a short story was to begin with the effect and then work your way out.

The would-be writer of horror stories may be tempted to stop right here and say: That's a lousy list of bears, fella. There isn't a werewolf or a vampire to be had. True enough. Not even an escaped mummy hunting for tanna leaves. My humble advice is to leave these bears to their well-deserved rest. They've been done to death. There are undoubtedly a few twists left in the Old Guard, but not many. Even the endlessly proliferating comics market is turning away from them in favor of more contemporary subjects—but more on that later.

Another caution is in order at this point: Don't think that because you have selected a scary bear, the rest of the story will be a snap. It won't be. Horror isn't a hack market now, and never was. The genre is one of the most delicate known to man, and it must be handled with great care and more than a little love. Some of the greatest authors of all time have tried their hands at things that go bump in the night, including Shakespeare, Chaucer, Hawthorne *(My Kinsman, Major Molinaux* is a particularly terrifying story, featuring a #9 bear), Poe, Henry James, William Faulkner *(A Rose for Emily),* and a score of others.

So where is the market today? For straight fiction, it's mainly in the men's magazines. But the writer who feels he can approach *Playboy* or *Cavalier* or *Penthouse* or *Adam* with a 1930's-style blood-pulp-and-sex thriller is going to find the market has progressed beyond that to a reasonable point of sophistication—good for the professional who wants to work seriously in the genre, bad for the amateur who thinks he can mix a couple of sea monsters with an Atlantic City beauty contest and come up with a few hundred bucks. And so, before a listing of some possible markets, a few practical hints on selling horror to the men's magazines:

1. Don't feel obligated to add sex to your story if there isn't a sex angle there to begin with. We've both been to the corner drugstore and know that pin-ups are a stock in trade, along with articles that deal with the sex life of the American male. But a fair propor-

tion of fiction steers clear of women entirely, dealing with "escape" subjects instead: survival situations, science fiction, crime, suspense . . . and horror.

2. Read the market. To be perfectly blunt, your chance of selling a story to a men's magazine you haven't read is probably no more than 2%, even if your story is another *The Lottery.* Get rid of the idea that all men's magazines are the same. Find out who is buying stories from two to four thousand words, who is buying out-and-out fantasy, who has a penchant for psychological horror, who is publishing good stories by people you never heard of.

3. Take a hard, critical look at your own story and try to decide if it's better, worse, or about equal to the fiction being published in the magazine you're considering. The realization that your brainchild may not be up to *Playboy*'s standards may be a bitter pill, but it's better than wasting postage in a lost cause—especially when you could be selling your story to another editor.

4. Throw away Poe and Lovecraft before you start. If you just screamed in agony, wait a minute and let me expand a little on this one. If you're interested in the horror story to begin with, you were (and possibly still are) an avid reader of Edgar Allan Poe and Howard Phillips Lovecraft. Both of these fine writers were rococo stylists, weaving words into almost Byzantine patterns. Both wrote some excellent short-short stories. *(The Tell-Tale Heart* by Poe can be read in ten minutes, and Lovecraft's *In the Tomb* is not much longer—yet the effect of both stories is never forgotten), but both did their finest work in longer form. *The men's magazines don't buy novelettes.* The average length of accepted fiction is 2500-4000 words. Neither will they buy much, if any, fiction written in the styles of Poe or Lovecraft. In spite of the antique charm both hold for modern readers, most editors regard the

style as outdated and bankrupt. If you're still screaming and cradling your wounded manuscripts, I'm sorry. I'm only telling the truth. If it's Poe or Lovecraft, send it to a fanzine and be content with your contributor's copies.

A great many writers begin with the mistaken notion that "the Lovecraft style" is essential to success in the field. Those who feel this way no doubt pick up the idea by reading the numerous Lovecraft-oriented anthologies on sale. But anthologies are not magazines, and while the idea is no small tribute to H.P.L.'s influence on the field, it's simply not so. If you're looking for alternatives (ones that are adaptable to the men's magazine format), I'd recommend John Collier, Richard Matheson, Robert Bloch (who began as a Lovecraft imitator and has made a successful switch to a more modern style), and Harlan Ellison. All of these writers have short story anthologies on the market, and a volume of each makes a wonderful exercise book for the beginner.

5. When your story is ready for rewrite, cut it to the bone. Get rid of every ounce of excess fat. This is going to hurt; revising a story down to the base essentials is always a little like murdering children, but it must be done. If the first draft runs 4000 words, your second should go about 3000. If the first is around 3000, you can still probably get down to about 2500 by tightening up the nuts and bolts. The object here isn't to shorten for the sake of shortening but to speed up the pace and make the story fly along.

Almost all of the men's magazines are excellent markets for the beginning horror freelancer. They need lots of material, and most of them could care less if you're an unknown. If your story is good, and if you pick the right market, you can make a sale. Here is a list of *some* possible men's magazine markets. Check your *WRITER'S MARKET* and *THE LITERARY MARKET PLACE* for further details: *Cavalier, Escapade, Adam, Knight, Best for Men, Men's Digest, Rascal, Sir!, Oui, Penthouse,* and *Playboy.*

I have a particular warmth for *Cavalier,* because they published my own first marketable horror stories. Both Doug Allen and Nye Willden are warm and helpful, and if your story is good, they'll publish it. They report in four to six weeks and pay from $200 to $300 depending on length and previous number of stories published. The best length is around 4000 words.

Escapade is another good market to try. They have upgraded their fiction considerably over the last year, and are willing to pay top dollar for quality stories. *Adam* and *Knight* are the flagship magazines of a whole line of publications, including the *Adam Bedside Reader.* Your story will be considered for publication in any and all of their publications. *Adam* has been one of the most consistent publishers of science fiction, horror, and like *Cavalier,* they pay more to authors who consistently submit salable material. 3000 words is a good length here. If your story has sex interest and is still quality, I'd say send to *Adam* first.

Best for Men and *Rascal* is another chain outfit. Shorter fiction sells well here: 2500 words is about average. Sex interest is preferred, but still not necessary if the story holds up without it.

Penthouse, Playboy and *Oui* are all quality markets, and all pay well—well enough to attract "name" authors much of the time. But all three accept freelance material on occasion. Probably the most useful thing I can say about the three of them is don't bypass them if you think your story is really top-drawer stuff. Start at the top. You may find a $1000 check from *Playboy* waiting for you in the mailbox some morning—or $400 from *Penthouse.*

There is another market for the horror freelancer that should be discussed before sending you back to your typewriter, and that is the rapidly proliferating comic magazine market. Most of these are a good deal like the DC line of comic books that was published in the 1950's. At that time they were called "the new trend" comic books.

The "new, new trend" magazines aren't in the comic racks with *Superman* and *Batman,* as a rule. You'll find them with the standard magazines, and in standard magazine size. A black-and-white comic panel accompanies each advancing scene.

I can hear the purists in the audience starting to grumble right now—what has all that blood-and-guts claptrap got to do with me? I'm a *writer,* not a lousy comic book scenarist.

Well, the purists rarely make enough money to pay overdue library fines in the freelancing business, but if you're still not convinced, at least take the time to look at a few of the new wave comic magazines before passing them up. They rarely reach the plateau of *Art,* but they're far from trash. The artwork is often superb, and while the writing is more often just competent than really good, it is rarely as awful as that churned out in some of the other specialized markets. And the magazines have their own fanatic hordes of the faithful—fans that often know more about the arcane lore of terror than the writer himself. In a recent issue of *Creepy,* a college student took a writer severely to task for putting a witch-burning into his story of the Salem witchcraft hysteria of the 1660s. No Salem "witch" was burned, the reader quite rightfully pointed out.

Again, reading the market is essential. Go out to your local newsstand and pick up a dozen or so at a swipe. Your chances for success without reading the market first is zero. Your second step should be a query letter, which also serves as a note of introduction. Mention any sales you have made in the horror field to other markets.

The editor will probably ask you to submit several "summary" stories. A summary should run no more than 300 words, and you can include anywhere from one to a dozen in a package. You may get a go-ahead on all of them, only two or three, or (sadly) none at all.

Following a go-ahead, the story must be expanded so it will fill 6, 7, or 8 pages in the final magazine copy, and it must be written in TV script form so that the assigned artist can collaborate.

The same rules that apply to the men's fiction markets go down here. Sex is okay if it isn't overplayed; there is no comics' code to regulate magazine-size comic periodicals. But keep it tasteful and leave it out altogether if it doesn't play a central part in the story. Avoid all the tired old bears; leave them for the staff writers to re-hash.

Here are some magazine titles for the comic market. As you can see, they're all chain publications: WARREN PUBLISHING COMPANY (Magazines Published: *Creepy, Eerie, Vampirella);* SKYWALD PUBLISHING CORPORATION (Magazines Published: *Psycho, Nightmare, Scream,);* MARVEL COMICS GROUP (Magazines Published: *Tales of the Zombie, Dracula Lives!, Monsters Unleashed, Vampire Tales);* EERIE PUBLICATIONS, INC. (Magazines Published: *Weird, Horror Tales, Terror Tales, Witches' Tales, Tales from the Tomb, Tales of Voodoo).*

The Warren Publications are the most open to freelance inquiries and contributions; they were first in the field and still publish the best material. They use from fifteen to eighteen stories per month (to get an idea how good the form can be when it's working, see *Dead Man's Race* in *Creepy* #54, story by Jack Butterworth and art by Martin Salvador). Second choice for good horror material would be the Marvel Comics Group magazines, which are an offshoot of the more conventional and tremendously successful Marvel comic books, such as *Spiderman* and *Incredible Hulk*.

Skywald is fairly new to the trade, and at this writing they seem the most vital—constantly moving ahead, breaking new ground, and using consistently innovative stories. Be warned, however, that the freelancer is in strong competition here with a "bullpen staff."

There are also a few strictly horror magazines on the market, mostly holdovers from the old pulp days, but they are generally in the reprint business and payment for originals ranges from twenty-five to a hundred dollars.

Americans have always loved a good horror story, and in these days when everyone is mourning the "death" of short magazine fiction, it's good to know that, in this field at least, the beast is still alive and kicking. And snarling. And drooling . . .

Stephen King's Horror Has a Healing Power

by Andrew M. Greeley

It is very easy to be upset with horror writer Stephen King, for not only has he turned out his annual, successful terrifier, he has also produced a remarkable nonfiction work in which he discusses the meaning and the appeal of the horror story. If you want to appreciate the full range of Mr. King's talents, read *CUJO* to be horrified and *DANSE MACABRE* to understand why you were horrified.

The former is a real blood-chiller with a little bit of the supernatural scariness that has marked such earlier works as *THE SHINING* and *CARRIE*. But most of the terror comes from something that is quite "natural": a wonderfully loving and friendly St. Bernard dog. The dog follows a rabbit into a hole in the ground where he is bitten by rabid bats and then proceeds to destroy four people, including the father of the family to which he belongs and an adoring four-year-old boy. Mr. King makes this gruesome story come alive with a strange mixture of frightfulness and poignancy.

But I ask myself as I write these lines and the reader doubtless asks as he reads them, why read a book about a rabid dog who unintentionally destroys relatively innocent humans? Isn't there enough ugliness in the world?

Yet we devour Mr. King. We shiver as Carrie obliterates her high school graduating class and as the fire-starter wipes out half of the Central Intelligence Agency and as the woman in *CUJO* beats the St. Bernard dog to death, trying unsuccessfully to save the life of the little boy. What kind of ghouls are we?

Mr. King's answer is ingenious and, I believe, persuasive. If I may simplify and paraphrase him, he believes we are all only too well aware of the secret terrors that hide just beneath the surface of everyday life. We may not quite be surrounded by vampires as the people in *'SALEM'S LOT,* but we know that there are evil and destructive forces, at least as deadly as vampires, and more pervasive than rabid dogs, which can easily do us in. We delight not so much in reminding ourselves that the terrors exist as we do in reassuring ourselves that we are capable for the moment of surviving them. Our fascination by the horror story, suggests Mr. King, is because in reading the story we are reassured that there is hope that we may continue to survive the forces of evil a little bit longer.

Unlike some other horror writers who lack his talents and sensitivity, Stephen King never ends his stories with any cheap or easy hope. People are badly hurt, they suffer and some of them die, but others survive the struggle and manage to grow. The powers of evil have not yet done them in. It is little enough, but it is all there is, Mr. King seems to be saying. The mother and father in *CUJO* have lost their four-year-old, but as the book ends they seem to be finding one another. In this respect, at any rate, the horror story is profoundly religious. It celebrates sometimes only tiny smidgens of hope, but hope, like goodness and love, needs only to exist to finally win.

Monsters in Our Midst

by Robert Bloch

One day, almost ten years ago, I received a long-distance phone call from a writer named Stephen King.

He didn't have to identify himself to me. My admiration of his work had already been quoted on the dustjacket of his first-published book, *CARRIE,* and we'd exchanged correspondence when he sent me an inscribed copy of *'SALEM'S LOT.* Already he was being hailed as a best-selling novelist and an emerging media personality.

Now, King told me, he was about to pay a forty-eight-hour visit to Hollywood to discuss a film project. Would my wife and I join him for dinner during his stay, and could I extend the same invitation to Richard Matheson and his wife as well?

I could and I did. The following week we met at a hotel and spent an enjoyable evening together.

Stephen King proved to be a likeable young man, free of the affectation and pretension which sometimes characterizes the *arriviste* author. Since that time I've had the pleasure of visiting with him at various science fiction conventions where, as his celebrity increased, he was besieged by hordes of fans and admirers. To the best of my knowledge he hasn't changed; fame and fortune didn't impair his patience, his candor, or his unfailing good nature. He gives time and energy to the demands of public appearances and generously praises his fellow writers. On the face of things he still appears to be a devoted husband, fond father, and the product of a small-town background who shares the ordinary interests of his generation—rock music, sports, television, and the films and comic books of the Fifties which infiuenced his formative years. Once a schoolteacher, he's obviously more literate and knowledgeable than many of his peer group, but taken on the whole he seems to be a normally respectable human being.

All of which may be true, except for one slight difference. The moment I met Stephen King I recognized him for what he was—a monster.

They say it takes one to know one, and I cheerfully concede the point. I'm a monster too, like virtually every writer in the field of dark fantasy.

On the face of it we're a mixed lot, we purveyors of terror, horror and suspense. If you were to assemble photographs of our baleful brotherhood and show them to readers unaware of our occupation, I venture to guess that very few would recognize us for what we are.

Nevertheless, Matheson recognized him for what he was, and so did I.

We know our monsters—and what shaped them—for these were the forces that shaped us all.

The first dead giveaway is the sense of humor. It's always present—that defense mechanism we designed over the years to insulate us from the insults of those who automatically attack anyone they suspect of being "different."

In today's society—no less than in Poe's time, or Lovecraft's life-span—the youngster who takes too great an interest in reading is suspect by his fellows. The child who is sickly, awkward or lacking in coordination runs the risk of becoming an outcast on the playground, the last one to be chosen for a group-sports team. Even if he displays some athletic aptitude it doesn't compensate for his peculiar preoccupation with books. Any physical deviation is greeted with gibes. Only wimps wear glasses; anyone unusually short, unusually tall, too fat or too skinny must be prepared to defend himself against being labelled a freako. And an abnormal affinity for the arts brands him as a nerd.

Hence the development of that sense of humor. It served us as both a shield and a weapon; we used it either to protect our self-esteem or to attack our tormentors. With it we coped with the casual cruelty of childhood companions, turning upon them with a verbal volley capable of annihilating both boors and bullies.

But there's more to life than mere physical security. One wants to be liked, appreciated, even admired. And we monsters usually find a way.

The route we take may vary; some of us discover it through our own personal fantasies, others come upon it as a result of the imaginative stimulus resulting from reading, but in the end it comes down to one common solution. We learn how to tell stories.

And if we develop a knack for storytelling we find that people are willing to listen or even to read our efforts. With luck we may even be paid for our efforts. The cloud under which we labored turns out to have a silver lining; for a favored few that lining may prove to be gold, or—as in the case of King—platinum.

The skill we bring to our work can range anywhere from minor talent to major genius. Given the latter there are no limits to creativity.

Properly applied it can explain the world as it appears to be, or reshape it to our heart's desire; we can even replace it with a brand-new world if we so decree. Within the construct of our choice we may appear as ourselves, as masters or victims of fate, or don multiple masks as hero or villain, comic or tragic. If there's an element of autobiography in our fiction we have the power to justify ourselves, to reward or revenge.

Thus it is that the youthful inmate of a workhouse in nineteenth-century England can appear in his novels as a put-upon product of poverty who, through courage, good conscience, and a little bit of luck, emerges triumphant in the end. A country bumpkin from the hinterlands or Hannibal, Missouri, moves from obscurity to fame as an Innocent Abroad, then in later life becomes a clown-turned-cynic who forsakes humor for pessimistic philosophy and rages against the human race. A shy, stammering, sexually-confused victim of human bondage becomes a worldly, world-traveled sophisticate; an Irish expatriate goes blind but illuminates literature with his personal vision of a modern *ODYSSEY;* an invalid in a cork-lined room recreates a lifetime with his remembrance of things past.

Multiple choices, multiple fancies. Given such freedom, why is it that some of us select the monster role? Why frighten rather than enlighten, why dwell upon and within a domain of darkness, dread and death? Why did Poe become the imp of the perverse; what impelled rationalist Lovecraft to create a cosmology containing Cthulhu?

I'm neither a philosopher nor a psychiatrist, and I must opt for the easy explanation. On the basis of personal belief and observation, I'd say that those of us who direct our storytelling into darker channels do so because we were perhaps a bit more mindful than most regarding our childhood confusions of identity, our conflicts with unpleasant realities and our traumatic encounters with imaginative terrors. Although there are significant exceptions, it would appear that the majority of writers who deal with the supernatural have repudiated the tenets of organized religion. In so doing they may have lost the fear of hellfire but they've also sacrificed any hope of heaven. What remains is an all-too-vivid fear of pain and death and a final, total, eternal oblivion.

Just what does all this have to do with Stephen King?

A great deal, I think. I don't have access to the intimate details of his life, factual or fantastic. But I do know a monster when I see one, and I can at least offer by way of explanation a half-educated guess, based largely on my acquaintance with his work.

Something—a broken home, lack of security in parental affection, sibling rivalry, a siege of illness, problems on the playground, or any combination of the above—would provide the standard psychotherapeutic solution.

Are the genes the source of genius? If so, then its development is sparked by the adversities enumerated above. Armed with a wry and mordant sense of humor and a gift of communication developed over long years of reading and writing, Stephen King's professional *persona* emerged.

How do I know this? Because it's there, all of it, in his work.

Stephen King's novels and stories are populated by troubled children—children who possess or who develop wild talents. From *CARRIE* onward we meet them, these seeming losers whose special abilities become instruments of creativity or destruction, of salvation or revenge.

Adults, too, are often outcasts who usually triumph, even in defeat.

All dramatize their differences, recapitulating the personal progress of the ill-adjusted individual who by dint of perseverance learns to employ uniqueness to his own ends.

No one in our time has learned these lessons better than Stephen King. While predecessors like Poe and Lovecraft came into full command of their fantasies they appeared to have an uncertain grasp upon realities; they had difficulty in dealing with everyday characters and situations.

King, however wild his fancies, roots his work in the real world of today. His "normal" characters speak and think in the gritty language and slang idioms of the present generation. Thus a symbiosis is set up; horror feasts upon the humdrum, and commonplace circumstances nourish perverse perils.

It's a winning combination, and it has won him the accolades of critics and the rewards of commercial success. Both are well-deserved.

And so, Stephen King, I feel that I speak not only for myself but for my fellow monsters when I say, "Welcome to the club."

You've paid your dues.

A Girl Named Carrie

by Bill Thompson

There was a panel at one of the annual fantasy conventions, and the heavy hitters were holding forth: King, Straub, Streiber, Morrell, et al. Once again I heard Steve King tell the Bill Thompson story: the near acceptance of an earlier script; the cautious optimism about *CARRIE,* the munificent $2500 advance. It's a story Steve has told and written often and one I certainly never tire of.

After the seminar, Peter Straub accosted me: "Bill, you're becoming a rumor in your own time."

It was a good line, and when Chuck Miller and Tim Underwood proposed I write an introduction to the new book on the King legend, I was frankly delighted. Authors aren't the only ones with egos; we editors welcome the occasional creative burst as well.

Steve King's gift of nearly perfect recall will per se make the narration of my side of the connection relatively pale. He's pretty much told it as it happened. But for the record, here's what really happened . . .

Doubleday in 1970 was the Pentagon of publishing. Editors were grouped according to book category, so one office (blue carpet) may have been religious books; another (orange carpet) children's books. I was part of Special Projects (green carpet) and five of us were to concentrate on refining and expanding Doubleday's enormous backlist: the non-fiction books that may never nudge a best-seller list, but will continue to sell steadily over the years. You know the books: *BOWLING SECRETS OF THE PROS; HOW TO REPAIR YOUR FOREIGN CAR; BEST LOVED SONGS, RECIPES, POEMS* (fill in the blank) *OF THE AMERICAN PEOPLE.*

The *real* editors (beige carpet) tended to sneer at us; after all they worked with the likes of Irving Stone, Alistair MacLean, Arthur Hailey, or any of the dozens of Doubleday established best-sellers. *Their* books were advertised; their authors toured; their books got book club selections and huge reprints. We were the drudges who toiled at *CULTIVATING CARNIVOROUS PLANTS* and *HOUSE PLANTS IN COLOR.*

The fact that our drudge books often subsidized the *real* books that didn't make it onto the best-seller lists (or didn't earn back an advance) was not really important to any except the Green Bay Packagers, as we were called. So we became a sub rosa publishing company, sneaking in the fiction manuscripts we'd come to feel passionate about. Need I tell you it took guile, politicking, and lobbying efforts far exceeding our counterparts in the trade book division?

We special projects editors were all book people; we were readers, respecters of the written word, admirers of the authors who did it well. We were often asked to supply reports for one of the "real" books, since our reports, if good, not only supported a sponsoring editor but reflected commercial acceptance; if bad they could be safely ignored or burned.

I was such a reader on Loren Singer's *PARALLAX VIEW* and gave a good report on that unusual novel. The sponsoring editor was Doubleday's token hippie, a brilliant man who chafed at corporate bureaucracy, and who would sweep in with a red-lined opera cape (often with eyes that matched). When he left Doubleday, he requested I be assigned to *PARALLAX VIEW*, by then successfully published.

Some time later, I received a letter simply addressed to the Editor of *PARALLAX VIEW*. It was a query letter from an author named Stephen King who suggested he had a script in tone not unlike *PARALLAX VIEW* and perhaps I might want to see it.

Send it on, I replied. And so he did. The script was called *GETTING IT ON* and dealt with a high school class taken over by one of the students and a gun. It was a masterful study in character and suspense, but it was quiet, deliberately claustrophophic and it proved a tough sell within the house. I'd asked Stephen—for by now we were on a first name basis—for changes which he willingly and promptly made, but even so I couldn't glean sufficient support and reluctantly returned it. Steve King at this time was a high school teacher or a laundry worker (he's been both) and could not afford a phone on either salary, and so we wrote each other letters. These and other letters were ripped off from the Doubleday files and they were probably not nearly as trenchant or perceptive as I remember, but a rapport was established between this particular author and this particular editor. We gave good letters.

Stephen King, who'd been writing since he was 12, just happened to have some more manuscripts lying idle and after the initial disappointment of *GETTING IT ON*, tried me on the others. (Since he blew his cover recently, it comes as no surprise to find these earlier books were subsequently published as original paperbacks, as the works of one Richard Bachman.)

But it still wasn't magic time. The scripts weren't strong enough for the first novel break-out, and they went back, although oddly enough, the rejections strengthened our personal connection.

Some months later, our correspondence having faltered, I sent him a country music calendar. Country wasn't trendy then, but he and I were both buffs and I thought he'd enjoy knowing Earl Scruggs' birthday. But I also wanted to hear from this talented writer whose letters I enjoyed and who was going to make it as a published author.

The reply was a thank-you-for-the-calendar, and er-ah-you-wouldn't-want-to-see-another-manuscript, would-you?

The script was *CARRIE,* and it was magic time.

Once again, I asked Steve to make some changes prior to going to contract. Bear in mind we'd gone through this at least once before with *GETTING IT ON (RAGE)* and a contract never materialized. Bear in mind that manuscript changes before contract are speculative work on an author's part, a kind of masochistic stroking to a fantasy that just might become real. Once again, Steve promptly and willingly revised the script.

There's been a lot of guff written and spoken about the editorial process. Who *really* writes the book—the synergistic and interlinear relationship between author and editor and like that. Basically the editorial process means understanding what the author wants to do and helping him get there. With *CARRIE,* I don't think at any time before or after, have I as editor been so in tune with the author's concept of a book. Steve and I knew what *CARRIE* was supposed to do for and to the reader, and because we both were on exactly the same wavelength regarding this pathetic and lethal young girl, the revisions we discussed made sense. Carrie had to be believable in the face of an unbelievable plot; she had to be sympathetic even as she wiped out the better part of a town; we had to care about her. And because that was what the book was always supposed to be, and because author and editor were in complete non-combative agreement about what the book was supposed to be, the editorial process worked. Sometimes it does; sometimes it doesn't. Liking and respecting one another also helps.

I was determined to see *CARRIE* published, but this time I downplayed reactions from editorial colleagues in favor of the profit-center types—sales, publicity, subsidiary rights. When the rights director's eyes lit up, and when the advertising manager called it a "cooker," I knew we were home free.

Steve and Nelson Doubleday will read here that the approved advance on *CARRIE* was $1500 (not really too mingy for a first novel in 1970). I upped it to $2500 and sneaked it through. Steve still didn't have a phone, and a letter—for this news—would take too long, so I sent him a telegram. *CARRIE* was officially going to be published.

Steve would come to New York to sign the contract. Usually, contracts are mailed back and forth, often hurriedly, because contracts mean checks. But the *CARRIE* contract really was so much more than a document that something celebratory seemed in order, and what could be more festive than a lunch in the big city. Naturally the author would pay for his transportation; after all, the publisher was buying the lunch.

It was an odd feeling, meeting this man I'd come to know and care about personally and professionally for the first time. We'd been through so much together.

That sounds nutty, I know, but it was true. Nadine Weinstein, my assistant who had fallen on each Steve King letter and manuscript with the same enthusiasm I had, would join us. She felt she knew Steve well, too. We didn't know that Steve had arrived in New York at 7 a.m., having borrowed money for bus fare and having rattled around New York all morning after riding all night. (Knowing Steve, he hung around book stores or the library.)

He arrived in the lobby around noon. The Doubleday receptionist was a frosty Junior Leaguer type who would have been selling hats at Bendel if she wasn't a receptionist. She nearly always smelled something bad, and authors cooled their heels a discreet distance from her desk before being escorted Behind The Scenes. When she called to say "A Stephen King" was here, I went out to greet him. This giant of a man was looming there. I'm 6′ 2″, and he made me feel small. He was also very hairy, with a beard that clearly lived a life of its own; so did his smile and his handshake. Stephen King had come to town.

There have been many lunches since that one, many contracts. The letters, alas, have pretty much stopped, since Steve now has a phone; but the smile, the beard (in season) and the handshake endure. So does the talent, which is really what it's all about.

Welcome to Room 217

by Ramsey Campbell

I know two hotel anecdotes about Steve King. One is my favorite souvenir of Baltimore, where the hotel staff were either entering into the spirit of Halloween or aiming to give members of the World Fantasy Convention the welcome that seemed appropriate. The lady at Reception who obviously suspected Steve of not being able to pay for his hotel booking because he didn't have a credit card was dressed, as I remember, as a pumpkin. I can think of no better introduction to a weekend of fantasy than the spectacle of the most popular author in the field being suspected of insolvency by a lady pumpkin. That's one anecdote; the other comes from Birmingham, England, where Steve King nearly was.

(o god that room in the Imperial mustn't think about it talk about something else)

He was to be guest of honor at the British Fantasy Convention in 1978, until the surgeon intervened—or rather, until the aftermath of a vasectomy did. I shall leave the details to your imagination, not least because I don't want to put off any potential subjects of the operation, which I believe is a good thing. I should know, having had two of them. (I'm sure I'm wrong to think that to make certain the second time, the surgeon used a chainsaw.) However, there's no truth to the rumor

(rumor doesn't sound like room don't think about the room that changed)

that Steve and I ever thought of collaborating on a vasectomy novel, especially not if the Guild of Master Vasectomists makes it worth our while not to do so. A pity about those wasted titles, though: *THE UNKINDEST CUT, THE BALL IS OVER, SCRAGGING THE SCROTUM, NOBBLED IN THE NUTS, DEFERENS DEFERRED* . . . . But I was talking about Birmingham and Steve King as the guest who never was.

I can't now lay my hands on the appreciation of him that I wrote for the program booklet, but I believe I suggested that King is to the present what Matheson was to the fifties, *'SALEM'S LOT* rediscovering the logical terrors of *I AM LEGEND*, the Overlook Hotel threatening to overtake Hell House as the least desirable venue for an overnight stay (high praise indeed from me, *HELL HOUSE* being the last work of fiction that actually made me wish I hadn't stayed up late reading it to the end). I also claimed, I think, that part of the secret of Steve's success (besides his gift for storytelling, whose equal I have yet to find in contemporary fiction) might lie in the way his fiction holds up a distorting mirror to popular themes: The American Novelist Returns Home in *'SALEM'S LOT*, The Artist Struggles With Alcoholism in *THE SHINING*, The Ugly Duckling Strikes Back in *CARRIE*, Local Boy

Makes Good in *CUJO* and *THE DEAD ZONE* . . . . Of course by this stage the distortions are so severe as to be dismaying, but surely that's one of Steve's most remarkable achievements—that he manages to reach so many readers by giving them (in Hitchcock's words) what they think they don't want, telling them what they would rather not admit they know. That, incidentally, is one factor that distinguishes good horror fiction from escapism. It's also more worthwhile than simply appealing to the side of the reader that wants to gawk at car accidents. There's considerably less of the latter appeal in Steve's work than he sometimes lets himself be persuaded there is, and far more of the nobler stuff.

If the sincerest tribute one can offer another writer is to imitate him, perhaps I should point out a couple of tributes of mine. *THE PARASITE* was written in the spirit of discovering whether I could learn from *THE SHINING*, as Peter Straub told me he had—whether I could achieve large-scale supernatural effects, full frontal terrors. I think mine was only a moderate success, and so a few years later I designed "Down There" as a tribute to Steve and his work. What imp of the perverse distracted me from noticing that the story's chief fatality was called Steve? Freudians no doubt will make of that what they choose.

I was involved in one other tribute to Steve King, and if one believes the stories, that one

(just a story just a ghost story just a mistake people ought to overlook o god overlook)

is still going wrong, lingering like the phone numbers Steve has scattered through his home town (I've lost count of how many ex-directory numbers I've rung only to be told tartly that no, this is no longer Stephen King's). But surely the stories are a joke, just like the prank that gave rise to them.

The idea was, you see, that when Steve arrived at the Birmingham hotel he should discover that he was booked into room 217. But there was no suite of that number, and certainly nothing less than a suite would do. So, like Kubrick in his film of the book but for quite different reasons, we decided to have the number changed on the door of the suite. Then Steve's vasectomy grounded him, and the number wasn't changed, and so nothing could have happened at the hotel, could it? Surely any rumors meant that the hotel staff were trying to outdo the British Fantasy Convention in imagination, however un-British that might be. Why, the hotel records don't even show the name of the guest some people claim booked the suite.

Whoever was to change the numbers must have told his colleagues why. Several of them read Steve King, but what's surprising about that? Does a bear shit in the woods? The chambermaid who claimed she was making up the suite for Mr. Bachman

(the man who would be king no the man with no face o god)

certainly was a fan of Steve's, and so can't we conclude that her admiration and imagination got the better of her? Perhaps the thought of entering a bedroom that was to have been Steve's proved too much for her, or the thought of venturing into the bathroom of a suite that had almost been 217. She must have been thinking about that, for she says that as the door to the corridor closed slowly behind her without her having touched it, she was sure she caught sight of the number 217 on the door.

She told herself not to be foolish, she says. She made herself go quickly into the bathroom to prove that there was nothing—made herself do so even though the shower curtain hid the whole of the bath. She heard her footsteps click over the linoleum like the ticking of a clock that was counting the seconds it took her to reach the curtain. The fluorescent lighting gave a small buzzing twitch as she closed her hand on the edge of the chilly plastic. She took a breath that tasted of new soap, and then she snatched the curtain back.

The bath was empty. That was such a relief that she had to support herself with one hand against the damp tiles above the bath. She only just restrained herself from mopping her forehead with one of the fresh towels she was supposed to hang up on the rail. She laughed at herself then, and told herself she'd stay off books that scared her for a while, read Shaun Hutson instead. She switched off the bathroom light and went along the hall to the bedroom, to change the sheets.

She couldn't get hold of the doorknob at first; her fingers slipped. She wiped her hand on her uniform and tried again. This time the doorknob turned, though it was wet. It reminded her that the tiles above the bath had been damp even though the last guest had checked out of the suite days earlier. Then she realized that she'd noticed something else without being aware at the time that she had. There were wet patches on the hall carpet—patches like footprints leading from the bathroom to the bedroom.

They must have been made a while ago. If they'd only just been made there couldn't have been much to the feet that had made them. All at once she decided not to go into the bedroom after all, at any rate not by herself. She bit her lip and said a prayer and let go of the doorknob. Just as she let go, she felt the doorknob turn the rest of the way.

Something on the other side of the door was turning it. Before she could run down the hall, which was only a few paces long and yet the outer door seemed so far away, the bedroom door swung open, and

(no god no not the drowned woman just a story i promise i won't read anything like that again only the Bible)

when the hotel staff heard her screams, a carpenter had to unscrew the hinges before they could get into the suite, she was huddled so immovably against the outer door.

She was in the Birmingham hospital for weeks. When she started talking to her visitors they learned that she remembered nothing since she'd unlocked the door of the suite that wasn't 217. She seemed happy enough, especially once a nurse gave her a Bible, and nobody might have known what she thought she saw beyond the bedroom door if the hospital public address system hadn't happened to page a John Smith. She began to scream then

(o god the dead zone carries on never flags never flagg)

and cower against the pillow, and babble until they thought she would never stop.

Whatever she saw in that room, surely she couldn't have seen all she claimed: a dying young girl whose death seemed to reach for her and draw her into the dark, a cellar trapdoor yawning as the dark fell over it and a voice called from below "Come down," a man in a white jacket who told her she'd always been the chambermaid, a man wearing an anorak whose hood seemed to contain nothing but blackness and two glaring eyes, someone reaching up to his own face with a spade-claw hand, a closet creeping open to let out a sound of vicious growling, a head in a refrigerator, the mouth stuffed with feathers . . . . All that, and a voice saying "Always more tales"? Could any door conceal so much?

If a door really opened, we try to reassure ourselves, surely it was only in her mind. But that explanation is by no means as reassuring as it seems. Whatever happened in the hotel suite, it was more than imagination. Something beyond imagination was needed to make her listeners see in their own minds all the words she babbled, *in parentheses, printed in italics.*

Perhaps she was simply making a tribute to Steve King, beside which mine seem amateur and clumsy. Still, I did my best. Here's to Steve. Let's raise a can of Bud to him. Long may he continue to open doors in the Gothic structures of our minds.

Thanks to the Crypt-Keeper

An Appreciation of Stephen King
by Whitley Strieber

It is a hot summer night in the year 1954. A full Texas moon glares down over the sleepy little city of San Antonio. The hour is late; even the katydids have stopped chirping. On my block not a light is showing. The big old houses stand silent in the heat, choked by the baroque foliage, huge vines twisting up the walls, rats scuttling along the gutters. There is no sound but for a stifled sigh and the faint playing of a radio. Light flickers in one of the rooms, then blazes. Shouts are heard, the smack of a hand against bare flesh. My copy of the August issue of *The Crypt of Terror* flutters down to the lawn. It has been torn to pieces by my outraged and uncomprehending father.

My enjoyment of horror became permanent on that night. I realized that it was forbidden and despised; by reading it I declared myself to the world as a rebel, a member of a secret cabal of screwed-up kids who were cheerful at funerals, who giggled when ordered to say a prayer at the sound of an ambulance siren, who weren't above putting a dead rattlesnake in bed with their sister to see if the EEEEYAAAHHHs scattered across EC Comics were accurate renderings of the sound of horror.

Watching the beginning of *Creepshow* I detected parallel experience. Somewhere back there Stephen King must have gone through something similar, at least in spirit. He's written that he was a fan of EC Comics, so we have to thank the Crypt-Keeper—and the Old Witch and the others, for that matter—for a great deal.

Horror fiction is the essential fiction of rebellion in modern times. In Stephen King's work it is the rebellion of the middle against all extremes. On one level his books are about supernatural—or at least, inexplicable—horrors. On another, they are about injustice. When I was a young man Norman Thomas told me that "the republic stops where the secrets start," and said that the greatest political problem of my generation would be the tendency of bureaucracy to hide behind classification laws. *FIRESTARTER* is a book of rage against the cancerous spread of secrecy in our government. Its message is that governmental secrets diminish the life of the ordinary man. In its fury and its driving narrative power it stands far above the more conventional novels on the subject, with their vapid warnings and constricted prose.

What excites me about King's work most is the drive, the passion that keeps breaking through. Every time I read one of his novels I am struck once again by the notion that his is a true voice. Because of this there is a ring of conviction in his books that makes them not only important and politically satisfying, but more fun to read than you'll find elsewhere in modern fiction.

I picked up *CARRIE* in hardcover at Doubleday's

in New York a few weeks after it was published. I didn't know Stephen King at the time, but the first three sentences of the novel told me that he had come to horror the true way: he wasn't writing for money; this man was passionate about his material. He was writing about the outrageous state of the world, and giving me a terrific thrill when Carrie did just what I had wanted to do when the basketball team made me eat my nerdpack and then crushed my glasses.

Ideally, I would be able to say that I sat there stunned, realizing that a great talent was before us. But I didn't. I was young, struggling, poor, and fool enough to buy hardbacks anyway. I put the book aside and forgot about it. Some time later I saw the film and enjoyed it. Still, I didn't fully understand what I was dealing with.

Then I read *'SALEM'S LOT* and I finally realized that this guy wasn't just a genuine horror novelist, but something real special. Someone who reads a lot of horror is always in danger of becoming jaded. Back in '75 and '76 I was reading far more horror than I do now, almost as much as I did when I was ten. Whether I was jaded or not, *'SALEM'S LOT* did what it was supposed to do to me. I was sitting in the middle of my bed at two o'clock in the morning when I crossed through the dark forest with the kids, and something was there, and we all knew it, and it was not going to go away, and this was real.

And it's still there.

The great tales of horror wait for us forever in the back of our memories, ready to give service when needed. Those of us who need a good horror story to escape for a little while from life give thanks for the lingering chills, the characters who don't die, the scenes which can be relished even years later. And always, there is the ancient and fundamental service of the novel: like the best of what has come before, Stephen King's work is moral fiction. No matter how fashions and time change the world, for this reason his books will persist.

The wonder of it is, of course, that you also get the fun. Stephen King has provided me with more and better lurking fears than any other single writer I can think of. I must admit that it was Lovecraft who made me uneasy about Whippoorwills, but I've never been frightened by tentacled excrudescences, I find them just a bit funny. Give me a little girl who might cause me to burst into flames if I express unconstitutional sentiments in her presence, or a cat that actually does what all cats want to do and can't—yet.

The question of why horror is popular has been asked too many times, but it's been answered correctly so infrequently that I'd like to have a go at it here in the context of Stephen King's work. People suffer and feel powerless. Life is not pretty. Nature is against most of us. The washing of cars causes rain and the planting of gardens drought. But washing the car *and* planting the garden doesn't help. Then the house simply burns down. And in the end we all get killed.

Part of good horror is the "it's not happening to me" syndrome. I am here, in this bedroom, reading all of these fascinating misfortunes, and they are *more horrible* than the fact that the dog left his calling card in one of my good shoes again this morning. These deaths are lingering agonies far worse than anything I need expect, even if I go down in a jet and burn to death amid a jumble of agonized fellow-passengers.

I am here, safe in this bedroom. And they are out there in the *DEAD ZONE,* suffering. Stephen King has guided me through this dreadful place, and he's been a good guide. He never actually gave me one of those headaches but he tried, and I appreciated that, how hard he tried. He probably took a migraine or two while writing the book. But he never abandoned me, he stayed with me, guiding me sweetly along—and then shoving me into the next fright like a good friend should.

I am here, safe in this bedroom. Maybe something awful is going on outside that window. Maybe a psychotic is climbing up the house with a meathook in his hand.

But, even if that's true, what he's going to do to me will not hurt as much as what Jack Torrance is going to do to his wife with that axe, because Jack is *so slow* and the psycho will have to be quick to catch me.

We are all running, always, from real fears. King can scare us because he knows how. I've heard him describe his feelings upon walking across a certain unpleasant railroad bridge. He's described his dislike of beds with dust ruffles, a dislike I share, and for the same reason. If you lift that dust ruffle—as you must—every night, one of these nights the statistics are going to wipe you out. You are going to be staring into the barrel of a .45—or worse, down the length of a long, long fingernail.

My relationship with Stephen King has been confined to meetings at conventions. Conversations tended to be wary, with both of us worried that the other might discover just how strange we really are. I've at times been aware of the fact that I was in the presence of a very acute and somewhat dangerous mind. Stephen King is suspicious of artifice. For some reason, that knowledge makes me want to dress up in fancy suits and order old wines when with him, while he slops even more Black Label down his t-shirt. I can tell that he sees through me and I suspect that might I see through him. What do I see? Well, a lot of the fear is genuine. He writes about what he knows. Once I saw him in a plane, sitting in the first row close to the door, in a state of deep meditation. I was farther from the door, I suspect, only because he had reserved the closer seat before I called the airline.

And what were we doing there, clutching our bellies in that airplane? I was up front for two reasons: one, if it's a survivable crash and there's a fire, the people in the front have the best chance of getting out. If it's a nonsurvivable then front is better too—you get a nice, clean impact death. You do not have to die in agony, spattered with flaming jet fuel you can't beat out, choking in smoke and terror with hundreds of others, leaving your fingernails embedded in the windows.

I cannot speak for King. Maybe he isn't as fearful as I think. But somehow I don't see him striding into the bedroom and saying to hell with the dust ruffle. Or sitting in the front of the plane simply because it's more convenient.

The average guy recognized that King was important a long time ago, and made him into a bookselling phenomenon. Among cognoscenti in the field he's considered a master. But his work is also important both as literature and as cultural matter. He writes from the heart of the American experience. There is something in his voice that fits our American ear very well. We feel comfortable with a guy like this telling us a good story, and we know that he comes to us with truth. We like justice, and to see it done fulfills one of our deepest longings. King talks American and even though he might now be as rich as he can be, he was once down at the bottom and he knows what it is to be an ordinary member of our society.

His language, his situations, reflect this strange and glittering culture accurately. If by some odd chance the people of the future read, and they want to learn about America in our time—not the history, but the smell and taste and feel of it—they will certainly turn to Stephen King for guidance.

God knows what they will think of us. But one thing is sure: they are going to get an unforgettably good scare.

Fantasy as Commodity and Myth

by Leslie Fiedler

If we accept the standard dictionary definition of fantasy as "imaginative fiction dependent for effect on strangeness of setting (as other worlds and times) and of characters (as supernatural or unnatural beings). . . ," it seems clear that in America at least it has become the reigning genre of the moment. Certainly popular narrative—both in print and the post-print media—has come over the past couple of decades to be more and more dominated by two sub-varieties of the genre: Horror and Science Fiction.

Despite their appeal to contemporary sensibility, neither, of course, is of recent origin. Horror, indeed, is almost as old as the modern novel itself: representing the first backlash against the newfangled mimetic mode established in the mid-eighteenth century by Samuel Richardson, with its disavowal of the "marvelous," and the "wonderful" characteristic of Medieval and Renaissance Romance. Instead of evoking, like those earlier forms of prose narrative, "other times" and "supernatural or unnatural beings," Richardson's novels portrayed ordinary people confronting the small crises of everyday domestic life—in a mode later called "realism" but known originally as "verisimilitude." Moreover, his experiment *worked;* which is to say, his *PAMELA* and *CLARISSA* became immediate best-sellers, thus proving once and for all that for many readers the "familiar" was as appealing as the "strange."

But apparently not for all readers nor for very long; since before the eighteenth century was over, the Gothic Romance or the Tale of Terror had begun to appear: a kind of neo-fantastic fiction which abandoned the recognizable present in favor of an exotic past, in an attempt to restore the waning popularity of the "marvelous." As might have been expected, however, in the aftermath of the French Revolution, when the failed dream of Reason was breeding monsters in the dark undermind of Europe, the fantastic was reborn in sinister form, as terrifying nightmare rather than idyllic dream.

In part, surely, for this very reason, the earliest Gothic narratives (even M. G. Lewis's ridiculous–marvelous minor masterpiece, *THE MONK*) failed to recapture the evergrowing mass audience from the popular sentimental-domestic novel. The former were in fact largely the product of the kind of writers we would call nowadays "avant-garde." Like later alienated artists, they perceived themselves and were perceived as being deliberately provocative, dedicated to *"epater la bourgeoisie,"* which is to say, to shocking their own mothers and the genteel clergymen who guided their taste.

Certainly it was out of just such a group of radical bohemians, including Lord Byron and Percy Shelley—poets in flight from a world which did not understand or sympathize with their literary aspirations and deviant life-style—that the first and still widely known Tale of Terror emerged, Mary Wollstonecraft Shelley's *FRANKENSTEIN, OR THE NEW PROMETHEUS*. But not until our own century—and the invention of motion pictures—did even that dark fable of a rejected monster turning on his master pass fully into the public domain, from which it promises never to depart. In the decades immediately following its publication, Mrs. Shelley's novel was not held in very high esteem, since a reaction had set in against Gothicism, eventually resulting in hostile burlesques of the genre like Jane Austen's *NORTHANGER ABBEY*.

Though the parodists did not succeed in laughing it out of existence, by the late Victorian Era macabre fiction had come to be considered disreputable *shlock*. To the genteel it seemed vulgar and gross, to apostles of "high seriousness," frivolous make-believe; and to the critical establishment a regrettable regression: a turning back from the straight path of literary progress, which had led from the puerile fabrication of the superstitious Dark Ages to the mature realism of an enlightened time. This attitude persists still in the Marxist world of Eastern Europe, where "social realism" is enforced by fiat and censorship; while in the bourgeois West, though "realism" of all varieties has been in disfavor since the rise of the modernist art novel, popular fantasy is equally condemned.

By the end of the nineteenth century, at any rate, not just Dark Fantasy but all hardcore fantasy had been ghettoized: demoted to the Nursery, on the one hand; and on the other, remanded to circulating libraries and railroad bookstalls. Fairy tales could be and were written still (think of George MacDonald, Lewis Carroll and Hans Christian Andersen) but only if supposedly addressed exclusively to children, and Gothic Horror was left to modest hacks (think of Rider Haggard and Bram Stoker) content to be loved by the yahoos but despised or condescended to by the official guardians of literary standards.

In the 1930's—in the depths of the Great Depression when all images of disaster seemed relevant and true—those few works of horror which had somehow survived the critic's scorn (neither *DRACULA* nor *SHE,* for instance, had ever been out of print) were translated into motion pictures by gifted but unpretentious film-makers like James Whale and Tod Browning; and thus were made available to an audience immensely larger than that which had consumed them in print. They still had to stand hat in hand, however, at the backdoor of culture, as it were; implicitly acknowledging that they knew their place as "mere entertainment," unworthy of being taken seriously like High Literature or even Art Films. It was, therefore, chiefly at Midnight Halloween shows, or after awhile on "Fright Night" on TV, that they survived. Yet, perhaps precisely because of this, they have refused to die from our deep imaginations, in which all of us remain children, for therapeutic reasons we do not understand.

Even when they first appeared, however, the movie versions of nineteenth-century Horror Pop were regarded with hostility by concerned parents, who tried valiantly indeed to keep their children out of the theatres where they were being shown. Abetted by self-righteous reviewers and timid exhibitors, they eventually drove many of them from the screen; so that Tod Browning, for instance, the greatest master of the genre, was forced into early retirement. After World War II matters grew even worse, as parents convinced that imaginary violence created rather than reflected real violence, launched a full-scale attack against all forms of Horror previously available to children. Comic books were their first target, and they eventually drove E.C. Comics, the most horrific examples of the genre, out of business completely. But they did not stop there, going on to expurgate even *GRIMM'S FAIRY TALES,* snatching unbowdlerized copies from the hands of their presumably innocent sons and daughters—and, of course, forbidding them to go to suspect movies, not just the monster flicks but Walt Disney's animated cartoon versions of Grimm—and even *Donald Duck.*

It was a time of repression, but the far-from-innocent kids of the 50s fought back; surreptitiously indulging in the literature of horror, even as they listened to the rock music disapproved of by their fathers and mothers. Nor did their tastes change when they came of age in the 60s. Indeed, at that point they became the core of a new kind of audience for the hitherto ghettoized forms of pop. It was not because they knew no better that such college-bound or college-educated offspring of the most privileged classes preferred the old comic books (along with the newer even more outrageous "head comics" modeled on them) to the classic works urged on them by their English teachers—or the monster films of the 30s (along with more recent thrillers patterned after them, like George Romero's *Night of the Living Dead*) to the pretentious foreign films with subtitles which their parents considered superior to Hollywood junk. Rather it was because—as pioneers of what they called the "counter culture"—they thought they knew *better* than their parents what was good for them and their society.

The formerly despised pop forms had for them the added appeal of the taboo, providing not only the traditional *frisson* of fear but the added titillation of guilt—the thrill of peeking through the keyhole at an obscenity more shocking in an age of sexual liberation than anything merely erotic. Nor has horror ceased to function for us as pornography even now when the Counter Culture has become the Over-the-Counter Culture; and the taste of the dissident minority of the 60s dictates reigning fashion. Yet without quite ceasing to be experienced as porn (in part, indeed, for that very reason) Weird Fiction has in the last decades of the twentieth century turned into a best-selling commodity in the supermarket of popular culture—like T.V. Dinners, "Natural" Cereals, and Diet Pepsis; or rather perhaps more like mood elevators, anti-depressants and what we call these days, "recreational" drugs.

Most successful of all have been works which combine the horrific and the lubricious, like Ira Levin's *ROSEMARY'S BABY* and William Peter Blatty's *THE EXORCIST*, which first in print and then in film demonstrated during the 70s the failsafe box office appeal of the R-rated uncanny. More recently, however, the chief beneficiary of the mass audience's hunger for eroticized Dark Fantasy has been Stephen King, whose first best-selling novel, *CARRIE*, had the good fortune to be realized on the screen by Brian De Palma, a director who had served his apprenticeship making low budget skin-flicks. It manages to touch all the bases: moving from a shot of a naked teenage girl having her first menstruation in a shower (somehow the combination of blood, running water and sanitary plumbing has a special appeal for contemporary movie fans) to a scene in which a corpse breaks out of its newly made grave.

While it is not quite true—as some of his more ardent fans assert—that King has thus single-handedly and overnight, as it were, made Horror a best-selling genre, it cannot be denied that no other writer in the genre had ever before produced so long a series of smash successes, in hardcover, paperback and on the screen; so that he has indeed finally become—in his own words—a "brand name" like Vaseline or Coca Cola. We have, in any case, come a long way from the early nineteenth century, when Charles Brockden Brown, the first American author of Tales of Terror, and his immediate successor, Edgar Allan Poe, died neglected and scarcely known.

A friend of mine said you know you're being scary when you can feel the malevolent grin begin to creep up your face—and he's right. Humor and horror are close together. Both come from the same aggressive impulse and in both cases we laugh or scream because we're happy it isn't us.

I don't think anybody laughs at anything that isn't inherently aggressive or hurtful or painful.

We have a history of being drawn to horror. Maybe it's because we're mortal and we keep trying to fit our minds around the concept of dying.

—Stephen King

Surviving the Ride

by Clive Barker

"The tygers of wrath are wiser than the horses of instruction."
—William Blake: *The Marriage of Heaven and Hell.*

First, a confession: I have no thesis. I come to these pages without an overview to propound; only with a substantial enthusiasm for the work of Stephen King and a *potpourri* of thoughts on fear, fiction, dreams and geographies which may bear some tenuous relation to each other and to King's fiction.

Theoretical thinking was never a great passion of mine, but ghost-trains are. And it's with a ghost-train I begin.

It's called—ambitiously enough—*L'Apocalypse.* To judge from the size of the exterior, the ride it houses is an epic; the vast, three-tiered facade dwarfs the punters who mill around outside, staring up with a mixture of trepidation and appetite at the hoardings, and wondering if they have the nerve to step out of the heat of the sun and into the stale darkness that awaits them through the swinging doors.

Surely, they reassure themselves, no fun-fair ride can be as bad as the paintings that cover every inch of the building suggest: for the pictures record atrocities that would have turned de Sade's stomach.

They're not particularly good paintings; they're rather too crudely rendered, and the gaudy primaries the artists have chosen seem ill-suited to the subject matter. But the eye flits back and forth over the horrors described here, unable to disengage itself. In one corner, a shackled man is having his head sliced off; it seems to leap out at us, propelled by a geyser of scarlet blood. A few yards from this, above a row of arches that are edged with canary-yellow lights, a man watches his bowels being drawn from his abdomen by a Cardinal in an advanced state of decomposition. Beside the entrance booth, a crucified woman is being burned alive in a chamber lined with white-hot swords. We might be tempted to laugh at such *grand guignol* excesses, but we cannot. They are, for all the roughness of their presentation, deeply disturbing.

I've never ridden *L'Apocalypse*. I know it only as a photograph, culled from a magazine some dozen years ago, and treasured since. The photograph still speaks loudly to me. Of the indisputable glamor of the horrible; of its power to enthrall and repulse simultaneously. And it also reminds me—with its sweaty-palmed punters queuing beneath a crystal blue sky for a chance at the dark—that nobody ever lost money offering a good ride to Hell.

Which brings us, inevitably, to the architect of the most popular ghost-train rides in the world: Mr. Stephen King.

It's perhaps redundant, in a book celebrating Stephen King's skills, for me to list his merits at too great a length. We, his readers and admirers, know them well. But it may be worth our considering exactly *what* he's selling us through the charm and accessibility of his prose, the persuasiveness of his characters, the ruthless drive of his narratives.

He's selling death. He's selling tales of blood-drinkers, flesh-eaters, and the decay of the soul; of the destruction of sanity, community and faith. In his fiction, even love's power to outwit the darkness is uncertain; the monsters will devour that too, given half a chance. Nor is innocence much of a defense. Children go to the grave as readily as the adult of the species, and those few Resurrections that circumstance grants are not likely to be the glory promised from the pulpit.

Not, one would have thought, a particularly commercial range of subjects. But in King's hands their saleability can scarcely be in question. He has turned the horror *genre*—so long an underdog on the publishing scene—into a force to be reckoned with.

Many reasons have been put forward for King's popularity. A common element in most of the theories is his *plausibility* as a writer. In the novels—though rather less in the short stories—he describes the confrontation between the real and the fantastic elements so believably that the reader's rational sensibilities are seldom, if ever, outraged. The images of power, of loss, of transformation, of wild children and terrible hotels, of beasts mythological and beasts rabid and beasts human—all are dropped so cunningly into the texture of the world he conjures—morsel upon morsel—that by the time our mouths are full, we're perfectly willing to swallow.

The net effect is akin to taking that ride on *L'Apocalypse,* only finding that the dummies on either side of the track, enacting over and over their appalling death scenes, closely resemble people we know. The horror is intensified immeasurably. We are no longer simply voyeurs, watching some artificial atrocity unfold in front of our eyes. We are intimately involved with the sufferers. We share their traumas and their terrors. We share too their hatred of their tormentors.

This is by no means the only approach to writing dark fantasy, of course. Many authors choose to plunge their readers into the world of the subconscious (which is, surely, the territory such fiction charts) with scarcely a glance over their shoulders at the "reality" the reader occupies. In the geography of the *fantastique,* for instance, Prince Prospero's castle—sealed so inadequately against the Red Death—stands far deeper in the world of pure dream than does the Overlook Hotel, whose rooms, though no less haunted by violent death, are far more realistically evoked than Poe's baroque conceits.

There are, inevitably, losses and gains on both sides. Poe sacrifices a certain accessibility by his method; one has to embrace the fictional conventions he has employed before the story can be fully savored. He gains, however, a mythic resonance which is out of all proportion to the meagre pages *The Masque of the Red Death* occupies. He has, apparently effortlessly, written himself into the landscape of our dreams.

King's method—which requires the establishing of a far more elaborate fictional "reality"—wins out through our commitment *to* that reality, and to the characters who inhabit it. It also earns the power to subvert our sense of the real, by showing us a world we think we know, then revealing another view of it entirely. What I believe he loses in the trade-off is a certain *ambiguity.* This I'll return to later.

First, a couple of thoughts on subversion. It has been argued, and forcibly, that for all the paraphernalia of revolution contained in King's fiction—the weak discovering unlooked-for strength and the strong faltering; the constant threat (or promise) of transformation; a sense barely hidden beneath the chatty surface of the prose, that mythic elements are being juggled here—that, despite all this apocalyptic stuff, the author's world-view is at heart a conservative one. Is he perhaps a sheep in wolf's clothing, distressing us with these scenes of chaos in order to persuade us to cling closer to the values that his monsters jeopardize?

I admit to having some sympathy with this argument, and I admire most those of his tales which seem to show the world irredeemably changed, with no hope of a return to the comfortable, joyless, death-in-life that seems to be the late twentieth century ideal. But if there is evidence that gives weight to such argument, there is also much in King's work which is genuinely subversive: imagery which evokes states of mind and conditions of flesh which, besides exciting our anxieties, excites also our desires and our perversities.

Why, you may ask, do I put such a high value upon subversion?

There are many reasons. The most pertinent here is my belief that fantastic fiction offers the writer exceptional possibilities in that direction, and I strongly believe a piece of work (be it play, book, poem) should be judged according to how enthusiastically it seizes the opportunity to do what it can do *uniquely*. The literature of the fantastic—and the movies, and the paintings—can reproduce, at its best, the texture of experience more closely than any "naturalistic" work, because it can embrace the complexity of the world we live in.

Which is to say: our minds. That's where we live,

after all. And our minds are extraordinary melting pots, in which sensory information, and the memory of same, and intellectual ruminations, and nightmares, and dreams, simmer in an ever-richer stew. Where else but in works called (often pejoratively) *fantasies* can such a mixture of elements be placed side by side?

And if we once embrace the vision offered in such works, if we once allow the metaphors a home in our psyches, the subversion is under way. We may for the first time see ourselves as a *totality*—valuing our appetite for the forbidden rather than suppressing it, comprehending that our taste for the strange, or the morbid, or the paradoxical, is contrary to what we're brought up to believe, a sign of our good health. So I say—*subvert.* And never apologize.

That's one of King's crowning achievements. From the beginning, he's never apologized, never been ashamed to be a horror author. He values the *genre,* and if horror fiction is in turn more valued now than it was ten or twenty years ago it is surely in no small degree his doing. After all, the most obsessive of rationalists must find it difficult to ignore the man's existence: he's read on buses and trains; in Universities and Hospitals; by the good, the bad and the morally indifferent.

At this juncture it may be worth remembering that the dreams he is usually concerned to evoke are normally known not as dreams but as *nightmares.* This is in itself worthy of note. We have other classes of dreams which are as common as nightmares. Erotic dreams, for instance; dreams of humiliation. But it's only the dream of terror which has been graced with a special name, as though we recognize that this experience, of all those that come to us in sleep, carries some essential significance. Is it perhaps that in our waking lives we feel (rightly or wrongly) that we have control over all other responses but that of fear? Certainly we may use the word nightmare freely to describe waking experience ("the traffic was a nightmare," we casually remark), but seldom do our lives reach that pitch of terror—accompanied by the blood-chilling sense of inevitability—that informs the dream of dread.

In reading a good piece of horror fiction, we may dip into the dreaming state at will; we may even hope to interpret some of the signs and signals that nightmares deliver to us. If not that, at least there is some comfort in knowing that these images are *shared.*

(An aside. One of the pleasures of any fiction is comparing the intricacies of response with other readers, but this process takes on a wonderfully paradoxical quality when two horror enthusiasts are exchanging views on a favorite book or film. The gleeful detailing of the carnage, the shared delight, as the key moments of revulsion and anxiety are remembered: we smile, talking of how we sweated.)

There are many kinds of nightmare. Some have familiar, even domestic settings, in which commonplace particulars are charged up with uncanny and inexplicable power to intimidate. It is this kind of nightmare that King is most adept at evoking, and the kind with which he is probably most readily identified. It is in a way a natural progression from rooting outlandish horrors—*CARRIE; 'SALEM'S LOT*—in settings so familiar we might occupy them, to making objects from those settings—a dog, a car—themselves the objects of anxiety. I must say I prefer the earlier books by quite a measure, but that's in part because the Apocalypses conjured seem so much more comprehensive, and I have a practically limitless appetite for tales of the world turned inside out.

The other kind of nightmare is a different experience entirely and it is not—at least in the conventional sense—about threat. I mean the kind of dream voyage that takes you out of any recognizable context, and into some other state entirely. The kind that lifts you up (perhaps literally; for me such nightmares often begin with falling that turns into flight) and whips you away to a place both familiar and utterly new, utterly strange. You have never been to this place in your waking life, of that your dreaming self is certain; but there are presences here familiar to you, and sights around every corner that you will recognize even as they astonish you.

What actually happens on these voyages will run from the banal to the Wagnerian, depending on the dreamer's sense of irony, but the way this second sort of nightmare operates upon your psyche is totally different from the first. For one thing, the fears dealt with in the first sort are likely to be susceptible to analysis. They are fears of authority figures, or terminal disease, or making love to Mother. But the second kind is, I believe, rooted not in the specifics of the personality, but in something more primitive; something that belongs to our response as thought-haunted matter to the world we're born into. The images that come to overwhelm us in this region are not, therefore, projections of neurosis; they are things vast; contradictory; mythological.

King can conjure such stuff with the best of them; I only regret that his brilliance as a creator of domestic demons has claimed him from writing more of that other region. When he turns his hand to it, the effect is stunning. *The Mist,* for example, is a story that begins in familiar King territory, and moves through a variety of modes—including scenes which, in their mingling of the monstrous and the commonplace work as high, grim comedy—towards a world lost to humanity, a world that echoes in the imagination long after the book has been closed. In the final section of the story the survivors encounter a creature so vast it doesn't even notice the protagonists:—

> . . . Its skin was deeply wrinkled and grooved, and clinging to it were scores, hundreds, of those pinkish 'bugs' with the stalk-eyes. I don't know how big it actually was, but it passed directly over us . . . . Mrs. Reppler said later she could not see the underside of its body, although she craned her neck up to look. She saw only two Cyclopean legs going up and up into the mist like living towers until they were lost to sight.

There is much more of breathtaking imaginative scope in *THE STAND,* and in a more intimate, though no less persuasive fashion, in *THE SHINING* and *'SALEM'S LOT.* Moments when the terror becomes something more than a fight for life with an unwelcome intruder; when the horror reveals itself, even in the moment of causing us to recoil, as a source of fascination and awe and self-comprehension.

This is the root of the ambiguity I spoke of before, and to which I said I would return. *Wanting* an encounter with forces that will change our lives—that will deliver us once and for all into the regions of the gods ("I had a dream that I saw God walking across Harrison on the far side of the lake, a God so gigantic that above the waist He was lost in a clear blue sky." —*THE MIST*)—yet fearful that we are negligible things and so far beneath the concern of such powers that any confrontation will simply kill us.

Charting that ambiguity is, I would suggest, a function that the fantasy *genre* can uniquely fulfill. It is perhaps the liability of King's virtues that such ambiguity is often forfeited in exchange for a straightforward identification with the forces of light. King's monsters (human, sub-human and Cyclopean) may on occasion be *comprehensible* to us, but they seldom exercise any serious claim on our sympathies. They are moral degenerates, whose colors are plain from the outset. We watch them kick dogs to death, and devour children, and we are reinforced in the questionable certainty that we are not like them; that *we* are on the side of the angels.

Now *that's* fiction. We are not. Darkness has a place in all of us; a substantial place that must, for our health's sake, be respected and investigated.

After all, one of the reasons we read tales of terror is surely that we have an *appetite* for viewing anguish, and death, and all the paraphernalia of the monstrous. That's not the condition of the angels.

It seems to me vital that in this age of the New Righteousness—when moral rectitude is again a rallying-cry, and the old hypocrisies are gaining acolytes by the hour—that we should strive to avoid feeding delusions of perfectibility and instead celebrate the complexities and contradictions that, as I've said, fantastic fiction is uniquely qualified to address. If we can, we may yet keep from drowning in a wave of simplifications that include such great, fake dichotomies as good versus evil, dark versus light, reality versus fiction. But we must be prepared to wear our paradoxes on our sleeve.

In King's work, it is so often the child who carries that wisdom; the child who synthesizes "real" and "imagined" experience without question, who knows instinctively that imagination can tell the truth the way the senses never can. That lesson can never be taught too often. It stands in direct contradiction to the basic principles which we are suckled upon and are taught make us strong in the world. Principles of verifiable evidence; and of the logic that will lead, given its head, to terrible, but faultlessly logical, insanities.

I return again to the list of goods that King is selling in his fiction, and find my summary deficient. Yes, there is death on the list; and much about the soul's decay. But there's also *vision.*

Not the kind laid claim to by politicians or manufacturers or men of the cloth. Not the vision of the *better* economy, the *better* combustion engine, the *better* Eden. Those visions are devised to bind us and blind us. If we look too long at them we no longer understand what our dreams are telling us; and without that knowledge we are weak.

No, King offers us another kind of vision; he shows us adults what the children in his fiction so often take for granted: that on the journey which he has so eloquently charted, where no terror shows its face but on a street that we have ourselves trodden, it is not, finally, the stale formulae and the trite metaphysics we're taught from birth that will get us to the end of the ride alive; it is our intimacy with our dark and dreaming selves.

Writing has always been *it* for me. I was just sort of a nerdy kid. I didn't get beat up too much because I was big, played a little football and stuff like that. So mostly I just got this "King—he's weird. Big glasses. Reads a lot. Big teeth." I've thought about stopping—sometimes it seems to me I could save my life by stopping. Because I'm really compulsive about it, I drive that baby. . . .

—*Stephen King*

Two Selections from "Harlan Ellison's Watching"

I. In Which We Scuffle Through the Embers

If tomorrow's early edition of *The New York Times* bore the headline STEPHEN KING NAMED AS DE LOREAN DRUG CONNECTION, it would not by one increment lessen the number of Stephen King books sold this week. Goose the total, more likely.

If Tom Brokaw's lead on the NBC news tonight is, "The King of Chiller Writers, Stephen King, was found late this afternoon in the show window of Saks Fifth Avenue, biting the heads off parochial school children and pouring hot lead down the necks," it would not for an instant slow the rush of film producers to put under option his every published word. Hasten the pace, more likely.

If your cousin Roger from Los Angeles, who works for a food catering service that supplies meals to film companies working on location, called to pass along the latest hot bit of ingroup showbiz gossip, and he confided, "You know Steve King, that weirdo who writes the scary novels? Well, get this: he worked with Errol Flynn as a secret agent for the Nazis during World War II!" it would not drop the latest King tome one notch on the *Publishers Weekly* bestseller listings. Pop it to the top of the chart, more likely.

Stephen King is a phenomenon *sui generis*. I've been told he is fast approaching (if he hasn't already reached it) the point of being the bestselling American author of all time. In a recent survey taken by some outfit or other—and I've looked long and hard for the item but can't find it so you'll have to trust me on this—it was estimated that two out of every five people observed reading a paperback in air terminals or bus stations or suchlike agorae were snout-deep in a King foma.

There has never been anything like King in the genre of the fantastic. Whether you call what he writes "horror stories" or "dark fantasy" or "imaginative thrillers," Steve King is the undisputed, hands-down, nonpareil, free-form champ, three falls out of three.

This is a Good Thing.

Not only because King is a better writer than the usual gag of bestseller epigones who gorge the highest reaches of the lists—the Judith Krantzes, Sidney Sheldons, Erich Segals and V. C. Andrewses of this functionally illiterate world—or because he is, within the parameters of his incurably puckish nature, a "serious" writer, or because he is truly and in the face of a monumental success that would warp the rest of us, a good guy. It is because he is as honest a popular writer as we've been privileged to experience in many a year. He writes a good stick. He never cheats the buyer of a King book. You may or may not feel he brought off a particular job when you get to page last, but you *never* feel you've been had. He does the one job no writer may ignore at peril of tar and feathers, he *delivers*.

Sometimes what he delivers is as good as a writer can get in his chosen milieu, as in *CARRIE* and *THE SHINING* and *THE DEAD ZONE* and *THE DARK TOWER*. Sometimes he's just okay, as in *CUJO* or *CHRISTINE*. And once in a while, as in the *NIGHT SHIFT* and *DIFFERENT SEASONS* collections, he sings way above his range. (And those of us who have been privileged to read the first couple of sections of "The Plant," King's work-in-progress privately printed as annual holiday greeting cards, perceive a talent of uncommon dimensions.)

So why is it that films made from Stephen King's stories turn out, for the most part, to be movies that look as if they'd been chiseled out of Silly Putty by escapees from the Home For the Terminally Inept?

This question, surely one of the burning topics of our troubled cosmos, presents itself anew upon viewing *Firestarter* (Universal), Dino De Laurentiis's latest credential in his struggle to prove to the world that he has all the artistic sensitivity of a piano bench. Based on Steve King's 1980 novel, and a good solid novel it was, this motion picture is (forgive me) a burnt-out case. We're talking scorched earth. Smokey the Bear would need a sedative. Jesus wept. You get the idea.

The plotline is a minor key-change on the basic fantasy concept King used in *CARRIE*. Young female with esper abilities as a pyrotic. (Because the people who make these films think human speech is not our natural tongue, they always gussie up simple locutions so their prolixity will sound "scientific." Pyrotic was not good enough for the beanbags who made this film, so they keep referring to the firestarter as "a possessor of pyrokinetic abilities." In the Kingdom of the Beanbags, a honeydipper is a "Defecatory Residue Repository Removal Supervisor for On-Site Effectation.")

The conflict is created by the merciless hunt for the firestarter—eight-year-old Charlene "Charlie" McGee, played by Drew Barrymore of *E.T.* fame—that is carried out by a wholly improbable government agency alternately known as the Department of Scientific Intelligence and "The Shop." Charlie and her daddy, who also has esper abilities, though his seem to shift and alter as the plot demands, are on the run. The Shop has killed Charlie's mommy, for no particularly clear reason, and they want Charlie for their own nefarious purposes, none of which are logically codified; but we can tell from how oily these three-piece suiters are, that Jack Armstrong would never approve of their program. Charlie and her daddy run, The Shop gnashes its teeth and finally sends George C. Scott as a comic-book hit man after them; and they capture the pair; and they run some special effects tests; and Charlie gets loose; and a lot of people go up in flames; and daddy and the hit man and the head of The Shop all get smoked; and Charlie hitchhikes back to the kindly rustic couple who thought it was cute when she looked at the butter and made it melt.

The screenplay by Stanley Mann, who did not disgrace himself with screen adaptations of *THE COLLECTOR* and *EYE OF THE NEEDLE*, here practices a craft that can best be described as creative typing. Or, more in keeping with technology, what he has wrought now explains to me the previously nonsensical phrase "word processing." As practiced by Mr. Mann, this is the processing of words in the Cuisinart School of Homogeneity.

The direction is lugubrious. As windy and psychotic as Mann's scenario may be, it is rendered even more tenebrous by the ponderous, lumbering, pachydermal artlessness of one Mark L. Lester (*not* the kid-grown-up of *OLIVER*!). Mr. Lester's fame, the *curriculum vita,* that secured for him this directorial sinecure, rests upon a quagmire base of *Truck Stop Women, Bobbie Jo and the Outlaw* (starring Lynda Carter and Marjoe Gortner, the most fun couple to come along since Tracy and Hepburn, Gable and Lombard, Cheech and Chong), *Stunts* and the awesome *Roller Boogie.* The breath do catch, don't it!

Like the worst of the television hacks, who tell you everything three times—Look, she's going to open the coffin!/She's opening the coffin now!/Good lord, she opened the coffin!—Lester and Mann reflect their master's contempt for the intelligence of filmgoers by endless sophomoric explanations of things we know, not the least being a tedious rundown on what esp is supposed to be.

The acting is shameful. From the cynical use of "name stars" in cameo roles that they might as well have phoned in, to the weary posturing of the leads, this is a drama coach's nightmare. Louise Fletcher sleepwalks through her scenes like something Papa Doc might have resurrected from a Haitian graveyard; Martin Sheen, whose thinnest performances in the past have been marvels of intelligence and passion, has all the range of a Barry Manilow ballad; David Keith with his constantly bleeding nose is merely ridiculous; and Drew Barrymore, in just two years, has become a puffy, petulant, self-conscious "actor," devoid of the ingenuousness that so endeared her in *E.T.*.

And what in the world has happened to George C. Scott's previously flawless intuition about which scripts to do? It was bad enough that he consented to appear as the lead in Paul Schrader's loathsome *Hardcore;* but for him willingly to assay the role of John Rainbird, the ponytailed Amerind government assassin, and to perform the part of what must surely be the most detestable character since Joyboy's mother in *The Loved One*, Divine in *Pink Flamingos* or Jabba the Hut, with a verve that borders on teeth-gnashing, is beyond comprehension. It has been a while since I read the novel, but it is not my recollection that the parallel role in the text possessed the McMartin Pre-School child molester mien Scott presents. It is a jangling, counter-productive, unsavory element that is, hideously, difficult to sweep from memory. That it is in some squeamish-making way memorable, is not to Scott's credit. It is the corruption of his talent.

Dino De Laurentiis is the Irwin Allen of his generation, coarse, lacking subtlety, making films of vulgar pretentiousness that personify the most venal attitudes of the industry. He ballyhoos the fact that he has won two Oscars, but hardly anyone realizes they were for Fellini's *La Strada* and *Nights of Cabiria* in 1954 and 1957—and let's not fool ourselves, even if the publicity flaks do: those are *Fellini* films, not De Laurentiis films—long before he became the cottage industry responsible for *Death Wish*, the remakes of *King Kong* and *The Hurricane*, the travesty known as *Flash Gordon*, *Amityville II* and *Amityville 3-D*, *Conan the Barbarian* and the embarrassing *King of the Gypsies*.

But Dino De Laurentiis is precisely the sort of intellect most strongly drawn to the works of Stephen King. He is not a lone blade of grass in the desert. He is merely the most visible growth on the King horizon. Steve King has had nine films made from his words, and there is a formulaic reason why all but one or two of those films has been dross.

II. In Which We Discover Why the Children Don't Look Like Their Parents

Pinter works, though he shouldn't; and I'll be damned if I can discern why; he just does. Bradbury and Hemingway don't; and I think I can figure out why they don't, which is a clue to why Stephen King doesn't, either. Xenogenesis seems to be the question this time around, and if you'll go to your Unabridged and look it up, I'll wait right here for you and tell you all about it when you get back.

Times passes. Leaves flying free from a calendar. The seasons change. The reader returns from the Unabridged.

Now that we understand the meaning of the word Xenogenesis, let us consider why it *is* that King's books—as seemingly hot for metamorphosis as any stuff ever written by anyone—usually wind up as deranged as Idi Amin and as cruel as January in Chicago and as unsatisfying as sex with the pantyhose still on: why it *is* that the children, hideous and crippled offspring, do not resemble their parents.

First, I can just imagine your surprise when I point out that this thing King has been around in the literary consciousness a mere ten years. It was just exactly an eyeblink decade ago that the schoolteacher from Maine wrote:

> Nobody was really surprised when it happened, not really, not at the subconscious level where savage things grow. . . . Showers turning off one by one, girls stepping out, removing pastel bathing caps, toweling, spraying deodorant, checking the clock over the door. Bras were hooked, underpants stepped into. . . . Calls and catcalls rebounded with all the snap and flicker of billiard balls after a hard break.

> . . . Carrie turned off the shower. It died in a drip and a gurgle. . . . It wasn't until she stepped out that they all saw the blood running down her leg.

Second, I'll bet none of you realized what a fluke it was that King took off so abruptly. Well, here's the odd and unpredictable explanation, conveyed because I happened to be there when it happened. (Who else would tell you this stuff, gang?)

Doubleday had purchased *CARRIE* for a small advance. It was, in the corporate cosmos, just another mid-list title, a spooky story to be marketed without much foofaraw among the first novels, the "learn to love your brown rice and get svelte thighs in 30 minutes" offerings, the books one finds in the knockoff catalogues nine months later at $1.49 plus a free shopping bag. But King's editor read that opening sequence in which the telekinetic, Carrie White, gets her first menstrual experience before the eyes of a covey of teenage shrikes, and more than the lightbulb in the locker room exploded. Xeroxes of the manuscript were run off; they were disseminated widely inhouse; women editors passed them on to female secretaries, who took them home and gave them to their friends. That first scene bit hard. It was the essence of the secret of Stephen King's phenomenal success: the everyday experience raised to the mythic level by the application of fantasy to a potent cultural trope. It was Jungian archetype goosed with ten million volts of emotional power. It was the commonly-shared horrible memory of half the population, reinterpreted. It was the flash of recognition, the miracle of that rare instant in which readers dulled by years of reading artful lies felt their skin stretched tight by an encounter with artful truth.

Stephen King, in one apocryphal image, had taken control of his destiny.

I'm not even sure Steve, for all his self-knowledge, has an unvarnished perception of how close he came to remaining a schoolteacher who writes paperback originals as a hobby and to supplement the family income in his spare time when he's not too fagged out from extracurricular duties at the high school.

But just as Ian Fleming became an "overnight success" when John F. Kennedy idly mentioned that the James Bond books—which had been around for years—were his secret passion; just as *DUNE* took off in paperback years after its many rejections by publishers and its disappointing sale in hardcover, when Frank Herbert came to be called "the father of Earth Day" and the novel was included in *THE WHOLE EARTH CATALOG;* just as Joseph Heller, Joseph Heller's agent, Joseph Heller's publisher and the Eastern Literary Establishment that had trashed *CATCH-22* when it was first published, began trumpeting Heller's genius when *another* literary agent (not Heller's), named Candida Donadio, ran around New York jamming the book under people's noses, telling them it was a new American classic; in just that inexplicable, unpredictable, magic way, Doubleday's in-house interest spread. To *Publishers Weekly,* to the desk of Bennett Cerf, to the attention of first readers for the film studios on the Coast, to the sales force mandated to sell that season's line, to the bookstore buyers, and into the cocktail-party chatter of the word-of-mouth crowd. The word spread: this *CARRIE* novel is hot.

And the readers were rewarded. It *was* hot: because King had tapped into the collective unconscious with Carrie White's ordeal. The basic premise was an easy one to swallow, and once down, all that followed was characterization. That is the secret of Stephen King's success in just ten years, and it is the reason why, in my view, movies based on King novels never resemble the perfectly decent novels that inspired them.

In films written by Harold Pinter as screenplay, or in films based on Pinter plays, it is not uncommon for two people to be sitting squarely in the center of a two-shot speaking as follows:

> CORA: (Cockney accent) Would'ja like a nice piece of fried bread for breakfast, Bert?
>
> BERT: (abstracted grunting) Yup. Fried bread'd be nice.
>
> CORA: Yes . . . fried bread *is* nice, in't it?
>
> BERT: Yuh. I like fried bread.
>
> CORA: Well, then, there 'tis. Nice fried bread.
>
> BERT: It's nice fried bread.
>
> CORA: (pleased) Is it nice, then?
>
> BERT: Yuh. Fried bread's nice.

Unless you have heard me do my absolutely hilarious Pinter parody, or have seen every Pinter play and film out of unconstrained admiration for the man's work—as have I—then the foregoing copy cannot possibly read well; nor should it, by all the laws of dramaturgy, *play* well on-screen. But it does. I cannot decipher the code; but the cadences work like a dray horse, pulling the plot and character development, the ever-tightening tension and emotional conflict, toward the goal of mesmerizing involvement that is Pinter's hallmark.

We have in this use of revivified language a sort of superimposed verbal continuum at once alien to our ear and hypnotically inviting. To say more, is to say less. It *does* work.

But if we use the special written languages of Bradbury and Hemingway as examples, we see that such "special speaking" does *not* travel well. It bruises too easily.

Perhaps it is because of the reverence lavished on the material by the scenarists, who are made achingly aware of the fact that they are dealing with *literature*, that blinds them as they build in the flaws we perceive when the film is thrown up on the screen. Perhaps it is because real people in the real world don't usually speak in a kind of poetic scansion. Perhaps it is because we love the primary materials so much that *no* amount of adherence to source can satisfy us. But I don't think any of those hypotheses, singly or as a group, pink the core reason why neither Bradbury's nor Hemingway's arresting fictions ever became memorable films. When Rock Hudson or Rod Steiger or Oskar Werner mouth Bradburyisms such as:

> "Cora. Wouldn't it be nice to take a Sunday walk the way we used to do, with your silk parasol and your long dress swishing along, and sit on those wire-legged chairs at the soda parlor and smell the drugstore the way they used to smell? Why don't drugstores smell that way any more? And order two sarsaparillas for us, Cora, and then ride out in our 1910 Cord to Hannahan's Pier for a box supper and listen to the brass band. How about it? . . . If you could make a wish and take a ride on those oak-lined country roads like they had before cars started rushing, would you *do* it?"

or Gregory Peck or Ava Gardner carry on this sort of conversation from Hemingway:

> "Where did we stay in Paris?"
> "At the Crillon. You know that."
> "Why do I know that?"

"That's where we always stayed."

"No. Not always."

"There and at the Pavillion Henri-Quatre in St. Germain. You said you loved it there."

"Love is a dunghill. And I'm the cock that gets on it to crow."

"If you have to go away, is it absolutely necessary to kill off everything you leave behind? I mean do you have to take away everything? Do you have to kill your horse, and your wife and burn your saddle and your armor?"

what we get is the auditory equivalent of spinach. The actors invariably convey a sense of embarrassment, the dialogue marches from their mouths like Prussian dragoons following Feldmarschall von Blücher's charge at Ligny, and we as audience either wince or giggle at the pomposity of what sounds like posturing.

This "special speaking" is one of the richest elements in Bradbury and Hemingway. It reads as inspired transliteration of the commonplace. But when spoken aloud, by performers whose chief aim is to convey a sense of verisimilitude, it becomes parody. (And that Bradbury and Hemingway have been parodied endlessly, by both high and low talents, only adds to their preeminence. They are *sui generis* for all the gibes.)

The links between King and Bradbury and Hemingway in this respect seem to me to be the explanation why their work does not for good films make. That which links them is this:

Like Harold Pinter and Ernest Hemingway, Ray Bradbury and Stephen King are profoundly allegorical writers.

The four of them *seem* to be mimetic writers, but they aren't! They *seem* to be writing simply, uncomplicatedly, but they aren't! As with the dancing of Fred Astaire—which seems so loose and effortless and easy that even the most lumpfooted of us ought to be able to duplicate the moves—until we try it and fall on our faces—what these writers do is make the creation of High Art seem replicable.

The bare bones of their plots . . .

A sinister manservant manipulates the life of his employer to the point where their roles are reversed.

An ex-prizefighter is tracked down and killed by hired guns for an offense which is never codified.

A "fireman," whose job it is to burn books because they are seditious, becomes secretly enamored of the joys of reading.

A young girl with the latent telekinetic ability to start fires comes to maturity and lets loose her power vengefully.

. . . bare bones that have underlain a hundred different stories that differ from these only in the most minimally variant ways. The plots count for little. The stories are not wildly inventive. The sequence of events is not skull-cracking. It is the *style* in which they are written that gives them wing. They are memorable not because of the thin storylines, but because the manner in which they have been written is so compelling that we are drawn into the fictional universe and once there we are bound subjects of the master creator.

Each of these examples draws deeply from the well of myth and archetype. The collective unconscious calls to us and we go willingly where Hemingway and Bradbury and Pinter . . . and King . . . beckon us to follow.

Stephen King's books work as well as they do, because he is writing more of shadow than of substance. He drills into the flow of cerebro-spinal fiuid with the dialectical function of a modern American mythos, dealing with archetypal images from the pre-conscious or conscious that presage crises in our culture even as they become realities.

Like George Lucas, Stephen King has read Campbell's *THE MASKS OF GOD,* and he knows the power of myth. He knows what makes us tremble. He knows about moonlight reflecting off the fangs. It isn't his plots that press against our chest, it is the impact of his allegory.

But those who bought for film translation *'SALEM'S LOT, CUJO, CHRISTINE, Children of the Corn* and *FIRESTARTER* cannot read. For them, the "special speaking" of King's nightmares, the element that sets King's work so far above the general run of chiller fiction, is merely white noise. It is the first thing dropped when work begins on the script, when the scenarist "takes a meeting" to discuss what the producer or the studio wants delivered. What is left is the bare bones plot, the least part of what King has to offer. (Apart from the name *Stephen King,* which is what draws us to the theater.)

And when the script is in work, the scenarist discovers that there isn't enough at hand to make either a coherent or an artful motion picture. So blood is added. Knives are added. Fangs are added. Special effects grotesqueries are added. But the characters have been dumbed-up, the tone has been lost; the mythic undercurrents have been dammed and the dialectical function has been rendered inoperative. What is left for us is bare bones; blood and cliché.

It is difficult to get Steve King to comment on such artsy-fartsy considerations. Like many other extraordinarily successful artists, he is consciously fearful of the spite and envy his preeminence engenders in critics, other writers, a fickle audience that just sits knitting with Mme. Defarge, waiting for the artist to show the tiniest edge of hubris. Suggest, as I did, to Steve King that *Cujo* is a gawdawful lump of indigestible grue, and he will respond, "I like it. It's just a movie that stands there and keeps punching."

How is the critic, angry at the crippling of each new King novel when it crutches onto the screen, to combat such remarks? By protecting himself in this way—and it is not for the critic to say whether King truly believes these things he says in defense of the butchers who serve up the bloody remnants that were once creditable novels—he unmans all rushes to his defense. Yet without such mounting of the barricades in his support, how can the situation be altered?

Take for instance *Children of the Corn* (New World pictures). Here is a minor fable of frightfulness, a mere thirty pages in King's 1978 collection *NIGHT SHIFT;* a one-punch short story whose weight rests on that most difficult of all themes to handle, little kids in mortal jeopardy. Barely enough there for a short film, much less a feature-length attempt.

How good is this recent adaptation of a King story? *Los Angeles* magazine began its review of *Firestarter* like so: "This latest in a seemingly endless chain of films made from Stephen King novels isn't the worst of the bunch, *Children of the Corn* wins that title hands down." That's how bad it is.

Within the first 3½ minutes (by stopwatch) we see four people agonizingly die from poison, one man gets his throat cut with a butcher knife, one man gets his hand taken off with a meat slicer, a death by pruning hook, a death by sickle, a death by tanning knife . . . at least nine on-camera slaughters, maybe eleven (the intercuts are fastfastfast), and one woman murdered over the telephone, which we don't see, but hear. Stomach go whooops.

Utterly humorless, as ineptly directed as a film school

freshman's class project, acted with all the panache of a grope in the backseat of a VW, *Children of the Corn* features the same kind of "dream sequences" proffered as shtick by Landis in *An American Werewolf in London,* De Palma in *Carrie* and *Dressed to Kill,* and by even less talented of the directorial coterie aptly labeled (by Alain Resnais) "the wise guy smart alecks." These and-then-I-woke-up-and-it-had-all-been-a-bad-dream inserts, which in no way advance the plot of the film, are a new dodge by which Fritz Kiersch, *Corn*'s director, and his contemporaries—bloodletters with view-finders—slip in gratuitous scenes of horror and explicit SFX-enhanced carnage. This has become a trope when adapting King's novels to the screen, a filmic device abhorrent in the extreme not only because it is an abattoir substitute for the artful use of terror, but because it panders to the lowest, vilest tastes of an already debased audience.

It is a bit of cinematic shorthand developed by De Palma specifically for *Carrie* that now occurs with stultifying regularity in virtually *all* of the later movies made from King's books.

I submit this bogus technique is further evidence that, flensed of characterization and allegory, what the makers of these morbid exploitation films are left with does not suffice to create anything resembling the parent novel, however fudged for visual translation. And so fangs are added, eviscerations are added, sprayed blood is added; subtlety is excised, respect for the audience is excised, all restraint vanishes in an hysterical rush to make the empty and boring seem scintillant.

Children of the Corn is merely the latest validation of the theory; or as *Cinefantastique* said in its September 1984 issue: "King's mass-market fiction has inspired some momentous cinematic dreck, but *Children of the Corn* is a new low even by schlock standards."

Of the nine films that originated with Stephen King's writings, only three (in my view, of course, but now almost uniformly buttressed by audience and media judgments) have any resemblance in quality or content—not necessarily both in the same film—to the parent: *Carrie, The Shining* and *The Dead Zone*.

The first, because De Palma had not yet run totally amuck and the allegorical undertones were somewhat preserved by outstanding performances by Sissy Spacek and Piper Laurie.

The second, because it is the vision of Kubrick, always an intriguing way of seeing, even though it is no more King's *The Shining* than Orson Welles's *The Trial* was Kafka's dream.

The third, because David Cronenberg as director is the only one of the field hands in this genre who seems artistically motivated; and because Christopher Walken as the protagonist is one of the quirkiest, most fascinating actors working today, and his portrayal of Johnny Smith is, simply put, mesmerizing.

But of *Cujo's* mindlessness, *Christine*'s cheap tricks, *Firestarter*'s crudeness, *'Salem's Lot*'s television ridiculousness, *Children of the Corn*'s bestial tawdriness and even Steve's own *Creepshow* with its intentional comic book shallowness, nothing much positive can be said. It is the perversion of a solid body of work that serious readers of King, as well as serious movie lovers, must look upon with profound sadness.

We have had come among us in the person of Stephen King a writer of limitless gifts. Perhaps because Stephen himself has taken an attitude of permissiveness toward those who pay him for the right to adopt his offspring, we are left with the choices of enjoying the written work for itself, and the necessity of ignoring everything on film . . . or of hoping that one day, in a better life, someone with more than a drooling lust for the exploitation dollar attendant on Stephen King's name will perceive the potential cinematic riches passim these special fantasies. There *must* be an honest man or woman out there who understands that King's books are about more than fangs and blood.

All it takes is an awareness of allegory, subtext, the parameters of the human condition . . . and reasonable family resemblance.

Good writing in itself is a pleasure, and it can seduce you into the story. I'm not very concerned with style, but I *am* concerned with the balance. Language should have a balance the reader can feel and get into—rhythm to the language as it moves along. Because if the reader is seduced in the story, then it carries him away.

—*Stephen King*

The Unexpected and the Inevitable

by Michael McDowell

It was with some hesitation that I agreed to write about Stephen King's work. I was trained as an academic, with an eye towards analysis and criticism, but now I have only contempt for the sapping methods of literary "appreciation" taught in colleges and graduate schools. The idea of analyzing a volume of writing that I think very good seems unappealing and pointless. Increasingly, I find myself in the critical vein that either gushes, "Oh God it's great you've got to read it!" or moans, "Can you believe that anybody would publish this," or is silent from indifference. So that I think the best—and probably most helpful—reaction to King's work is a simple, "Oh God I've read everything, and I haunt the bookstores waiting for the next one."

Certainly, that is the common reaction.

Another hesitation is that my view of King and his work is probably skewed. In the first place, I know the man, and like him very much. For another thing, I am a writer of occult fiction myself, and therfore read King with a more specialized eye than his usual admirer. Usually, in fact, to be read by another writer is like having a carpenter over. He's not going to admire your taste in decoration, he's going to be looking at how you *built* the house. You try to show him the new living room furniture, and he wants to know what kind of cement you put in the foundations. When I read Stephen King, I'm looking to see how he puts the damn books and stories together, and what makes them stand so straight and solid.

This innate, technical evaluation is in operation every time I read a book of fiction. (For pleasure, I have to make do with books on astronomy and particle physics.) I pick up a book with a promisingly lurid cover. On page twelve I've guessed not only the premise, but five important plot points, and the ending. I always know what's coming next. Discordances of tone grate. Misshapen or improbable dialogue sounds in my mind like Hanna-Barbera voices. It's a great tribute to King that by some point in the story, I no longer think about the cement in the cellar foundations and don't care how tight the sashes are in the window frames. I'm simply propelled room to room through the narrative, as by an energetic host, gaping and wary and fearing. It can take me a great while to finish one of King's books, simply because he transforms me into a timid reader. "Oh God," I think, "he's not going to do *that,* is he?" I put the book down for a space, till I have courage to pick it up again and make sure that, indeed, he *is* going to do it.

He always does, of course. No wet fuses. And the climaxes are exactly right. The dynamite is laid, stick by stick, and every one of them goes off, in a precise, rhythmic pattern.

Which brings me to the point of this little essay.

Stephen King's rhythm.

It is what stands out most for me in the books, it is what makes me sweat with jealousy when I read him, it is what—I suspect—makes the narratives so enormously effective.

It has become increasingly apparent to me that books rise or fall by the rhythm of the narrative. A story can carry you along—despite lapses in grammar, probability, or tone—if the rhythm is right. This rhythm is manifest in many ways, and in different measurements—that is to say that there are rhythms that are apparent on a scale of kilometers (an entire book), and rhythms that are manifest on a scale of centimeters (a sentence or two), and everything in between. In fact, a novel may be looked at as a series of interlocking rhythms. Five sentences that are rhythmically just right form a good paragraph; five good paragraphs, set up just so, make a good section to be separated by asterisks; six good sections make a very good chapter; and then all you have to do is write thirty of those, arrange them in the right order, smooth down the lumps, and now you have a good, rhythmic book—one that propels the reader forward. Prologue to *fin*.

People out there who don't write books, or who write books thoughtlessly, are saying, "That can't possibly be how it's done." But it is. It's how Stephen King writes, and I know because, one, it's how I write and I recognize the phenomenon when I see it; and two, he's told me so.

Of course you can't freehand a chart of arcs and say, "Well, here's the shape and rhythm of my new novel." But you can have a story in mind, and start writing it. The rhythm begins to develop on its own accord. It's astonishing how quickly it's established—usually for me by the end of the second chapter. And every book's rhythm is different, just as the tone of every book is different. Then, as you proceed further and further into the story, the rhythm becomes more complex, and more demanding. You can't always feel when it's right, but by God, you surely do know when it's *wrong*. When it's wrong—and you're conscientious—you stop and fix it, and then you go on. At the end, you sit down, read the book through—not for spelling errors, not for the rightness of the dialogue or the plausibility of motivation—but to make sure that it reads well. Which is to say, to make certain that the rhythm is right.

Some scenes, you'll invariably find, are overlong considering their importance. This would mean that a reader would spend longer with them than he should. It's a fault most obvious in transitions between disjointed sections. So you trim them back so that the amount of space they take up on the printed page is commensurate with their relative importance to the narrative.

On the other hand, some important scene may not be given its proper weight in the story simply because you wrote it too briefly. Then, even if you got everything in the first time, you have to write a few more pages, simply so that the reader will be slowed down a bit during the important bits.

Of course, there are no hard and fast rules about length *versus* importance. You know when it's wrong, and you can have a pretty good idea when it's right. If you write as much as King does (or as I do), the process of meting out space in a narrative becomes second nature. You don't often get it wrong. There's a little mental tape measure that reads off in pretty exact measurements. "This scene ought to get twelve pages. This transition ought to be three paragraphs and a snatch of dialogue. This can't be more than a page and a half."

To illustrate:

A few months ago, Stephen King asked me to read through the manuscript of his new novel, *MISERY,* and tell him what I thought. I gladly acceded to the request, and devoured the book. I liked it very much, and saw many things to praise, and very few to object to. I made one small suggestion for a refinement of cruelty, and King said, "Very nice. I'll add it. Anything else?"

"The climax needs one more beat," I said. "I have no idea what it should be, but you need about six more pages of *something.* To slow it down. Because now it's over too quickly. Just a beat, that's all."

"I felt that," King replied. "But I was hoping I was wrong. I wasn't. I'll fix it."

And I know that he will have fixed it by the time the book is published. Because I've never come across even so small a lapse as that in one of his published books. I was gratified to find that error in rhythm, in fact, because it showed me that he had to work (even if only a little) to establish his perfectly rhythmic narratives. It wasn't *all* sheer and casual talent.

What this also shows, I think, is that the process of creating a rhythm actually exists. When I said that *MISERY'*s climax needed an extra beat, King knew exactly what I was talking about. A build-up needs a pay-off, and the pay-off has to be in proper proportion to the build-up. Otherwise, the story is unbalanced, and in some way the reader will be dissatisfied. All through King's books, there are smaller build-ups and pay-offs, culminating in a final pay-off that balances everything that came before. One great arc encompasses all the smaller ones. The pattern may be worked out subconsciously, or by instinct, but it's still no accident.

I remember when a consciousness of this kind of narrative rhythm first came into focus for me. It wasn't after studying literature through four years of college and three of graduate school. It was reading *THE SHINING*. And it was the scariest moment in the book, the point at which the boy Danny, having willed away the vision of the dead, drowned woman in Room 217, finds her bloated hands round his neck.

> Time passed. And he was just beginning to relax, just beginning to realize that the door must be unlocked and he could go, when the years-damp, bloated, fish-smelling hands closed softly around his throat and he was turned implacably around to stare into the dead and purple face.

What happens next?

What happens next is that we get a new chapter. And it's not a chapter telling us what happens to Danny, and whether he's killed, whether he's only injured, whether he's able to will the ghastly residue away. It's a chapter dealing with Jack's parents.

I never read ten pages so quickly in my life, desperate to know what had become of the boy.

And when I found him again, at the beginning of the *next* chapter, Danny had bruises on his neck and was half-catatonic—but he wasn't dead.

At that point, I put the book down, and I said, aloud, "What a cheap device!"

Then I immediately incorporated the technique into the book that I was writing at the time.

Now, of course, the trick seems obvious. Bring the narrative to a fever of suspense—and then maintain that suspense by switching focus to an unrelated incident. While some poor victim hangs over the edge of the cliff by a fraying rope, pebbles spilling into his face, we switch to his distressed girlfriend begging a skeptical park ranger for assistance in finding him. The boyfriend can hang there for quite a while, in fact, till we get back to him. It's a cheap use of rhythm, but done correctly, it works. And it may be done *so* well, in fact, that the manipulated reader feels nothing but a straightforward anxiety for the poor victim at the end of the rope.

For me, the great lesson of that narrative sequence from *THE SHINING* was the importance of rhythm. I'm faintly embarrassed that it took this sledgehammer example of the thing to show me that. Now, I'm happy to say, I can be appreciative of much subtler sequence rhythms in King's work.

I much admire *Rita Hayworth and Shawshank Redemption,* the first of the four novellas that comprise *DIFFERENT SEASONS,* and as I read it, I was astonised by the delicacy of the construction. To nearly any reader, it is apparent that the climax of the story will be the attempt of Andy Dufresne to escape from Shawshank prison. The middle part of the story consists of various legal attempts that Dufresne makes to avoid or to shorten his term in prison. His trial. His model prisoner attitude. His discovery of the real murderer. Each of these fails, as we know it will. Then, at last, he's left with only one solution—an escape from the prison. What we've been waiting for. Something clever, something harrowing.

And of course, I assumed, a great deal of suspense would be tied up in whether he makes it or not.

Here again, King astonished me.

Only three-quarters of the way into the narrative, I came across this paragraph:

In 1975, Andy Dufresne escaped *from* Shawshank. He hasn't been recaptured, and I don't think he ever will be. In fact, I don't think Andy Dufresne even exists anymore. But I think there's a man down in Zihuatanego, Mexico named Peter Stevens. Probably running a very new small hotel in this year of our Lord 1977.

When I read that paragraph, I looked up from the book puzzled and shocked. I flipped to the end of the story, and saw that there was a good quarter of the narrative to go. Why give away the fact that Dufresne makes his escape, and survives? How would the rest of the story maintain a balance of suspense against what had come before?

The answer should have been obvious—the narrative maintained suspense through rhythm.

What I thought would come next was a detailing of the escape. But I was wrong.

What came next was the *discovery* of the escape by the consternated officials of the prison, told in completely satisfying detail. But still we didn't know *how* the escape was accomplished. And it is this that comes next, the narrator's methodical analysis of what *must* have happened, because it couldn't have happened any other way. Then at the last, a coda—the narrator's release from prison, and his resolve to join up with Dufresne in Mexico.

Thus, three very satisfying sections of narrative follow the "give-away" of Dufresne's successful escape, and each of them is a payoff for something set up earlier in the book. The corrupt prison officials' comeuppance. The method of Dufresne's harrowing escape. And—what came as a pleasant surprise—the resolution of the narrator's future.

None of these passages would have been half so

effective if we'd been troubled with wondering whether Dufresne would succeed with his escape. That question put to rest in a brief paragraph, we're able to relish the solution of three more questions.

Rita Hayworth and Shawshank Redemption has a lovely, audacious shape, and I can't believe that it requires another writer to appreciate it fully.

There is another example of bold rhythm in *Apt Pupil*, the second and longest novella in *DIFFERENT SEASONS*. The very title of the piece leads us to believe that Todd will be instructed in Nazi Dussander's evil, and (because King never pulls his punches), we realize well before the end that Todd will take his rifle to the edge of the freeway and begin picking off motorists—in a feeble imitation of the concentration camps' commanders' power to decide, casually and arbitrarily, who is to live and who to die. That snipering will be the Apt Pupil's graduation exercise, and it will end the story. That's the Inevitable Conclusion to the story.

But I know that while King delivers the inevitable, he never delivers it in quite the way I expected it. If I'm waiting at the front door, waiting for the bell, he goes around to the back, and knocks.

So what, I wondered, would be the Surprise to temper the Inevitability?

Here's how *Apt Pupil* ends:

> *"I'm king of the world!"* he shouted mightily at the high blue sky, and raised the rifle two-handed over his head for a moment. Then, switching it to his right hand, he started towards that place above the freeway where the land fell away and where the dead tree would give him shelter.

It was five hours later and almost dark before they took him down.

In other words, the snipering happens, but we don't see it. But all our worst imaginings—of what misery a young man with a rifle above a freeway can cause in the space of five hours—are excited by that simple, final sentence. This long story ends with a jolt precisely commensurate with what has gone before.

I remember when I first read that, I was shocked by its cold brevity. Then disturbed—because I sat back and thought to myself, "All right, just how many people did he kill, and who were they, and if I had been driving along that freeway, would he have picked *me* out for death?"

And then I nodded a little nod of professional acknowledgment to King, who had done it again. Provided me with the unexpected and the inevitable.

King likes horror movies. King has written them, and for every script he's written, he's probably seen three hundred. In a film, it is an easy matter to give the viewer a jolt. The hapless victim—let's make her a girl this time—climbs naked out of bed and peers through a darkened window, checking out that strange noise outside. She sees nothing. She turns back to her boyfriend, and says, "I didn't see any—" At that moment of course, a great hairy arm crashes through the window, grabs her around the throat, and a moment later, she spills backward through the sash in a shower of glass, never to be seen again. Later the boyfriend dies as well. (This is another in the "Fuck and Die" school of film production.)

Ominous music leads up to the jolt, the jolt comes in a *sforzando* of strings, and the audience gasps and represses (or does not repress) its screams.

But how do you do the equivalent in a book?

To *see* a hand crash through the window when you're not expecting it is not the same thing as to read, "She turned away from the window and reassured her boyfriend that there was nothing outside. Then a great hairy arm crashed through the window and caught her around the neck."

Not the same thing at all.

The difficulty is this. In a film, you can have five minutes of real (or is it "reel"?) time leading up to the climactic moment, and then the climactic moment takes less than a second. You have no control over the speed or the sequence of the action.

You can't do that in a book, because you can't control a reader's pace. You can't say, "All right, Gentle Reader, here's a slow part where I'm building suspense. Wait a minute, I'm still building—feel that terror mount?—a couple of paragraphs more, just to make sure you're good and primed, and now—and now—*voy-la!*— here's the surprise! Here's the great hairy arm through the window, and my God, weren't you scared?"

I've read books like that. I've even said hypocritically nice things to authors who write after that fashion, and if I'm not damned for *that,* I won't be damned for anything.

You just can't do it the way the movies can.

Or can you?

King obviously can, because his books are genuinely frightening. They deliver honest jolts. And they do it—have you guessed?—through rhythm.

There are ways of slowing a reader down and speeding him up. They are, in their way, quite technical, and have to do with the length of sentences, the length of words within those sentences, with the length and the alternation of the paragraphs the sentences make up.

A succession of long paragraphs, each composed of long sentences with great big words in them, is a lulling read. A good writer can make such a passage almost hypnotic. Then a one-line paragraph can jolt you right out of that trance. From the same sequence in *THE SHINING*, dealing with Danny's exploration of Room 217:

> A long room, old fashioned, like a Pullman car. Tiny white hexagonal tiles on the floor. At the far end, a toilet with the lid up. At the right, a wash-basin and another mirror above it, the kind that hides a medicine cabinet. To the left, a huge white tub on claw feet, the shower curtain pulled closed. Danny stepped into the bathroom and walked toward the tub dreamily, as if propelled from outside himself, as if this whole thing were one of the dreams Tony had brought him, that he would perhaps see something nice when he pulled the shower curtain back, something Daddy had forgotten or Mommy had lost, something that would make them both happy—
>
> So he pulled the shower curtain back.
>
> The woman in the tub had been dead for a long time . . .

Notice particularly how the last sentence of the paragraph describing the bathroom runs on, repetitious and soothing and dreaming. Then that's cut off by a single line of simple action—"So he pulled the shower curtain back"—which is given a paragraph of its own. Then the next paragraph begins in a terrible, matter-of-fact way—and that's the jolt.

When I say that the method for achieving this jolt is technical, I'm not suggesting that King did anything other than sit down at his keyboard and type out those very words, first draft, as they appear there. The technique is in his brain, and probably he doesn't know any way to write except in this casually efficient and effective manner. But to have constructed that passage in any other way would not have been either as efficient or effective. King's technique placed the words, the sentences, the paragraph breaks, the very punctuation in the manner that would precisely maximize the current of the jolt.

There are times when this rhythm is so important that the words themselves almost don't matter—when the sound of the words in the brain and their length and their alternation is to be considered much more than any specific meaning they convey. In the above passage, I would put the sequence, "as if this whole thing were one of the dreams Tony had brought him, that he would perhaps see something nice when he pulled the shower curtain back, something Daddy had forgotten or Mommy had lost, something that would make them both happy," into that category. The repetitious, stringalong nature of the passage is the giveaway—at least to me, who use it frequently—that it's the lulling rhythm at work on the reader here, and not the actual content of Danny's groping mind.

By the same token, there are ways of speeding a reader up.

One-sentence paragraphs is one. Short sentences within those short paragraphs.

Even sentence fragments to serve as paragraphs.

Rapid alteration of dialogue, with no adverbs (". . . , he admonished balefully") and as few identifying tags as possible (". . . , said the dead saleslady").

Put so badly, these sound—once again—like the cheapest of the cheap devices. But they work, and good writers use them. From the first page to the last.

And, contrariwise, bad writers don't use them. A bad writer may tell a story, and the story he tells may be a good one. But if he can't control the reader, the good story he tells won't be told well, and the reader won't be satisfied. I really do believe it is as simple as that.

Someone once asked me what I thought horror fiction did. What its purpose was. (King is asked this question frequently as well. It is only a very little less annoying that "Where do you get your ideas?") I don't know what he stipulated as the purpose of horror fiction, but I replied that when I wrote horror fiction, I tried to take the improbable, the unimaginable, and the impossible, and make it seem not only possible—but inevitable.

That is to say, the writer of horror fiction propels—or tries to propel—the reader up in a spiraling succession of improbabilities, and convince him that there is no other way that the story could unfold. That he presents the reader, at every turn, with a surprise—that after a moment's consideration becomes an inevitability.

You want the reader to say to himself, "Oh God that was a surprise, and a scary one, and I should have seen it coming, but I didn't, and yes—the author is right—it couldn't have been any other way." (This is, of course, only a little better than reciting the splendid review that the *New York Times* is going to accord your next work.)

This combination of the Unexpected and the Inevitable is, I think, what King probably does best. The foundation for the success of our belief in his narrative is laid, as has been often said, in the crushing normality of his settings and characters. I would add also that his characters' thoughts are crushingly normal as well. That's why we believe in them. The action unfolds with a semblance of worldly verisimilitude, and then the unexpected intrudes. The descriptions of the horrors tend to be flattened rather than heightened: "The woman in the bathtub had been dead for a long time . . ." (This is surely better, one can see, than "The terrified boy stared at the naked, corrupting, purulent, *grinning* corpse of what had once probably been a cheerful middle-aged woman . . ." Which is how some writers of horror fiction write, I'm sorry to say.) King's flatness in these descriptions accords the horrors the same legitimacy as his characters' lawn-mowers, and their thirst for a cold Pabst, and their tedious marital squabbles.

It is this rhythm of the mundane and the unnatural—the *crushingly* mundane and the *stupefyingly* unnatural, I think I can say—that provides the power of King's horror. That the same language is used for both gives a terrible credence to the reality of the unnatural. I admire Lovecraft—and considering King's tributary story *Jerusalem's Lot,* it appears that he did too. It may be that he still does, but there seems to me to be little left of that progenitor in King. No obscure eldritch adjectives, no *unthinkable* monstrosities, no *unnameable* deities, no *indescribable* horrors, and no straggling dead man's ravings to end a story as the flapping obscenity sweeps down out of the sky and bursts through the shutters. King's characters may go mad, King's narration does not. It remains clear-eyed, matter-of-factual, observing entirely too much for the reader's comfort.

(What King still has in common with Lovecraft is the overwhelming sense of place. Castle Rock is not as overtly sinister as the valley of the Miskatonic, but nasty things happen there. And if there's not an actual map of Castle Rock on King's bulletin board, I've a pretty good idea that if he were set down in that mythical municipality, he'd be able to get from the TasTee Freeze to the Dew Drop Inn without asking directions from a homicidal cop.)

In this regard, the alternation of the mundane with the unnatural, King employs a kind of flatness—an absence of rhythmic alternation. When the corpse trundles on in a King novel, there are no Bernard Herrmann strings in the background, but the same Muzak that was playing before plays on, to disconcerting effect. In this case, it is the *absence* of a perceptible rhythm that lends its heightening effect.

I don't really think it would matter if not a single reader of King's work understood, in a technical way, how his books are built on interconnecting and intersecting rhythms. For despite his narrative expertise, King's books work for most in a way that they perceive as visceral. And, as I say, I no longer belong to the camp that analyzes, draws apart, deduces formulae and sketches diagrams. I'm happy to say I'm on that side that passes around a book (not a reviewer's copy, but one paid for with American currency at a book store or a supermarket or a shop that sells cigars and lottery tickets) and says, "Hey listen, you got to read this, and I promise you, it'll give you fucking nightmares."

There are big things that scare people, like dying, which is the really big casino. Most people get scared anytime you venture into taboo territory. While we've become more explicit about things like sex, we've really tightened up on death and disfigurement. Those things scare people a lot because we put such a premium on being handsome and young.

—Stephen King

The Good Fabric: Of Night Shifts and Skeleton Crews

by William F. Nolan

The good fabric of things sometimes has a way of unraveling with shocking suddenness. —*Stephen King*

Over the past two decades Stephen King has published 17 novels (including the five by Richard Bachman) and some 70 shorter works of fiction. Thus far, into 1985, 52 of these shorter works have been collected by King in *NIGHT SHIFT* (20 stories), *DIFFERENT SEASONS* (4 novellas with 2 earlier stories incorporated into them), *THE DARK TOWER: THE GUNSLINGER* (5 stories) and *SKELETON CREW* (20 stories and a novella).

King's longer works continue to merit extensive coverage, but his short stories have been critically ignored. Unjustifiably so, since King is a modern master of the short story and his work in this category deserves separate consideration. Therefore, bypassing the novels and novellas, I shall limit myself, in this study, to the 40 shorter works in his two main collections, *NIGHT SHIFT* and *SKELETON CREW.*

For purposes of tracing the author's year-by-year development in terms of theme, locale and characters, the stories are examined in chronological order, as King wrote them, and not in the order in which they appear in his collections.

☐ *The Reaper's Image* deals with a death mirror; those who gaze into its shining depths are never seen again. King wrote this story in 1965 and though the plot is thin, lacking suspense, the imagery, dialogue and characterization are all remarkably professional for an 18-year-old. Even at this early age, he displays the talent of a born storyteller.

☐ *Jerusalem's Lot* was written two years later, as a class project, when King was a college sophomore. He called it "an outrageous Lovecraft pastiche," and it is indeed that. But this story is much more than a stylish bow to H. P. Lovecraft. It marks King's first use of the Maine locale he would make his own, and it prefigures his second major novel, *'SALEM'S LOT,* published in 1975. Additionally, it is written with a skill far beyond the reach of most college students. Again, the born storyteller in action; an early flexing of creative muscle.

☐ *Cain Rose Up,* concerning a student who turns campus sniper, was also written while King was in college. Printed when he was 21, it proved that he could handle a contemporary theme of urban horror with force and firm stylistic control. A total departure from Lovecraft.

☐ *Here There Be Tygers* (1968) offers an early example of King's wry humor. This taut little fable, dealing with a teacher-devouring tiger in the boys' room at grade school, owes an obvious debt to the dark whimsy of John Collier.

□ *Strawberry Spring* (1968), like *Cain Rose Up,* is another effective urban horror tale. No fantasy here; the events are realistically based. The first-person narrator tells us about a killer, Springheel Jack, who stalks his victims at a New England Teachers' College. King displays firm mood control in this poetic shocker.

□ *Night Surf* (1969) offers a chilling preview of King's expansive science fiction novel, *THE STAND* (1978). In each, a killer flu has ravaged the world. The characters dramatized here are cynical, hard-edged teenagers living at the edge of death on a beach in southern Maine. A starkly brutal doomsday tale.

□ *Graveyard Shift* (1970) takes us into the dank, rotting subcellar of an old rat-infested mill in the backwoods of Maine. The rats get bigger as the narrative unfolds in a story rich in sensory detail.

□ *I Am the Doorway* (1971) is science fiction horror, dramatizing the deep-space effects of a Venus probe on a returned astronaut. He's back home—the Florida Keys—but he's not alone. Technically clever and chillingly effective.

□ *Battleground* (1972) offers a perfect example of King's ability to render total fantasy in matter-of-fact terms. We believe, absolutely, that the miniature soldiers who have made a battleground of a penthouse apartment are capable of killing the adult protagonist. King employs his tiny helicopters and explosive rockets to deadly purpose. We might laugh at these frenzied little guys, but we're damned glad they aren't after *us*.

□ *The Mangler* (1972) is a masterwork of mechanized horror. King is second to none in his ability to bring machines to soul-chilling life on a printed page. His actual working experience in an industrial laundry lends special depth to this unsettling drama of a demoniac

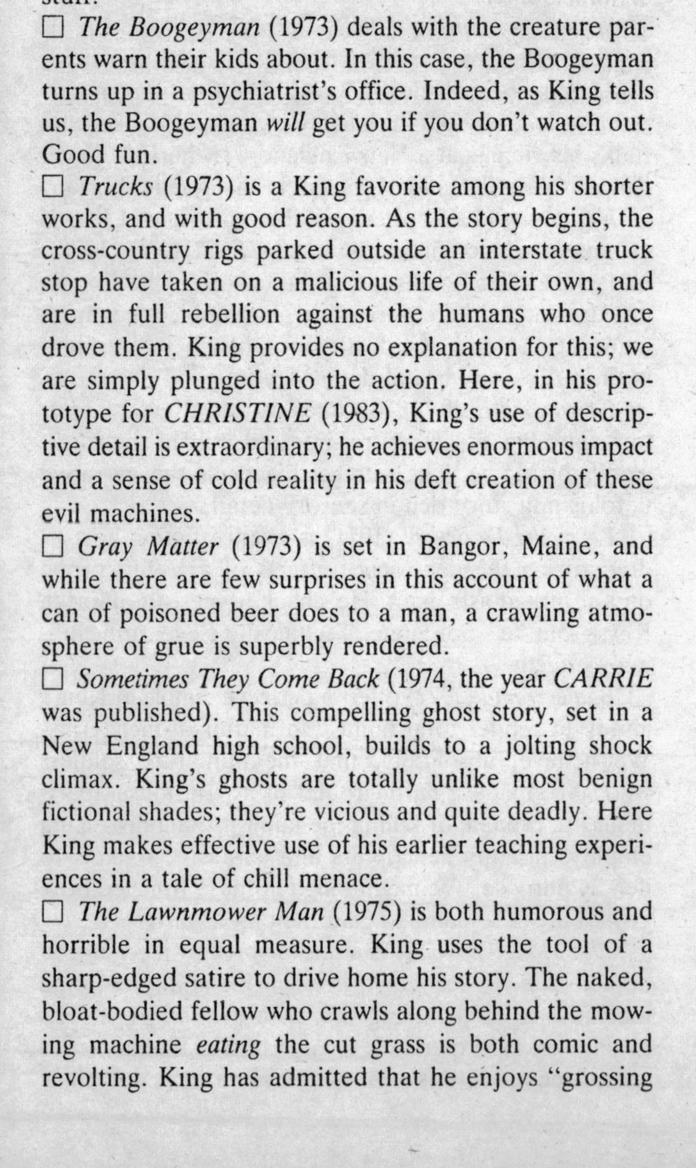

steam-pressing machine on a killing rampage. Strong stuff.

☐ *The Boogeyman* (1973) deals with the creature parents warn their kids about. In this case, the Boogeyman turns up in a psychiatrist's office. Indeed, as King tells us, the Boogeyman *will* get you if you don't watch out. Good fun.

☐ *Trucks* (1973) is a King favorite among his shorter works, and with good reason. As the story begins, the cross-country rigs parked outside an interstate truck stop have taken on a malicious life of their own, and are in full rebellion against the humans who once drove them. King provides no explanation for this; we are simply plunged into the action. Here, in his prototype for *CHRISTINE* (1983), King's use of descriptive detail is extraordinary; he achieves enormous impact and a sense of cold reality in his deft creation of these evil machines.

☐ *Gray Matter* (1973) is set in Bangor, Maine, and while there are few surprises in this account of what a can of poisoned beer does to a man, a crawling atmosphere of grue is superbly rendered.

☐ *Sometimes They Come Back* (1974, the year *CARRIE* was published). This compelling ghost story, set in a New England high school, builds to a jolting shock climax. King's ghosts are totally unlike most benign fictional shades; they're vicious and quite deadly. Here King makes effective use of his earlier teaching experiences in a tale of chill menace.

☐ *The Lawnmower Man* (1975) is both humorous and horrible in equal measure. King uses the tool of a sharp-edged satire to drive home his story. The naked, bloat-bodied fellow who crawls along behind the mowing machine *eating* the cut grass is both comic and revolting. King has admitted that he enjoys "grossing out" his readers and here the technique works splendidly.

☐ *The Ledge* (1976) is a tour de force in suspense, the cold-blooded tale of a crime lord's revenge on the man who took his wife. King puts you on a 5-inch-wide concrete ledge encircling a windswept building 43 stories above the city streets in a sequence nerve-wracking enough to induce permanent nightmares. You don't *read* this one—you sweat it out!

☐ *I Know What You Need* (1976) is told from a feminine viewpoint (she's a campus coed in Maine) and deals with the use of psychic power in sustaining a neurotically dangerous relationship. A low-key thriller with expert control of mood and tone.

☐ *Children of the Corn* (1977) is set in the farming country of Nebraska and details the fate of a tourist couple trapped by a band of teen cultists who worship a Corn God (He Who Walks Behind the Rows). Reminiscent of Golding's *LORD OF THE FLIES,* it shocks and convinces.

☐ *One for the Road* (1977) forms a dark coda to *'SALEM'S LOT,* with its red-eyed vampires still on the prowl for victims in southern Maine. The story is told in first-person, during a blizzard, and King manages a remarkable sense of weather; you can feel the blowing snow against your skin. A gripping narrative.

☐ *The Man Who Loved Flowers* (1977) is light and lyrical in its deft portrayal of a hammer-killer endlessly seeking his lost love. Again, King gives us some very real weather—a lovely summer in New York. There is irony here as King reveals darkness within light.

☐ *Quitters, Inc.* (1978) is another tour de force, dealing with a protagonist determined to kick the smoking habit. He signs up with a clinic which uses extremely ruthless methods to effect its cures. This one is not credible, but King gives it a good shot.

☐*The Last Rung on the Ladder* (1978) is a moving, powerfully effective mainstream tale of a close brother-sister relationship climaxed by tragedy. Superb story-telling.

☐*The Woman in the Room* (1978) is the all-too-real mainstream portrait of a son who gives his cancer-ravaged mother the gift of death. An emotionally shattering story, told with a quiet, steely intensity and based directly on King's feelings about his own mother who also died of cancer.

☐*Nona* (1978) follows a young man on a murder spree in the Castle Rock area of Maine. (The town of Castle Rock, used by King in many of his stories, is fictional but is based on real towns in the Bangor area.) The story's title character may or may not be real; she is the dark force setting the murders in motion and may only be alive in the twisted mind of the young killer. strong stuff.

☐*The Monkey* (1980) concerns a toy that brings death to those who hear it clash its cymbals. Though written with power and force, the story lacks interior logic. (Why didn't the protagonist simply *destroy* the monkey?) Also, it suffers from over-length.

☐*The Wedding Gig* (1980) is successfully offbeat—a jazz/murder tale set in a small town near Chicago in 1927. King's swift, hard-boiled approach perfectly fits the action.

☐*Morning Deliveries* (circa 1980) presents us with a character fully as bizarre as "The Lawnmower Man." This weirdo gleefully delivers poison and deadly spiders with the morning milk. A dark little vignette that originally formed a section of an aborted King novel.

☐*Big Wheels: A Tale of the Laundry Game* (1980) is also part of the same unfinished novel and is equally strange. Set in rural Pennsylvania, it follows the fate of two school chums whose sudden reunion leads to death and murder. Odd and fascinating.

☐ *The Jaunt* (1981) was admittedly inspired by Alfred Bester's novel *THE STARS MY DESTINATION* and is one of King's rare excursions into science fiction. Set in a futuristic New York spaceport, with a family about to undergo a "jaunt" to Mars, it traces the history of jaunting and ends on a note of raw shock-horror.

☐ *The Man Who Would Not Shake Hands* (1981) is, to my mind, a failure in that its basic premise is unworkable. King's title character has been put under a curse: his touch causes death. Therefore, he refuses to shake hands. At the climax, he dies by shaking hands with himself. Oh, come on, Steve! This one is downright silly.

☐ *The Reach* (1981) deals with an old woman who has spent her entire life on a remote island in Maine and who finally decides to cross the winter-frozen reach (the body of water separating island from mainland) as her final act. Her snowbound crossing represents our passage from life to death and King invests the sequence with tremendous power. A story of emotional echoes, beautifully fashioned.

☐ *Survivor Type* (1982) is a real stomach churner. We share the day to day horror of a man trapped on a tiny island, without food, who begins to cannibalize himself, piece by piece, to stay alive. And when he *drools* over the prospect of eating his own fingers . . . . Well, yech! King's black humor helps ease the reader through it.

☐ *The Raft* (1982) is, without question, the most harrowing tale of terror I've yet encountered—and I've been reading extensively in this genre since the mid-1940s. For sheer gruesome impact, this one is unsurpassed in the King canon. The premise is simple:

four teenagers (two boys and their girlfriends) swim from a chilly fall beach out to a wooden raft floating quietly on a deserted lake in Pennsylvania. But something else also floats there: a water-thing that looks like a large black oil slick—with hypnotic powers and a ravenous hunger for human flesh. Here King is relentless and unsparing. The graphic description of one teenager's bloody demise, as he is sucked to bone-grinding death through a between-boards crack in the raft, is brilliantly revolting—the ultimate King gross-out. You'll never forget *The Raft.*

☐ *Word Processor of the Gods* (1983) deals with a failed writer (a King who *didn't* make it) who is given a second chance to reshape his life via a magic word processor. Deeply felt, and capped with a happy ending that is both valid and emotionally real.

☐ *Uncle Otto's Truck* (1983) sits today in a field fronting a woods road near Bangor, Maine. King, having driven by it many times, decided to build a story around it. He conjured up a neat little fantasy in which the gutted wreck comes to murderous life. The ending, involving an oil-filled corpse, is deliciously grotesque.

☐ *Mrs. Todd's Shortcut* (1984) is also factually based. King's wife, he claims, is always on the lookout for back-road shortcuts to their home in Bangor. Thus, Mrs. Todd is Tabitha King. In this bit of modern folklore, Mrs. T. finds the ultimate shortcut—into another dimension.

☐ *Gramma* (1984) is a balefully frightening mood piece in which an 8-year-old boy discovers that his dead grandmother was a witch, with powers beyond death. Terrific suspense.

☐ *The Ballad of the Flexible Bullet* (1984) suffers from an overlong narrative. It deals with elves who inhabit writers' typewriters and would have been far more

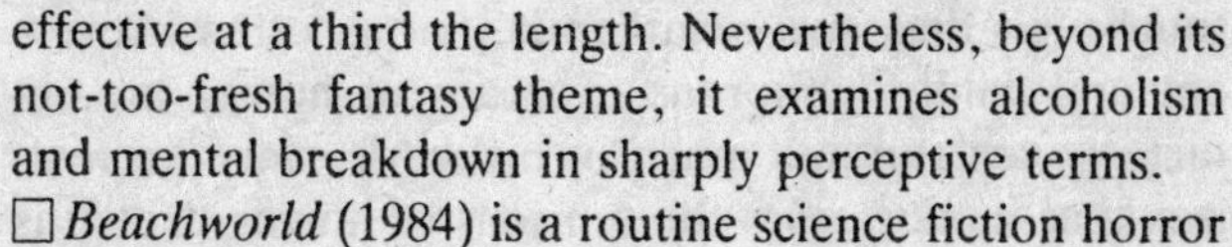

effective at a third the length. Nevertheless, beyond its not-too-fresh fantasy theme, it examines alcoholism and mental breakdown in sharply perceptive terms.

□ *Beachworld* (1984) is a routine science fiction horror tale set on a world of living sand. Not much of the King magic is in evidence here.

□ *The Revelations of 'Becka Paulson* (1984) is the bizarre study of a woman with a fragmenting mind. She talks with Jesus (who's on her TV set) and ends up electrocuting herself and her husband. Raw drama, expertly orchestrated.

These 40 stories form an impressive body of fiction and while it is King's work in the novel that has earned him his reputation and overwhelming commercial success, I feel that his short fiction is equally important. In fact, had he never written a novel, judged strictly on the basis of these 40 stories, King's place in the pantheon of horror fiction would be secure.

There is a depth of feeling in much of King that transcends the horror genre; he truly understands the Human Condition. He undercuts the bullshit. His people bleed emotionally as well as physically. They are real. We feel we have met them, loved them, feared them, suffered their losses and shared their triumphs. Also, he has an amazing perception of place and climate. Not just for his home state of Maine (though no writer has rendered it with greater poetic realism), but for the country stretching from ocean to ocean; he understands our attitudes and our culture, understands its slang, its politics, its hype, its brand names, its myths and misconceptions—and the Games People play. And he uses it all in his fiction, often writing directly out of the tensions of our times.

As a stylist, he has total sensory command of his material. With him, we see, hear, taste, smell and touch. His dialogue is authentic, biting, often irreverent and wildly humorous. Threads of humor are, in fact, woven through much of his work, since he realizes that humor eases the tensions of horror. Yet it is the horror we remember, the chill he evokes in all of us.

He's not *always* on target. He can be careless and awkward from time to time; he has a tendency to over-extend his ideas in terms of story length, and he is not above graphic excess to gain an effect. But these are minor flaws in an overall performance level that merits high praise.

As a popular writer, of course, we value his unique ability to scare the living daylights out of us. King, more than any other modern master of Dark Fantasy, knows how to activate our primal fears. He knows what frightens us because these same things frighten him. To a great extent, therefore, he's still a kid hiding under the covers, fearing the dark and the Things that dwell there.

I, for one, hope he never grows up.

In a way, with those early (unpublished) novels, I felt like a guy who was plugging quarters in the machine with the big jackpot. And yanking it down. And at first they were coming up all wrong. Then with the book before *CARRIE,* felt I got two bars and a lemon; then with *CARRIE,* bars across the board—and the money poured out. But the thing is, I was never convinced I was going to run out of quarters to plug into the machine. My feeling was, I could stand there forever until it hit. There was never really any doubt in my mind. A couple of times I felt I was pursuing a fool's dream, but those moments were rare.

—*Stephen King*

The Life and Death of Richard Bachman: Stephen King's Doppelganger

by Stephen P. Brown

The dawn is beginning to burn off the ground fog as you drive over the final hill on the winding New Hampshire road. On your left, a man wearing a burlap sack around his neck is standing in front of three weathered chicken coops that lean in lazy defiance of gravity. The fog is calf-high, its surface fraying and wisping into the morning air. The chickens clustered around the man's legs are just beginning to emerge from the fog, disembodied heads bobbing, appearing and disappearing as the man reaches into his sack for more seed to sling.

The sound of your car stopping causes the man to glance up. You get a brief glimpse of what seems to be a head without a face. A tattered ruin is stretched over the man's skull. The only recognizable feature is a single eye, fixed on you with truculent rigidity. Richard Bachman turns and hurries toward the farm house, seed sack banging against his hip. The door slams. The dawn is quiet again but for the chickens clucking irritably as they materialize from the thinning fog.

During the eight years that Richard Bachman was publishing his five novels, the New American Library would receive occasional inquiries: interested film producers, writers hunting for an interview or quote, and just plain fan letters. There weren't many of these, as Bachman's books rarely lasted more than a month on the Greyhound Terminal racks and they attracted virtually no attention. Those inquiries were forwarded to the author of the Bachman books, Stephen King. He constructed a typically Stephen King reason for Richard Bachman refusing to meet anyone—Bachman was a chicken farmer with a cancer-ravaged face and was understandably too shy for company. "The poor guy was one ugly son of a bitch," says King.

But the publication of *THINNER* in November 1984 was the beginning of the death of Richard Bachman. This was no ephemeral paperback original; NAL published it in hardback and promoted it heavily. *THINNER* was one of their featured books at the American Booksellers Convention in Washington, DC on Memorial Day, 1984. *THINNER* was also a book instantly recognizable as a King novel. It had been written in 1982 by a well-known writer at the peak of his popularity. With the exception of *ROADWORK* (written immediately after the completion of *'SALEM'S LOT*), the earlier Bachman novels had been trunk novels, early works where King's distinctive style was still partially unformed.

That distinctive style finally drove me to the Library of Congress in the fall of 1984. I had read all five Bachman novels and was about eighty percent convinced that it was Stephen King. A peek at the Bachman copyrights confirmed my suspicions. All but one of the books listed Bachman as a legal pseudonym, and listed King's agent, Kirby McCauley, as the holder of the copyright. The one exception, the earliest, *RAGE* had Stephen King's name on it. I sent King a letter detailing what I had found, and waited for a dissembling reply. Instead, the phone rang.

"Steve Brown? This is Steve King. Okay, you know I'm Bachman, I know I'm Bachman, what are we going to do about it? Let's talk."

There are very few writers in King's rarefied ultra-bestseller category who write more than one a year. Most of them follow the Robert Ludlum formula: one book a year, the paperback of the previous novel timed to show up in the stores at the same time as the current hardback. When a novel can generate seven million dollars in what King calls "rolling gross" (as did *PET SEMATARY),* then there are huge economic pressures at work. Publishers of ultra-bestseller writers live in fear that titles will be published too close together and interfere with each other's sales.

"Publishers have a superstition about publishing more than one book a year from a single author," says Kirby McCauley. "There are very few bestselling writers who write more than one book a year, and few of them have as much quality in their books as Steve does. He doesn't need the money any more, but he loves to write."

But King is an anomaly in this system. His millions of fans will buy and read his books as fast as they can. His sales and popularity continue to climb. Within a week of my original *Washington Post* article on Richard Bachman, *THINNER* shot to the top of the bestseller lists, from which it is just beginning to drop—sixteen weeks later, as I write. This at a time when *THE TALISMAN* was supposedly the King novel currently in print. With this kind of reassurance, Stephen King has just completed a complex deal that will allow four novels to be published during 1986 and 1987, *IT,*

THE TOMMYKNOCKERS, MISERY and *THE EYES OF THE DRAGON.*

Throughout most of his career, King, who comfortably writes two books a year, was forced to let his novels stack up like jets over O'Hare airport, or resort to the subterfuge of a pseudonym to get a few of the backlog into print. But King's fans couldn't care less about the qualms of publishing executives, they just wanted more King.

"I know how they feel," sighs King. "It's something that has nagged at me constantly, throughout my career. I was aware, eight years ago, that the production of my fiction was out of control; I've always been three or four books ahead. I've been feeling the frustration of having this stuff pile up for a long time. I'm wading against a tide of editors and publishers shaking their heads and saying: 'No, you can't do that.' "

"Why *can't* I do that?' I say.

"There'll be a glut on the market. You'll cut the sales legs from under the books.'

"Shit! If there was gonna be a glut on the market, it would have been the year that five movies came out. The critics were laughing about it: the Stephen King Movie-Of-The-Month. And all those paperback tie-ins . . . Then *PET SEMATARY* came out. The hardback sales of that book doubled anything I'd had before."

And so in 1977, under pressure, Stephen King begat Richard Bachman.

King was already becoming a household name in 1977. Brian De Palma's film version of *CARRIE* was out, with Sissy Spacek's transcendent performance pushing the movie into the national consciousness, and the name of Stephen King along with it. That year the paperback of *'SALEM'S LOT* had gone straight to the top of the bestseller lists, and *THE SHINING* had just come out in hardcover. But King had already completed first drafts of novels that wouldn't see print for years to come; books like *THE DEAD ZONE, CUJO* and *FIRESTARTER.* There were, as well, four other long-completed novels waiting in line for publication.

King decided he had to do something with one of the older completed books that he was fond of—*GETTING IT ON.* It was a different kind of book from his usual work and he was afraid that it "would become a book the parade had passed." He contacted Elaine Koster, his editor at New American Library (his paperback publisher from *CARRIE* to the present). Koster and NAL agreed to publish the book under an assumed name.

"I was emphatic about not wanting the book to be publicized," King says. "I wanted it to go out there and either find an audience, or just disappear quietly. The idea was not to just publish a book that I thought was good, but to honestly try to create another name that wouldn't be associated with my name. It was like having a Swiss bank account."

The manuscript for *GETTING IT ON* circulated around NAL's editorial offices under the name of Guy Pillsbury, King's grandfather. But it leaked out that Pillsbury was Stephen King. King withdrew, retitled and resubmitted the manuscript as *RAGE.*

"Then they called me up," King says. "They asked me what name I wanted on it. There was a Richard Stark book on my desk, and the Bachman-Turner Overdrive on the stereo. So I told them to call him Richard Bachman."

During the ensuing eight years, three other Bachman paperbacks were published: *THE LONG WALK, ROADWORK,* and *THE RUNNING MAN.* Bachman's career became an inverted parallel of King's. While Stephen King's audience grew, reaching the point where his name became an American icon as instantly identifiable as the CBS eye, Richard Bachman published in obscurity. Every other year a new Bachman novel would appear, flicker briefly on the book racks, and vanish. The major exception to this process was *THE LONG WALK*. That book developed a cult following in its own right, remaining in print for six years—surely a record for an unknown midlist paperback thriller. NAL put that book out of print only when the news of the author's identity began to leak out.

Then came *THINNER*.

In 1982, King finished a new supernatural thriller. At three hundred pages, it was fairly short when compared to the five hundred page novels he is known for. 1982 was the year that *THE RUNNING MAN,* the fourth Richard Bachman novel, was published. There were, as usual, many finished books in the Stephen King pipeline waiting their turn to be published. He decided to make *THINNER* a Bachman novel.

The publication of *THINNER,* in November 1984, marked the beginning of the end of Richard Bachman's career. It is a later work by a more experienced writer than the previous four, and stylistically is pretty obviously a King novel. It was published in hardcover, with heavy advertising, and lacked the anonymity of paperback original publication. There was even an enthusiastic letter sent to booksellers by editor Koster: "As the publisher of some of the finest horror novels ever written, it takes a lot to get me excited about a new horror writer. Such a writer has now appeared."

"I had been under a lot of pressure for a long time," says King. "NAL wanted me to come on over and do NAL hardcovers, which I had been reluctant to do. But, I thought, *THINNER* is a strong book. It's not like the other Bachmans. It's more like a Stephen King novel, and it has a chance to be commercial. I asked NAL if they wanted to do this book in hardcover, and they were very enthusiastic. They pushed it hard, partially, I think, because they wanted to show me what they could do with a hardcover. I originally went to New American Library full-time *because* they published the Bachman books. They published Bachman at a time when Doubleday was publishing me in hardcover. But it was through the Bachman books that I actually got to know *people* over there, real people. When my relationship with Doubleday became untenable, I was able to go to Doubleday and negotiate with the sure knowledge that if they passed on the deal I was offering them, that I would be able to go to NAL as Stephen King, because they'd been so good to my friend Richard Bachman."

New American Library managed to keep Richard Bachman's identity secret for eight years. This was a remarkable feat, considering the intense scrutiny King's every utterance is given by his legions of fans.

"I wanted to jump up and down and say, 'This is Stephen King!'" Elaine Koster remembers. "But I couldn't. We had many questions over the years, but we never led anyone to believe that it was Steve. We just stonewalled it, even though it would be to our advantage not to. It became a mission for me to respect Steve's privacy. We were so secretive that our chief executive officer, Bob Diforio, didn't even know."

One piece of subterfuge was the placement of a stranger's picture on *THINNER*'s dustjacket. That face, staring at the reader with detached amusement, is Richard Manuel, an old friend of Kirby McCauley's. Manuel lives in Roseville, Minnesota, a St. Paul suburb, where he works as a builder of energy-efficient homes.

"We had to find someone who lived a long way from New York," says McCauley. "There would have been a chance that someone in New York would recognize Richard Bachman walking down the street."

"I didn't tell anybody," says Manuel. "I was sworn to secrecy. Some friends called and said, 'Hey, Dick, there's a guy that looks like you who's writing books in New Hampshire.' Even my sister called and told me that."

But once *THINNER* had been published, secrecy became impossible to maintain. As a readily identifiable Stephen King novel, the book created a storm of rumor that began to form a cloud centered over Bangor, Maine.

"Before *THINNER,*" says King, "The books were dropping down a well. I get fifty or sixty fan letters a week, more if there's a movie or the paperback of something out. Bachman was getting two letters a month. I never thought much about working at keeping Bachman a secret. I didn't have to. But when *THINNER* came out, it was like carrying your groceries home in a shopping bag in the rain. Gradually the bag softens and begins to tear. Things start falling out."

During my talks with King while preparing my story, King felt he was under intense pressure. He was besieged by reporters, fans and booksellers.

"I ducked calls from Good Morning America," King says. "My hometown paper has been on my case. Some big bug at Walden's, B. Dalton's, one of the chains, called NAL and said, 'Look, we think he's King. If you tell us, we won't advertise it or anything, but we'll order another thirty thousand copies.' But NAL kept saying no, he's not him. ABC News and Entertainment Tonight have been bugging me every other day for the past two months. All of a sudden it began to pop up all over. It wasn't just from you, it was from everywhere, all at once. I'll keep denying it for a while, but I'm not in the same league as G. Gordon Liddy."

The beleaguered King released the basic information to his hometown paper, the *Bangor Daily News*, in February of 1985. From there the story spread erratically until on March third, *THINNER* appeared on the *New York Times* bestseller list. NAL immediately shipped out flyers to booksellers stating: "Stephen King writing as Richard Bachman." Plans were made for a one-volume reissue of the four out-of-print paperbacks. King is reluctantly allowing this to happen, but he is sensitive about the career of his spectral twin. He doesn't want to see a swarm of individual paperbacks crowding the shelves.

"I never felt the urge to let Bachman be anything but Bachman," King says. "We kept careful control to make sure the publisher couldn't go batshit with the books, if it all came out, unless we wanted them to. Frankly, I didn't want that. *THINNER* will go on selling as Richard Bachman. I'd like to see *THINNER* sold aggressively, because I'd want that for Dick's last book."

THINNER marked a change in King's attitude toward his alter-ego. No longer was Bachman the repository for unpublished early works, books that didn't fit well into King's career. Had the secret remained hidden, there were future plans for that New Hampshire chicken farmer.

"There is a book that I had thought would become the next Bachman novel," says King. "It's a novel called *MISERY*, and it's got that Bachman feel to it. So I thought: let's say that Bachman sells thirty thousand copies of *THINNER* in hardcover. Let's say that it doesn't become a bestseller, but it does pretty well. If I could have come back with another hardcover, I think I could have made the guy a bestseller in two or three years, completely on his own. Then a lot of people would have complained, saying: 'Hell! He writes just like Stephen King. He must be another imitator.' The Literary Guild took *THINNER* and I heard a comment from one of their readers that: 'This is what Stephen King would write like if Stephen King could really write.'"

It would be easy to say that Richard Bachman was simply a vehicle for King to move his earliest work out of the trunk. To a certain extent, that is true. Although he speaks of a "Bachman feel" to a novel, King does not overtly acknowledge Bachman as a separate persona with a distinct literary style.

"I only wrote one of the books, *THINNER,* with Bachman in mind," King says. "It was never a case like Donald Westlake used to say, that he wrote as Westlake on sunny days, and as Richard Stark when it rained."

But that chicken farmer with the ruined face has written four novels that are unlike King's own work. They are novels of simple stress, without the artificially high drama of the supernatural. Stephen King in a minor key.

"All of the Bachman books are sad books," says King. "They all have downbeat endings. I don't think the ending of a novel is particularly important, though a lot of people do. I'm more interested in how people react along the way. As far as I'm concerned, we're *all* going to come to an unhappy ending."

"They didn't fit into his career very well," comments Kirby McCauley. "He was known for his supernatural horror novels, and his fear was that he would lead his audiences astray. Steve thought of *CUJO* as more of a Bachman book. There was nothing supernatural about it, and it certainly had a downbeat ending. *THINNER*, retrospectively, should have been a Stephen King novel."

When viewed against the background of King's more well-known books, the first four Bachman novels seem thin and unpolished—with the exception of *ROADWORK*, a fine thoughtful novel by any standard. Yet they all have one classic Stephen King quality about them, the inability to tell a boring story.

Stephen King's page-flipping narrative drive, yanking the reader along with eye-straining velocity, is the engine that has powered his career. It is an invisible prose, where the reader is caught in the rush of events and forgets that words are being read. It is a quality as rare as it is critically underappreciated.

"I don't know why that is," muses King. "Sometimes I read the stuff aloud, and it's not there. Whatever it is that people like, it's not there to me. It's there when I write it, but it's not there when I pick it up. I've read in reviews for years that I don't *have* any style. With my kind of prose, I could be starving my ass off."

It is Stephen King's substance, not his supposed lack of style, that attracts readers. He has a gift for blocking out a scene, for bringing to life a character with a minimum of apparent effort. The most minor of his characters, the most mundane event, is always somehow interesting. King is obviously deeply affected by the fates of his characters, just as he is keenly aware of his audience. This passion, without a trace of cynicism, has made him a success, and is part of his motive for allowing these orphan novels of his to be published at all.

"I think the Bachman books are pretty lively," King says. "I felt very ambivalent about my life and my writing at the time. Partly because I went to college, which is never really a good thing for guys like me. I felt very strongly the difference between selling commercially, and selling because I loved what I was doing. I allowed the Bachmans to be published because I felt that nobody was going to get cheated. I thought that the books were very much alive, and that's not true of everything in my trunk. For example, there's a very long unpublished novel that is pretty bad. But if I thought the Bachmans were bad books, or if I was publishing them out of a sense of vanity, then I wouldn't allow them to go out under any circumstances."

The first half of *RAGE* was written in 1965, while a seventeen year old Stephen King was still in high school. Although he completed the book seven years later, most of his original high school prose remains intact. "I didn't rewrite it much," he says. "It's still there. It still has a smirky sophomore quality to it."

The remarkable thing about *RAGE* is that it's as good as it is. King's high school prose is indeed sophomoric, but considering that the book is written from a point of view of a high school student, the adolescent prose adds a powerful immediacy and verisimilitude to the narrative. As the following quote from the first page of *RAGE* demonstrates, even at the tender age of seventeen, King showed a gift for observation and a healthy disdain for literary niceties:

> The lawn of Placerville High School is a very good one. It does not fuck around. It comes right up to the building and says howdy. No one, at least in my four years at PHS, has tried to push it away from the building with a bunch of flowerbeds or baby pine trees, or any of that happy horseshit. It comes right up to the concrete foundation, and there it grows, like it or not.

The story is told by Charlie Decker, a high school boy who saunters into his algebra class one day and shoots the teacher dead. He takes her place at the desk, and confronts a now very attentive class. For a long afternoon Charlie holds the class hostage, while the streets outside fill with police and their bullhorns. During that afternoon, with the body of the teacher a constant reminder of how close they are to the sharp edge of the Abyss, the social structure of the class breaks down, then rebuilds into darker and more primitive patterns.

This is a theme that King would return to often, in his later work: isolate a random group of people, put them under stress, and see what kind of interrelationships would develop and dissolve. This theme was handled brilliantly in the novella *The Mist*, and reached its ultimate extension in *THE STAND*.

RAGE has the problems of an inexperienced writer. Charlie Decker is far too articulate for the kind of psychopathic boy he portrays. Although King carefully gives him the kind of brutal and terrifying family life that would create his kind of personality, Decker is too self-aware for believability. The story loses its focus toward the end when King attempts a miniature version of *THE LORD OF THE FLIES*.

But the unfolding drama inside that classroom is relentless and fascinating. The change in role of the various dominant high school personalities rings true, down to the kind of sympathy for the tormenter now known as the "Stockholm syndrome."

RAGE was originally submitted to Doubleday, where it ended up in the hands of Bill Thompson, the editor who "discovered" King. Doubleday almost bought it, but ultimately declined. This nevertheless brought King to Thompson's attention, and Thompson would become a formative editor and important influence on King's career as a commercial writer.

It is interesting to speculate on the direction King's career might have taken had Doubleday published *RAGE.* At the time King was desperately poor, a young writer with a family to support. He was eager to write any kind of fiction that editors would buy. Douglas Winter, in his book-length study *STEPHEN KING: THE ART OF DARKNESS* (NAL, 1984) quotes King on the subject:

"If Doubleday had published *GETTING IT ON (RAGE),* it would be easy to say that it would have changed everything, because the book was not a horror novel. But it really wouldn't have changed anything; because in the long run, the monster would have come out."

It does sound possible that *RAGE, THE LONG WALK, THE RUNNING MAN* and *ROADWORK* might have been published as Stephen King novels and *CARRIE, 'SALEM'S LOT* and *THE SHINING* as by Richard Bachman.

THE LONG WALK was the next Richard Bachman novel to be published, in 1979, the year *THE DEAD ZONE* came out. *THE LONG WALK* was the first novel that King completed, in 1967, when he was a twenty year old college freshman.

> An old blue Ford pulled into the guarded parking lot that morning, looking like a small, tired dog after a hard run.

With the opening sentence of his first finished novel, many of the tools of Stephen King's craft were already in place: the deceptively simple descriptive prose; the pungent and evocative simile; the urge generated in the reader to push on to the next line.

THE LONG WALK tells the story of a hundred boys, aged fourteen to sixteen, who take part in a brutal sporting event. They walk across Maine, from Canada to New Hampshire. The walkers are paced by soldiers in half-tracks whose duty it is to shoot and kill any boy whose pace drops below four miles per hour for longer than two minutes. The winner of the race—broadcast around the world with two billion dollars collectively wagered on the outcome—is the last one left alive, about four hundred miles down the road. There is no finish line.

Although the situation is arbitrary, and the glimpses of the near-future society that has created this contest are illogical, King's sense of relentless process carries the reader along with the accelerating pace his fans know well. The meat of the novel, as with *RAGE,* lies with the dozen boys who take on individual personality, and the crude social structure they develop among themselves as they walk.

This novel contains one of King's most terrifying accomplishments. After ten hours on the Walk, the boys enter their first night. The monotonous mundane horror of that night is endless and excruciating. By the time the walkers (and the readers) stagger into the dawn, we feel that we have just climbed out of Hell. But the Long Walk has just begun.

While Kennedy was in office, in the early Sixties, the country became briefly infatuated with the fifty-mile hike. Radio and TV stations organized them throughout the country.

"I had that in mind," King says. "I didn't have a car when I wrote that book. I was hitchhiking everywhere. I didn't finish my fifty-mile hike, though. I fell out after twenty miles."

The finest Richard Bachman novel, *ROADWORK* (and one of the four best novels King has written under either name), came out in 1981. *CUJO* had just been published. *ROADWORK* had been written in 1974, immediately following the completion of *'SALEM'S LOT.*

George Dawes is a middle-level executive at a large industrial laundry firm. When his son dies of a brain tumor as a child, Dawes is psychologically ruined.

> *Inoperable.*
>
> "The word echoed up the years to him. He had never thought words had taste, but that one did. It tasted bad and yet juicy at the same time, like rotten hamburger cooked rare."

The novel begins three and a half years after his son's death. Dawes has learned to cope with daily life, deluding himself that he is getting over it. But he is far from healed. Then a new problem is dropped into Dawes' lap, a problem that will push him all the way over the edge. A new freeway is planned that will require the use of the land on which rest both his business and residence. The problem of relocating the factory has been handed to him by his superiors, and the problem of relocating his home has been assigned to him by his wife.

As the freeway moves incrementally closer, upsetting Dawes' life with glacial inevitability (the book is subtitled, "A novel of the first energy crisis"), George Dawes finds that he cannot face the responsibility of his twin tasks. He makes the crucial decision not to decide. As the deadlines for these decisions approach and pass, all of Dawes' dormant anguish over the loss of his son resurfaces. He loses his job and his wife, and gradually descends into the pit. Dawes fixates on the freeway, plotting to destroy the construction site and spending eight hours a day driving back and forth across its one finished section. But this is all a blind. Dawes cannot face his mental weaknesses, and uses the freeway as a scapegoat in his search for something outside of himself to bear the responsibility for his own actions.

ROADWORK is a novel of cerebral fear. Every one of us has been confronted with a major decision, and wondered what would happen if we simply said, "The hell with it." It is painfully easy to empathize with George Dawes. Although marred by a too-obvious ending, this is the most powerful and satisfying of the Bachman novels. There are thematic similarities with another fine King novella, *Apt Pupil,* which shows a bright young boy's imperceptible metamorphosis into a freeway sniper.

"Yeah, *ROADWORK*'s my favorite, too," King says. "But I don't think it ever made a cent. It was probably bought by twelve people in bus stations with just that or the *ENCYCLOPEDIA BRITTANICA* or the Audubon bird book to choose between."

Unfortunately, quality and sales records often have little to do with each other.

"The Bachman books were so good on their own," says Elaine Koster, "that I was hoping they would become recognized. But when an author writes under a pseudonym, then he must face the marketplace just as any unknown writer does, regardless of the quality of the work."

In 1982, *THE RUNNING MAN* was published, the year *DIFFERENT SEASONS* came out, and the year that Stephen King and Peter Straub began writing *THE TALISMAN.* King says that he wrote *THE RUNNING MAN* "in one feverish weekend in 1971."

This is the least of the Bachman books.

The characterization is no more than functional, when compared to the sharply etched portraits King's fans have come to expect. It is political in tone, but it is the naive politics of a post-teenager. It is "power to the people," rather than an adult's more reasoned "how much power to which people, and what will be the consequences?"

THE RUNNING MAN is another barbaric-future-sport novel. Ben Richards is a poor man who has turned to gladiatorial competition in a last-ditch effort to feed his family. TV channels are filled with "game" shows based on real pain and death. Richards takes part in "The Running Man," the highest rated show. He is tracked through city streets by a professional team of hunters. The show follows his progress from week to week, and encourages viewers to participate with offers of fame and money for those who spot Richards and report his movements. Richards, inexplicably, uses his moment in the spotlight to trumpet environmental causes, to little effect, and with no regard to the logic of the story or to Richards' character.

Yet for all the book's faults, it builds without pause to a final chapter that must be among the most appalling scenes ever written. Even in this, his worst book, Stephen King can not only engross the reader, but gross him out in an astonishing display of visceral horror.

These first four Bachman novels were all early works. All but *ROADWORK* were true "trunk" novels, written before he began selling. They are downbeat novels of psychological terror, with nothing of the supernatural in any of them.

But then, eight years after *ROADWORK,* Stephen King finished writing *THINNER,* an unabashed supernatural Stephen King novel. The hardcover publication of this novel in November 1984, destroyed the anonymous career of Richard Bachman.

The protagonist of *THINNER* is an overweight lawyer named Billy Halleck. Halleck has accidentally killed an old Gypsy woman in a traffic accident. As he is leaving the courtroom where he has escaped culpability (but not guilt) for his actions, he is accosted by an ancient Gypsy man:

> 'Thinner,' the old Gypsy man with the rotting nose whispers to William Halleck . . . just that one word, sent on the wafting, cloying sweetness of his breath.'Thinner.' And before Halleck can jerk away, the old Gypsy reaches out and caresses his cheek with one twisted finger. His lips spread open like a wound, showing a few tombstone stumps poking out of his gums. They are black and green. His tongue squirms between them and then slides out to slick his grinning bitter lips.

From that moment on Halleck begins to lose weight steadily at the rate of a couple of pounds per day. The novel chronicles his disintegrating personal life and his desperate attempts to relocate the Gypsy and get the curse lifted. Halleck races against time as he approaches the state of an Auschwitz victim.

Billy Halleck's situation is inherently funny, and the book itself is amusing. Yet it is a real horror novel as well. *THINNER*'s odd fusion of opposites fascinates, and points the way toward a new direction in King's work. "It has a funny subtext about eating," says King. "It's about how everybody's eating, everywhere, all the time. It's about how we look, how we look to ourselves."

But, funny as some passages are, *THINNER* is not a humorous book. What happens to Billy Halleck is not at all funny to him. And the novel had its genesis in a serious episode in King's private life.

"I used to weigh 236 pounds, and I smoked heavily," King admits. "I went to see a doctor. He said: 'Listen man, your triglycerides are really high. In case you haven't noticed it, you've entered heart attack country.' That line is in the book. He told me that I should quit smoking and lose some weight. I got pissed and spent a very angry weekend off by myself. I thought about it, thought about how shitty they were to make me do all these terrible things to save my life. I went and lost the weight, and pretty much quit smoking. Once the weight actually started to come off, I began to realize that I was attached to it somehow, that I didn't really want to lose it. I began to think about what would happen if somebody started to lose weight and couldn't stop. It was a pretty serious situation, at first. Then I remembered all the things I did when I weighed a lot. I had a paranoid conviction that the scales weighed heavy, no matter what. I would refuse to weigh myself, except in the morning, and then after I had taken off all my clothes. I remember being so pissed off in the doctor's office, because he wouldn't let me take off my clothes and take a shit before I got up on the goddam scales. It was so existential that the humor crept in after awhile."

THINNER is breezy and somewhat slight when compared to books like *THE SHINING* or *THE STAND*. But it is a tremendously entertaining novel with a continuous narrative flow, filled with small gems of characterization. In the final section of the novel, King accomplishes a true tour-de-force in his depiction of a simple cherry pie as an object of the deepest, most unsettling horror. The novel ends on a deadly serious note that disturbs some readers, for all its subtextual humor.

"*THINNER* is a story about responsibilities," King says. "It's about coming to grips with your responsibilities, and what happens when you don't. If you avoid your obligations, then you always end up hurting your loved ones."

King is famous (or infamous, depending on which critic you listen to) for his use of the brand-name detritus of modern culture. Throughout his work, he invokes the names of our most familiar household products in a way that deepens the intense realism of his best fiction. In a wry acknowledgment of his own omnipresence in our daily lives, King uses his own brand name in *THINNER*: "You were starting to sound like a Stephen King novel for a while there . . ."

King is also famous for having created images of supernatural horror more powerful and vivid than anyone before him. Who can contemplate the concept of the vampire without recalling *'SALEM'S LOT*? But, more importantly, he has shown the ability to create human beings so depraved and evil in their own right, that the mere supernatural pales by comparison. Compare the Trashcan Man with Randy Flagg in *THE STAND*, for example. In *THINNER*, there is a tool that Billy Halleck uses against the Gypsy who cursed him: he acquires the services of a Mob overlord who brings "normal," evil human pressure to bear on the Gypsy, counteracting the supernatural curse with the far more terrifying "curse of the white man from town." With this device, King wittily and effectively returns to an old theme of his, a theme that forms the central core of much of his finest work: Though all the Powers of Darkness be arrayed against you, though the stench of Evil is turning the air green around you, nothing is so profoundly terrifying as a crazy white man.

People talk about reading between the lines. Any piece of horror fiction, whether it's in the form of a novel or in the form of a movie, has subtext. There are things in between those lines that are full of tension. In other words, horror fiction, fantasy fiction, imaginative fiction, is like a dream.

—*Stephen King*

Stephen King: The Good, the Bad and the Academic

by Don Herron

> Emerson wrote once that even a corpse is beautiful if you shine enough light on it.
>
> But that is horseshit.
>
> —*Charles Willeford, THE BURNT ORANGE HERESY*

Prologue—Summer, 1985:

For the first time in my life I visited one of Crown Books' discount stores, to pick up a copy of Stephen King's *SKELETON CREW*. I figured any book that cost $18.95, issued in first printing of half a million copies, would never be worth more than cover price—no matter how much money the guy's earlier books now sell for. Better get it at discount.

As I stood before mammonian stacks of top-ten bestsellers, with King's book first in line, a little guy with dark hair, dark eyes, came over and grabbed up a copy of *SKELETON CREW*, interrupting my idle reveries about the sorts of people who actually buy and read the current top ten.

"Stephen King—*this* is a great writer," the guy said.

"Yeah?"

"Yeah! Really great. *This* man can scare the death out of you." The guy gave me a searching look with his dark eyes. "There must be some *meaning* in that."

"Yeah?" I took the book to the cashier and paid for it.

Two used-book catalogues from fantasy dealers came in the mail.

Terence McVicker of Riverside, California, offered a truckload of King titles; in his description of a first edition of *CHRISTINE* (1983), he rhapsodized about King's writing:

> This book is the epitome of Stephen King's success, and talent; here we have damn near every cliché in the book; the highschool kid nobody likes, the highschool football player who befriends him, the beautiful girl who falls for the nerd and then when things are tragically breaking apart, falls in love with the football hero, and the focal-point of the story, that which every highschool boy wants, (yes! even more than the Girl!) a CAR! King takes all these overused and abused plot gadgets, puts them in his cranial blender, and, voila! we have our freshly polished and expertly mixed clichés which appear as new and original ideas. King's handling of characters, especially youthful ones, are the reason so many early teenagers can read him and say 'Yeah, I can get into that' . . . the tone in which he writes of those times, we of his generation can say 'Yeah' . . . the timelessness of his crises, appeals to everyone. *CHRISTINE* is one of his very best!

In his 55th catalogue, Dave McClintock of Warren, Ohio, offered merely four King items, noting:

> As those of you who follow the antiquarian book market are well aware, the Stephen King tulip bulb mania continues unabated. Even the local specialist in railroad books and literature gets his hands on a jacketless, water-damaged, and warped copy of the book club edition of *CARRIE* and thinks his ship has come in. Meanwhile, if one more teeny-bopper daughter of one more of my customers comes in this place and regales me, as she is in a state of pseudo-sexual arousal with glazed eyes and moist lip smackings, with each tiny detail, each writhe, of the death agonies of a character in the latest King book I shall STRANGLE the sweet little innocent with these bare little bookseller's hands.

Shortly after it opened I caught the Chevy Chase film *Fletch* in which Chevy as the investigative reporter-hero hesitatingly enters a darkened, menacing house, and as he stumbles through the living room ad libs, "*Cujo* . . .?"

Not long ago, I was listening to San Francisco's KRQR (The Rocker!) during DJ "Nasty" Nancy Walton's nightshift. Nancy usually poses a survey question to her listeners—where can you find the best pizza in the Bay Area? Who's the best songwriter on the rock scene today? This night she surveyed literature, specifically, what is the most recent book you've read? And what is the *best* book you've *ever* read? Titles I remember as favored by some listeners were *EVEN COWGIRLS GET THE BLUES*, *HITCHHIKER'S GUIDE TO THE GALAXY*, popular stuff like that, with one guy recalling *CATCH-22* as being the best of all time. But most of the call-ins came from teenage girls, and the majority of them voted for Stephen King's *THE STAND* as the greatest, and King himself unquestionably the greatest writer to ever live. One girl said the most recent book she had read was *PET SEMATARY* and the best book she'd *ever* read was *PET SEMATARY.*

Driving around San Francisco, I noticed in a couple of places a standing sidewalk sign for something called "John Lennon Murder Facts." Did it signal passersby to a lecture on the Lennon killing, *a la* the various conspiracy speakers on Kennedy-Kennedy-King (Martin Luter, Jr., not Stephen)? Or, more likely, was it just the name of one of our local punk rock bands (after the style of San Francisco's sassy "Dead Kennedys")? Frankly, I didn't have enough interest to find out. But I loved that sign. It featured Tricky Dick Nixon in his classic stance, arms raised in a V. On his right hand, *dexter,* is a hand puppet of Mr. Conservative himself, Ronald Reagan, while on his left hand, *sinister,* is a puppet of who else but Stephen King?

I began to have a recurring dream in which I walked into a bookstore to buy something to read and saw piles of *'SALEM'S LOT, FIRESTARTER, THE DEAD ZONE, DIFFERENT SEASONS, CYCLE OF THE WEREWOLF,* and *DANSE MACABRE* heaped from floor to ceiling. There was even a *THINNER DIET BOOK.* Every book in the store was written by Stephen King, with one exception—*HUMAN CEMETERY,* a novel of horror by Stephen King's *dog.* I bought a copy.

I. The Academic

When I first essayed the fiction of Stephen King for *FEAR ITSELF* (1982), King was immensely popular—today he is even more so. In those days if Sidney Sheldon had a novel at the top of the bestseller lists, a new book by King would not immediately replace it. But recently, to no one's surprise, *SKELETON CREW* shot straight to the number one spot on release, even though *most* story collections today are considered nothing but dead meat, in publishing circles. I don't think even a Sheldon novel could have stopped its momentum.

By 1982 there had been several films adapted from King novels, but the "newest Stephen King film" was not as yet a staple of our annual summer movie fare. Who knows, in a couple of years the present level of King activity may seem tame. The article "An Unstoppable Thriller King," *Newsweek,* June 10, 1985, reports that "Book companies traditionally publish no more than one book a year by a major author, for fear of diluting his audience . . . . But now [King] is about to challenge the system. Beginning in October 1986, King will release four books in just 15 months—*IT, MISERY, THE EYES OF THE DRAGON* and *THE TOMMYKNOCKERS.* King's publisher is confident this risky experiment will pay off. 'His fans have an insatiable appetite for his books . . . . This will be a Stephen King firestorm.' "

That ace drive-in movie critic out of Texas, Mr. Joe Bob Briggs, best summed up this incredible rush of interest in King in his review of the film version of *FIRESTARTER* for the week of May 27, 1984: "This is only Steve's second movie in two months and the fourth and fifth one in the last year. What's wrong, big guy, you send the typewriter out for repairs?"

Now Joe Bob would not have noticed, nor did *Newsweek* comment upon another aspect of the King phenomenon, in its way as interesting as the number of film adaptations and the strength of the book sales: the unprecedented surge of critical interest in King and his work. It's one of my great regrets that I missed a chance to be recognized as a prophet in my own time when some material got trimmed from my first essay, especially the paragraph where I wrote:

> . . . the academic impulse in general should serve King well. I can see papers in senior English classes on "High Schools as Settings in the Fiction of Stephen King" and "Strange Mental Powers in the Writings of Stephen King." I can imagine even a Masters thesis—hell, make it a Ph.D.—on "Wasps as a Symbol of the Sub-conscious in Stephen King's *THE SHINING*."

Since then no less than ten books concerning King's work have seen print, including a *STEPHEN KING CONCORDANCE*, and a large number of essays with snazzy titles like "Apocalypticism in the Fiction of Stephen King," "Stephen King and the Lovecraft Mythos," and "The Ultimate Horror: The Dead Child in Stephen King's Stories and Novels."

I saw it coming, you see. I have never read fiction as ready made for critical explication as King's. He has taught English at both high school and college levels, and he loads his work with themes, recurring *motifs*, cross-references. In essays and books he endorses the idea of the "sub-text"—important adult concerns about politics, relationships, or economics which invest an otherwise popular novel or film with serious intent. Thus, in *DANSE MACABRE* he sees 1950s alien invasion films as parables about the threat of Soviet takeover. The horrors experienced by the family in "The Amityville Horror," he suggests, are not *really* as worrying as any young family's concerns over buying a house—or, think of blood oozing from the walls as a badass case of broken plumbing. King's first novel *CARRIE*—which I think is a fine picture of the anguish the unpopular suffer during the teen years, and a rocking ballad to high school, prom night, and life here in the good old U.S.A., *when read for subtext*—is actually about the effects of the Women's Liberation movement on modern society; Carrie White, King says,. is "also Woman, feeling her powers for the first time, and like Samson, pulling down the temple. . . ."

It is an interesting phenomenon, this critical response to King, perhaps more interesting because it has not come thus far from the major mainstream critics or the working professors but from the same people who have been writing essays such as "Cats in the Fiction of H. P. Lovecraft" and "Lovecraft and Music" for the past couple of decades—the fantasy-horror fans who would like other people to know that the stuff they're reading is *real literature* too.

As far as I know, none of the major critics—whoever has inherited the mantles of T. S. Eliot or Ezra Pound or Edmund Wilson—has yet done anything more than perhaps mention King's name in passing, in much the same way a serious American historian might mention a popular figure such as Davy Crockett. The mainstream press has given King a lot of attention, but in terms of his mass appeal and the speed at which he is breaking barriers as to amount of money a person can actually make writing books. Generally, they have not taken King very seriously as a writer.

John Bloom, the man who writes the "Joe Bob

Briggs" movie columns, in a feature article accompanying his review of *Firestarter*, was quoted as saying:

> When I first started as film critic, I felt it was my responsibility to review everything that opened in this market. I was turning out columns with four or five straight reviews and then a couple of films like *Dead and Buried*. After a few weeks, it struck me as silly to review these as art. I wanted to find a way to treat them as they were meant to be treated, as product. Joe Bob was the result.

In this context, we find King's novels treated largely as product, with *Time* calling him "a master of post-literate prose." Syndicated in early June, 1985, the Cox News Service article by Patrick Taggart comments on the news that Richard Bachman *IS* Stephen King in this fashion, ". . . if you are a longtime subject of Stephen's literary Kingdom, you weren't at all misled by the Bachman ruse. *THINNER* is King through and through—from the premise, which involves a Gypsy's curses and hideous transformations of the human body—to the style, which remains a paragon of high hackery." Janis Eidus in *The New York Times Book Review* describes *THINNER* as "so burdened with cardboard characters that the terror and suspense never fully materialize. Instead, it becomes far more suspenseful to guess whether Mr. King/Bachman will ever tire of using the brand names he incessantly tosses about. We learn far more about Lacoste shirts, Rolex watches . . . than the people wearing them . . . . *THINNER*, for all its padding, can be seen for what it is—a pretty thin book." Even in *Twilight Zone*, the fantasy-horror field's own representative on national newsstands, the reviewer of *SKELETON CREW* in the August 1985 issue seems singularly bored with the task of describing another King book, saying it ranges from "the elegant . . . to the dumb . . . to the forgettable . . . to Yecch City . . . . And there's the scary, too. Of course, of course. Go ahead and read it—everyone else will. You'll like it."

The reaction against such indifference by the fantasy-horror King critics has been intense. In his introduction to *DISCOVERING STEPHEN KING* (1985) Darrell Schweitzer says, "In fact, King seems to have pleased almost everyone except conventional mainstream critics, who are immediately suspicious of anything which isn't *theirs* and which is successful (i.e., if Philip Roth sells, that's okay; if King does, his work must be trash) . . . . But, as often happens in these cases, nobody is listening to the conventional critics. On the scale King operates, *The New York Times Book Review* is a ridiculous provincial backwater. So, too, is the book review section of *Time*."

King, as the bestselling horror writer of all time, has been claimed as *ours* by fantasy-horror critics; a big gun they can whip out and blow away the opposition with. Even the relatively few horror critics who don't care for his work still seem to accept the validity of loading a horror novel with sub-texts centered in realistic human concerns. King is a writer who has plainly indicated that his fiction is about more than mere horror, he has explained his methods and his major concerns, and most critics in the field have taken these statements to heart, I think sometimes naively. I have profound doubts about the ultimate artistic value of the "sub-text" and even more suspicions regarding the current critical passion for King's work; in his *CAVALCADE OF THE ENGLISH NOVEL* (1943), Professor Edward Wagenknecht, in effect, summed up these feelings:

For many of the people who pretend to be study-

> ing literature in America today are not really interested in literature at all. They are interested in "ideas"; they are interested in propaganda. They simply cannot believe that the mind of a great creative writer does not work exactly like a professor's.

To the extent that anyone with critical aptitude can waltz through King's fiction and pull out major and minor themes with ease, then King's work is much like what you'd expect from a professor.

A professor, as well, who has many students listening with complete deference—Douglas Winter's *STEPHEN KING: THE ART OF DARKNESS* strikes me as remarkable because Winter never once disagrees with a King *dictum,* he does not suggest that one of the novels under discussion might, just possibly, have a minor flaw or two. In this respect it is typical of most of the new criticism, where the critics, like the audience of teenage girls who buy so many of the King books, find everything to be just wonderful. Since they are able to read of King's intentions in *DANSE MACABRE* or in his many published interviews, or even phone him up if need be to find out what a particular scene might mean, they become reporters instead of critics. Roger C. Schlobin wrote about the problems facing fantasy criticism in the 25th anniversary issue of *Extrapolation,* a leading critical journal on science fiction and fantasy; one observation he made struck me as particularly applicable to the writers on King: "Yet another factor that hampers quality scholarship is the sanctity accorded *anything* said by an author . . . . The impetus for such error, many might say, lies in the 'fan' tradition and in authors who have been worshipped and encouraged to pontification by the numerous fan conventions." Here we need not deal with symbols or meaning, we can actually deal with business. In his thirteenth footnote to the section on *DIFFERENT SEASONS,* Winter notes, apparently seriously, that

> As a result of money-oriented reviews, King sold the North American publication rights for *CHRISTINE* to Viking Press and New American Library in the spring of 1982 for an advance of royalties of one dollar from each publisher: "I'll take the royalties, if the book makes royalties, but I don't want to hear any more about Stephen King's monster advances." Interview with Douglas E. Winter. May 3, 1982.

Acceptance of this statement from a writer whose books earn millions of dollars seems incredible, since it conveniently ignores the more likely premise that the deal was made to effect a tax break, even possibly for the millions of dollars worth of publicity it would generate (more recently Scott Meredith has sold one of Arthur C. Clarke's sequels to *2001: A Space Odyssey* for an advance of 10¢, and what do you know, that deal got a lot of press coverage too). At this writing the latest news is that King recently sold two new books for $10,000,000—that's five million each, not one dollar, in case your math is shaky.

The conclusion that most of these critics seem to reach is that King, because he obviously is the most popular horror writer in history, must therefore be the *best* horror writer in history. Nine out of the top ten bestselling mystery novels of all time were written by Mickey Spillane. Would you want anyone who actually thinks Spillane is a better hard-boiled mystery writer than Dashiell Hammett or Raymond Chandler to teach your children in school?

From at least one critic coming out of the fantasy-horror field, I think a few points should be made, clearly.

II. The Bad

In his enthusiastic blurb for *CHRISTINE,* bookseller Terence McVicker put forth an opinion which most of the King critics somehow seem to agree with: Stephen King is such a talented writer that he can transmute clichés into "new and original ideas." The general feeling among these critics seems to be that if King writes a story in imitation of H. P. Lovecraft or *DRACULA* or *E. C.* comics then he is only paying tribute to his predecessors in the horror field, to stuff that was good *in its day,* you understand, though clearly not in a class with a *modern master* such as King.

I think this notion is nonsense. After reading over a dozen books in which King seldom sidesteps clichés, I think perhaps it is more likely that he just has very little original to say.

"When I conceived of the vampire novel which became *'SALEM'S LOT,*" King writes in *DANSE MACABRE,* "I decided I wanted to try to do the book partially as a form of literary homage. . . . So my novel bears an intentional similarity to Bram Stoker's *DRACULA* . . . . At the same time, because the vampire story was so much a staple of the *E. C.* comics I grew up with, I decided that I would also try to bring in that aspect of the horror story." In my essay for *FEAR ITSELF,* I called *'SALEM'S LOT* a grand catalog of every vampire situation and cliché, and it is—deliberately so. Douglas Winter in his *THE ART OF DARKNESS* notes that King repeats only *one line* of dialogue frm *DRACULA* directly in his own vampire novel; obviously, he was putting a lot of effort into which elements he would borrow directly, which obliquely. I ran off a long list of the scenes recycled from *DRACULA* and various vampire films in that first essay, plus a few of the many other allusions to horror material scattered throughout the book. I knew there was a ton of such stuff in *'SALEM'S LOT*—it's like a Masters thesis on traditional uses of the vampire in western literature and film—, but I'll admit that I was actually staggered one night when I finally saw the most likely source for the scene in which Mrs. Glick rises from the dead in the Cumberland County Morgue. I figured it was fairly creative for King to have this chunky, average women rise from the dead—a neat counterpoint to the usual beautiful women preyed upon by the vampires. Then I finally caught a latenight screening of *Blacula* on Oakland independent KTVU's "Creature Features," with its scene of a similarly average woman coming back to unlife on a morgue table and nabbing Elisha Cook, Jr. "Mrs. Glick!? Jesus!" I said to the TV set. And later in the same film, that scene where hordes of the undead come boring out from behind boxes in a warehouse also struck me as being more like the plague of vampires in *'SALEM'S LOT* than anything you'll find in one of the regular "Dracula" movies. Imagine. A writer who may have been influenced by *Blacula!* Give that guy a Pulitzer!

THE SHINING, of course, does pretty much the same sort of thing for haunted house lore, with added tributes to Poe, Robert Bloch, and others mixed in, while *THE STAND* admittedly is King's attempt to write something like Tolkien's *THE LORD OF THE RINGS* occurring in America. *CHRISTINE* is a King variant on the idea of animate evil machines—such as Theodore Sturgeon's earlier story *Killdozer,* once made into a movie for TV, or the 1977 film *The Car,* which King describes in *DANSE MACABRE.*

King's film *Creepshow* is his acknowledged imitation

of and tribute to those *E. C.* comics he read as a kid. In the last episode of the film, however, you'll find some borrowing from Bloch's story *The Beetles,* which ends as a dead man's "lips part, allowing a rustling swarm of *black Scarabaeus beetles* to pour out across the pillow." In the *Creepshow* sequence entitled "They're Creeping Up on You," King characteristically piles it on by having a swarm of *cockroaches* burst from the mouth, and then *explode* from the chest and eyes. It is a definitive example of King's *dictum:* if you can't achieve terror, go for horror; if you can't get horror, then gross 'em out—the sort of scene and theory that once prompted one horror critic in conversation to label King "The Gothicist as Gross-Out Artist."

In his "Notes" at the end of *SKELETON CREW,* King talks about his short novel *THE MIST,* and the rhythm of that story; he says "The real key to this rhythm lay in the deliberate use of the story's first line, which I simply stole from Douglas Fairbairn's brilliant novel *SHOOT.*" Fairbairn is one of the many writers King has expressed admiration for—another is Jim Thompson, known for *noir* paperback originals such as *POP. 1280*. In a review of Elmore Leonard's *GLITZ* for *The New York Times Book Review* King singled out Thompson as his favorite in the *noir*-suspense mode of which Leonard is now the star practitioner. For any King critic seeking the origins of the rapist-killer Frank Dodd sequences in *THE DEAD ZONE,* I'd suggest a glance at Jim Thompson's 1952 novel *THE KILLER INSIDE ME.*

Examples of this sort are endless—either acknowledged borrowing, scenes which King may easily have read and borrowed, or a premise so hackneyed—the gypsy curse in *THINNER*—that no one need claim to have originated it. That cat returning on awkward feet from the dead in *PET SEMATARY* may be found, more succinctly developed and I think more effectively used, in T.E.D. Klein's novelette *The Events at Poroth Farm,* first published in 1972. That striking image of a boy emerging from a swimming hole with a bloated leech attached to his testicles in King's novelette *The Body* derives from a Faulkner story. King's *The Monkey* plays the same theme as W.W. Jacob's more famous *The Monkey's Paw.* And remember Thomas Tryon, one of the writers who pioneered modern bestselling horror novels with his first two books *THE OTHER* and *HARVEST HOME*? When Tryon decided that he wanted to break away from the horror genre, with his fourth book he gave us *CROWNED HEADS,* four loosely connected novelettes based on famous Hollywood personalities. When King in 1982 decided to break away from the horror field and head toward the mainstream, at least for a moment, he gave us *DIFFERENT SEASONS,* four loosely connected novelettes of modern American life. Tryon's are much more skillfully woven together, and it's worth noting that one of them is based on Rita Hayworth—in view of King's *Rita Hayworth and Shawshank Redemption* in *DIFFERENT SEASONS.*

King disarms criticism frequently—being the first to call his prose style the literary equivalent of a Big Mac and large fries in his afterword to *DIFFERENT SEASONS.* What else can you say? Yet it is also in that afterword where King writes that he would be happy to be labeled a horror writer, along with Lovecraft, Leiber, Bloch, and others: ". . . I decided that I could be in worse company. I could, for example, be an 'important' writer like Joseph Heller and publish a novel every seven years or so, or a 'brilliant' writer like John Gardner and write obscure books for bright academics who eat macrobiotic foods and drive old Saabs with faded but still legible GENE MCCAR-

THY FOR PRESIDENT stickers on the rear bumpers." In *DANSE MACABRE* he comments further on his position as a highly paid and enormously popular writer:

> "You're not a writer at all," an interviewer once told me in slightly wounded tones. "You're a goddamn industry. How do you expect serious people to take you seriously if you keep turning out a book a year?" Well, in point of fact, I'm not "a goddamn industry" (unless its a cottage industry); I work steadily, that's all. Any writer who only produces a book every seven years is not thinking Deep Thoughts; even a long book takes at most three years to think and write. No, a writer who only produces one book every seven years is simply dicking off.

Now I don't doubt that even a long book may take only three years to write, but I would say it depends on what the writer is doing in the book. Everyone in the fantasy field knows it took J. R. R. Tolkien something like sixteen years to write his *THE LORD OF THE RINGS* (which is not much longer than King's *THE STAND),* but then Tolkien was creating a complex secondary worldscape, complete with its own histories, languages, and genealogies. He was using his readings in medieval and epic literature to pull out enduring myth types and then integrate them into his work. Today any reasonably adept professional writer in the fantasy field can sit down and, following Tolkien's example, turn out a "trilogy" modeled on *THE LORD OF THE RINGS.* We know that they can because we've seen their many imitations on the newsstands. It was just as easy for competent hacks in the 1930s and 1940s to turn out a hardboiled detective novel, after Dashiell Hammett and other writers for *Black Mask* magazine had established the formula.

I'm sure it didn't take King sixteen years to write *THE STAND*; he wouldn't have time. Instead, he borrowed Tolkien's plotline and just moved that already-pictured epic conflict of Good and Evil to America, where you don't need invented languages or new history: Mordor became Las Vegas, Gollum became Trashcan Man, and voila! he had a "new and original" book. Even his archcritic Douglas Winter notes that King's description of Randall Flagg at the moment of the big showdown "strongly echoes that of Sauron in the final confrontation of *THE LORD OF THE RINGS.*" If you're not going to originate new material, how long *can* a novel take? As for the framing device of *THE STAND,* the plague that wipes out most of humanity, King credits that to George R. Stewart's postapocalyptic science fiction novel *EARTH ABIDES.* No, it won't take sixteen years to write even such a lengthy book as *THE STAND,* if its component parts have been previously written elsewhere.

How long might it take to write something like King's recent *CYCLE OF THE WEREWOLF*? A couple of days? This short novel is notable only in that it provides an excuse for some more of Berni Wrightson's excellent illustrations, otherwise it has absolutely nothing new to offer. The description of the seasonal changes are nicely done, but how many millions of times have the seasons been described since man put pen to paper? The werewolf elements are completely standard issue. The fact that the werewolf is *really* a priest, and that a crippled kid is the one who must save the day, only add to the list of clichés.

I find it interesting that Joseph Heller answered King in advance, as it were, in his *Playboy* interview, June 1975. He commented that "There is a reading public in America that wants good, challenging books. That public is one of our national treasures." *Playboy* then asked his opinion about the "rest of the reading public and the 'popular' authors they support." Heller replied:

> There are two kinds of people doing what we'll call popular fiction. One kind is a hack, the producer of quick pornography, quick mysteries—opportunistic books. The hack knows he is writing junk. The other kind may not be an "intellectual" writer but believes that he or she is producing works as good as anything that has ever been written. This type of writer puts as much effort into the work as Beckett or Mann or any conscientious writer does. The readers of that type of book are not to be looked down upon, either. They're reading what, to them, is good literature.

Of course, in fairness to King, it should be noted that a writer as great as Shakespeare borrowed plots—*Hamlet,* for example: not bad for an imitation. Likewise, H.P. Lovecraft is deeply indebted to Poe and Lord Dunsany for many basic aspects of his work. Everyone who writes fiction has debts, no doubt about it. It may well be true that "there's no such thing as a new plot."

I think too that for a writer to reach King's level of popularity, his material *must* consist of the already familiar. Spillane's first Mike Hammer novel, *I, THE JURY,* obviously borrows from Hammett's *THE MALTESE FALCON* and swipes stylistic mannerisms from Chandler, and Spillane has said that the character of Mike Hammer is modeled very much on Race Williams, a gumshoe created by the lesser known Carroll John Daly, a contemporary of Hammett and Chandler from the detective pulp *Black Mask*. Spillane added some heavy sexual breathing and a little wholesale sadism to an already familiar formula and became the bestselling author of the 1950s, just as King has added the contemporary scene and the gross-out to standard horror fare to rival the bestselling writers of the 1970s and 1980s. In terms of content, films such as *Star Wars* and *Raiders of the Lost Ark* offer little except clichéd material, though they're done up in such a fever pitch of technical expertise that the audience really doesn't care.

I do not find King's expertise in horror effects as overwhelming as many other critics. In *THE DEAD ZONE* I believe he wrote a great novel—it has all his major interests and themes, even (an archetypical King device) a bad guy who, when introduced, is seen kicking a dog to death: the Kingian *works,* in short, but done with a sure hand, with no false notes, no characters *forced* into action to stimulate a sagging plot.

My favorite example of King being egregious comes from *'SALEM'S LOT*. Look at the paperback. It isn't until page 172 that school teacher Matt Burke tells hero Ben Mears that vampires are attacking the small Maine village they're living in. Mears has a crucifix, borrowed from his landlady at Burke's insistence, which he gives to the teacher. He listens to the man's story, but tells him by page 176 that people will think he's nuts if he makes this tale about vampires public. Nonetheless, Mears is willing to help Burke test this theory. After suggesting a plan or two, he returns to his rooming house, and begins musing over the many disappearances being reported.

Matt Burke has a heart attack after fighting off a vampire. In the hospital Ben Mears sees the teacher's recently acquired cross hanging with his clothes.

"I'm putting his cross around his neck," Ben said.
"Is he a Catholic?"
"He is now," Ben said sombrely.(p.229)

By page 237 Mears is urging his girlfriend Susan Norton to get a cross, "even if it only means gluing two sticks together."

"Ben, I still don't believe this. A maniac, maybe, someone who *thinks* he's a vampire, but—"
"Believe what you want, but make the cross."

At this point Mears still had had no firsthand encounter with a vampire, but he was taking the idea seriously—he talked a doctor into examining bodies in the morgue and was trying to get the village priest into the affair. Obviously, this is a smart guy, not about to take any chances.

Then comes page 265. Mears and Dr. Jimmy Cody are waiting at twilight in the morgue to see if the late Marjorie Glick will spring into undead animation.

It was 7:02.
Jimmy suddenly said, "Where's your cross?"
Ben started. "Cross? Jesus, I don't have one!"

Ben Mears, a man who has for several chapters been more cross-conscious than Jerry Falwell, doesn't have a cross? Right.

'SALEM'S LOT is an early novel, of course. In the more recent *THINNER* King presents us with only one competent character: Ginelli, a Mafia-style hit man, a man with a plan, a guy who hogties gypsies to trees with one hand, a fellow who never makes a false move. But toward the end of the book he wanders offstage for awhile; we learn later that he's been cut

down and cut up by the gypsies. Sorry, I didn't believe it. I *might* have been persuaded if the author had made some effort to show how it *could* have been done, but King didn't bother.

King related to Douglas Winter that the main complaint made about *CHRISTINE* comes from the disruption of narrative voice. In parts one and three the story is told in first person by Dennis Guilder, the football player, a convincing evocation of the way teenagers talk and think, another great portrait of high school life—King at his best. But the book's middle section simply doesn't work. It is rendered in third person so we can watch the car running over people at times Dennis wouldn't have been available as a witness. King says he intended to have the whole work in Guilder's voice, but the technical problems involving the second section proved too much for him, so he added the third person narration and published the book as is. Considering the quality of the first and third parts, I can wish that he had just sat on the book *a la* Heller for a few years, until he had figured a way to do it all up right.

I lost most hope for any sort of consistent improvement in King's creations of horror after seeing his appearance on "Late Night with David Letterman" a few years ago. Letterman asked him for the scariest scene in all of his books—you know, *the scene that scared even you.* King said that happened while he was writing the dead woman in the bathtub in *THE SHINING*—which I think is the highpoint of terror in his work to date, the credit that allows King serious consideration among the genuine masters of the terror tale. But King added that this was the *only* scene he'd written which actually scared him at the time of writing—almost as if he wasn't writing it, it was simply *happening* to him. I thought to myself, "Oh, no. This means he can't *control* it." I thought of Tobe Hooper and his incredible *Texas Chainsaw Massacre*—a film he has not since come within ballpark range of. I thought of all those mainstream literary figures such as F. Marion Crawford or Charles Dickens who would write just an *occasional* ghost story, usually to good effect.

The entire notion of a "professional horror writer" is a recent one. Most of the writers associated with horror were either amateurs such as M. R. James or H. P. Lovecraft, for the love of the art, or professional writers such as August Derleth or Robert Bloch who made a living largely by writing in other fields—Bloch, in particular, soon branched off from *Weird Tales* magazines in the 30s, to science fiction and mystery pulps and finally to film and television. The best horror stories, the recognizable classics, have not yet come from the newer crop of writers who apparently wake up every morning, drink coffee and eat breakfast, then sit down at the typewriter and attempt to get weird.

Primarily, King's comment to Letterman bothered me because I was greatly looking forward to *PET SEMATARY*, a novel King in interviews had been calling the most frightening thing he'd ever written, a book about burial practices, too terrifying to publish—a novel that sounded just terrific! I cried in print, "Bring it on!", figuring I might be able to give King the ultimate compliment on his work, to be found dead from a heart attack, slumped over some horrid chapter. Now I began to have doubts.

I bought *PET SEMATARY* as soon as it appeared, full cover price plus tax. I'd said I wanted to read the book, so I put my money down. I figured King had in this book a chance to create *anything at all,* something as original and unnerving as William Hope Hodgson's *THE HOUSE ON THE BORDERLAND*. But what do we find? Yet another invocation of the Wendigo, introduced to horror literature by Algernon Blackwood in 1910 and later incorporated into the Cthulhu Mythos by August Derleth. The possibilities for horror in funereal details and the American obsession with burial were by no means exploited to the fullest—if you doubt that, read Jessica Mitford's *THE AMERICAN WAY OF DEATH,* a non-fiction book on the subject. It has a gross-out chapter that puts King to shame. And I do think that these always-doomed families we find in Kings's novels, however realistically portrayed, may have already become as familiar and in their way as wearying as the doomed narrators in the Lovecraft-style horror story.

The last page of the novel is extremely well done, though—I think it's one of the best horror crescendos in the literature. I know, of course, that King is just reworking the dialogue from *'SALEM'S LOT,* part three, *The Lot (IV),* section 31, which ends:

> "Darling," she said.
> Reggie screamed.

But in *PET SEMATARY* King is really doing it right—a professional writer earning his money.

In reviewing *PET SEMATARY* for *Twilight Zone* June 1984, Thomas Disch noted that King's "conventional spatter-movie resolution" to the novel's theme of the dead living again was regrettable, but acknowledged that "It's doubtful, of course, whether the public wants to be harrowed. The blustering denouement King does provide is reassuring to readers precisely to the degree that it's conventional; it's King's way of telling us not to be upset: it was only a ghost story, after all." Disch strikes close to King's notion of subtext in his remark, "If the dead child had returned from the grave . . . disensouled, the horror would have been infinitely greater, because that loss would be a vivid correlative to a parental fear of a fate truly worse than death, the fear that one's child may be severely mentally impaired."

The Disch review seems especially important because he broaches the main issues and problems with King as a horror writer; he suggests that King should be writing something other than a typical horror novel to achieve the maximum effects that might come from his sub-text of reanimating your own dead child. I'd think everyone would agree that the issue of a retarded child is more important, because it is more realistic than the doubtful idea that people may rise from the grave—but should that make it a more important concern than the horrific conception of a corpse that walks *in a novel aimed at creating terror?* I think not.

The idea of sub-text as a desirable buttress for horror material in fiction or film seems to be serving two functions: it appeases the academic mind Wagenknecht spoke of, which seeks propaganda in everything it reads, and gives material which cannot carry its own artistic load something to fall back on. Tony Magistrale in *Extrapolation* vol. 26, no. 1, Spring 1985 offered the essay "Inherited Haunts: Stephen King's Terrible Children" in which the story *Children of the Corn* is seen as a comment on Vietnam. The hero is a Vietnam vet, the calendars in the village he and his wife drive into by accident end at 1964, the year we began active involvement in Southeast Asia, and "the 'disease of the corn' in this tale," Magistrale states, "while ambiguous throughout, can be interpreted in terms of American defoliation of the Vietnamese landscape, as well as the more symbolic cultural 'illness' of moral guilt and spiritual taint that accompanied American war involvement." This is a clever explication—I like it, and it may well be the intended deeper meaning King had in mind, if he had a deeper meaning in mind—but it reminds me of Raymond Chandler's essay "The Simple Art of Murder" and his notion that "writers who have the vision and the ability to produce real fiction do not produce unreal fiction." If you're good enough to write about Vietnam, why not write about Vietnam?

Several people in the horror field were convinced that *INVASION* by "Aaron Wolfe"—the ninth imprint of the now defunct Laser paperback books—was actually written by King. "Wolfe" was said to be a penname in the introduction. *I* certainly thought King was the author, and still would like to think so—despite the recent news that Dean Koontz is holder of the copyright and therefore the actual writer. It would be nice to think that King and Koontz are part of some elaborate and delightful coverup, because the book has so many King trademarks, such as a rural Maine setting with people listening to a radio station out of Bangor. The plot is the basic plot for King's *THE SHINING:* a man, his wife, and their young son are isolated alone in a remote place by winter snows, with an outside menace threatening them—and the man has a little history of mental unbalance. I was convinced King wrote it when I hit chapter 20 and the narrator thinks "I understood the symbology—both natural and psychological—that was operating in this affair. I had seen the parallels between these events in northern Maine and certain things I had endured in Southeast Asia . . . . It was like the war! It was Vietnam. It was, there in Maine, Vietnam all over again, the same pain, the same misunderstandings, the same mistakes, dammit!" If Koontz is the author, he was writing a novel of horror set in Maine, complete with sub-text, very much in the King mode (yet *before* King had established that mode). Give *that* guy a World Fantasy Award.

King in *DANSE MACABRE* devotes a lot of his attention to films which can be scanned for sub-text—*Dawn of the Dead, Invasion of the Body Snatchers*—wasting much space on mediocrities such as *The Amityville Horror* or *I Was a Teenage Werewolf,* while giving almost no notice to several of the truly great horror films. He writes, "There are films which skate right up to the border where 'art' ceases to exist in any form and exploitation begins, and these films are often the field's most striking successes. *The Texas Chainsaw Massacre* is one of these; in the hands of Tobe Hooper, the film satisfies that definition of art which I have offered, and I would happily testify to its redeeming social merit in any court in the country." Oddly, this is about all he has to say about *Chainsaw.*

For my money *Texas Chainsaw Massacre* is the greatest horror film thus far—horror as pure art. It has no sub-texts; it does not need any. Could you justify a film portraying murder by chainsaw by suggesting that it dramatizes the plight of hungry crackers down in Texas? It does not require justification. *Chainsaw* puts horror on the front line, where it belongs in a horror film, and becomes a buzzing, sweating, utterly relentless nightmare you live through in a darkened theatre. I know many, many people, especially among the more refined or intellectual circles, who refuse to see this movie—most of them simply because of its title. That is one of the finest tributes to terror that can be made: the name alone is frightening.

I was equally curious to hear what King would say about an earlier landmark of grotesque horror, Tod Browning's film *Freaks.* After a quick *Cliff Notes*-like summary of the plot (omitting the best scenes, such as the eery wedding feast or the moments when the dwarf blows a weird air through an ocarina), King concludes, "Browning made the mistake of using real freaks in his film. We may only feel really comfortable with horror as long as we see the zipper running up the monster's back, when we understand that we are not playing for keepsies." I could not disagree more. By using *real* freaks, by divesting his film of any weakkneed sub-texts, Browning created a masterwork that resonates powerfully, typified by its unforgettable line, "dirty, filthy, *freaks!*" Browning is not Stephen King; his film is about *freaks,* not about having a bad case of acne. Public response to it through the years demonstrates that it succeeds in its art. It was banned in America and England and has never been widely shown, but art does not need a large commercial audience to succeed in its own right.

Neither does great art need a sub-text. When Lovecraft's *The Colour Out of Space* appeared in *Amazing Stories* in 1927, it was instantly recognized as one of the scariest pieces he, or anyone, had written. Fritz Leiber has recalled that coming across such a depressing tale in a magazine otherwise devoted to the adventures of science genuinely rattled his perceptions, gave him the creeps. The inexplicable phenomenon portrayed in this tale, which rots away the countryside and the farmers living there, did not then have contemporary analogies in radiation sickness and nuclear blight. If anything, Lovecraft was prescient—he created a *text* to which a sub-text would be added years later by events in the real world. Typically, King chooses his sub-texts from events of the moment—as when he suggests that *'SALEM'S LOT,* written in the Watergate era, is as much about America's dread of political corruption as it is about vampires swarming into your living room. I think anyone can see that the roster of uptown brand names King rolls out in *THINNER* is a comment upon yuppie lifestyle and the substitution of *merchandise* for stronger emotional or social values. The sub-text in *THINNER* is much more interesting than the main text of gypsy curses and wasting doom, but I think neither will carry the novel very many years into posterity. Taking its sub-text from the moment, it becomes a book for the moment—what does it have to offer readers in a few decades except a list of brand name products and an uncompelling plot?

The underlying philosophy in King's works often does not seem supportive of his role as a master of horror. I noted in my earlier essay that King ends his best horror novel, *THE SHINING*, with a lame moral—when the cook Hallorann says to the young boy:

> "The world's a hard place, Danny. It don't care. It don't hate you and me, but it don't love us, either. Terrible things happen in the world, and they're things no one can explain . . . . The world don't love you, but your momma does and so do I . . . see that you get on. That's your job in this hard world, to keep your love alive and see that you get on, no matter what. Pull your act together and just go on."

In the novelette *The Ballad of the Flexible Bullet* from *SKELETON CREW*, King is a bit more brutal on this same theme in the lines, "YOU may wonder about long-term solutions; I assure you there are none. All wounds are mortal. Take what's given. You sometimes get a little slack in the rope, but the rope always has an end. So what. Bless the slack and don't waste breath cursing the drop. A grateful heart knows in the end that we all swing." This sentiment was expressed even better on a T-shirt recently, that declares, "LIFE SUCKS AND THEN YOU DIE."

For any sentiment other than the clichéd, you must look outside King's fiction. It struck me as ironic that Douglas Winter would end his introduction to his book on King *THE ART OF DARKNESS* with a quote that perfectly encapsulates the entire appeal of King's work: "We all had some fun tonight, considering that we're all going to die." *Great* thought—piercing, pithy, original. A quote from Stephen King? Well, no, comedian Steve *Martin* said it.

SKELETON CREW features a half-title page with the simple question, "Do you love?"—a question repeated in different tales in the book to varying effect. Still, it suggests a Rod McKuen of horror, a suggestion reinforced by a couple of really terrible poems King allows into the book. His poem to his son Owen is overly sweet, the sort of thing people write for local poetry contests, loading their verse with sentiment and love. Many of King's best stories in this collection—*Mrs. Todd's Shortcut, Word Processor of the Gods, The Reach*—have a similar gentle tone and message, practical if unoriginal advice from an obviously nice man. One of those teenage girls who called in to local radio station KRQR said that she liked *THE STAND* so much because it presented a positive picture of humanity—there may be hate, fear, and the threat of nuclear war, but there are a lot of okay people out and about, trying to do the best they know how. This is not a despicable sentiment.

For purposes of horror fiction, however, this emphasis is not one I can approve of. I once took part in a panel about horror at a Bay Area science fiction convention and almost gagged when the moderator stated, "I don't think horror should be *too* scary." But I note that King in *DANSE MACABRE* says something equally ridiculous: "Here is the final truth of horror movies: They do not love death, as some have suggested; they love life . . . . By showing us the miseries of the damned, they help us rediscover the smaller (but never petty) joys of our own lives." How utterly banal.

In his use of the routine and the clichéd, I find the most fault in King's fiction. Yet I note an odd reference in *THINNER* which produces much the same response, in context. Amid all those uptown brand names that mount up into terrible weight of useless materialism, what should we find but this allusion from King writing as Bachman:

> "And, Billy, I don't exactly consider pimples off-the-wall. You were starting to sound a little like a Stephen King novel for a while there . . . ."

Amid the Rolex watches and popular rock songs, the roll call of the safe and normal life most Americans lead today, why should the name of a man supposedly dedicated to the weird and horrific fit in so snugly, securely—and as Disch has suggested, *reassuringly*?

III. The Good

If King stood to horror only as Rod McKuen stands to poetry or as Mickey Spillane stands to mystery fiction: the bestselling modern representative in his respective field, then he would not be worth writing about. Few things are as completely uninteresting as most of the top ten bestsellers of yesteryear.

King has done some excellent work, however. The dead lady in the bathtub in *THE SHINING, she's* already received my accolades. *THE DEAD ZONE* is fine; I think too that it points to one of the most interesting features of King as a writer in the 1980s—in an era when fundamentalism is strongly on the rise, when an archconservative like Ronald Reagan roars into the Oval Office twice on incredible landslides, we find King writing in a liberal humanistic mode to a *huge* readership. *THE DEAD ZONE,* from the man who supported Gary Hart in the 1984 elections, is a needed antidote to the prevailing political climate.

When King is not suggesting he's better than Joseph Heller, I find his lesser stories have their moments. The entire sequence with Ginelli rousting the gypsies in *THINNER* was neatly done, good popular entertainment—the sort of competent nuts-and-bolts writing you expect from a pro writer.

King's best colloquial voice is fun to read too—I don't think it will put him in the ranks with Shakespeare, but I'm sure it is why so many people read him today. I'd say a comment like the following from *THINNER* is one type of definitive Stephen King:

> . . . Now he was sixteen years older and a *lot* heavier. And, as jolly old Dr. Houston had so kindly informed him, he was entering heart-attack country, The idea of having a heart attack halfway up the mountain was uncomfortable but still fairly remote; what seemed more possible to him was getting stuck in one of those narrow stone throats through which the trail snaked on its way to the top. He could remember that they'd had to crawl in at least four places.
>
> He didn't want to get stuck in one of those places.
>
> Or . . . how's this, gang? Ole Billy Halleck gets stuck in one of those dark crawly places and *then* has a heart attack! Heyyyy! Two for the price of one!

I think King also is aware of the dangers of becoming too saccharine with his "Do you love?" rhetoric. In *DANSE MACABRE* he notes that Ray Bradbury's "style, so attractive to me as an adolescent, now seems a bit oversweet." He reacts against the happy ending in some books with notes of profound despair—*CUJO, PET SEMATARY, THINNER.* It was King, though, who suggested that the young boy be allowed to live when *CUJO* was adapted for film. Otherwise, when only one or two of the characters meet bad ends, King is simply functioning at the norm for the horror field—as Disch said, a slasher finale is very much expected, and therefore safe.

Still, in a story like *Survivor Type* King steps beyond your typical unhappy ending into what I'd call relentless horror, as he strands a guy on an atoll where he is forced to autocannibalize himself in hopes of staying alive until he's rescued. This is not a story from a man who thinks horror shouldn't be too scary. It is more like the real thing. *Survivor Type* is one of the tales in *SKELETON CREW* the *Twilight Zone* reviewer characterized as "Yecch City"—an indicator that the mass market, even the mass market for the horror story, does *not* want relentless horror. But I'm glad King wrote this one out and got it published, for those of us who are devotees of that sort of thing . . . .

King generally is not subtle, but in two cases I've noticed he was, brilliantly so. His Lovecraft imitation *Jerusalem's Lot* from *NIGHT SHIFT* is your typical Cthulhu Mythos tale, with all the references to arcane books, tainted ancestry, and other trademarks of that form. Yet the protagonist of the story, living in Maine, is a northern *abolitionist,* publishing anti-slavery tracts. It is a fine twist on the well-known racism of Lovecraft, who occasionally signed his letters "Yrs. for cheaper niggers."

And, in *The Breathing Method* from *DIFFERENT SEASONS,* King creates an exclusive men's club where members come to read, relax, and tell stories. Inspired perhaps by the Grolier Club in New York, the Bohemian Club in San Francisco, or similar institutions, King evokes just the right air of comfort and clubbiness—again, a professional writer doing his job well. I find it refreshing, however, that he introduces into this traditional bastion of male companionship a tale based on *feminine* concerns—what happens when you get pregnant and there's no father in sight? Do you have the baby anyway? The juxtaposition of the solidly male club atmosphere and the woman facing pregnancy alone is deft; King never once jumps out and yells, "Look, gang, see this sub-text?!"

I'd say that King is at his best when he deals with small, personal matters. The depiction of what it is like to be a boy in the country in *The Body* is wonderful—not earthshaking material, not writing that is likely to make you forget any of the highpoints in world literature, but wonderful nonetheless, recalling many memories. I stand beside my original roster of "the best" from *NIGHT SHIFT: Children of the Corn* and *Sometimes They Come Back* selected as fine work by a writer hitting his stride; *The Boogeyman* selected because it so obviously had King's major concerns up front—in fact, in interviews since I wrote the first essay, King has repeatedly said his greatest fear is walking into one of his children's rooms and finding death; and *The Woman in the Room,* chosen because it was the most moving, and one of the few truly personal pieces in the book—written soon after King experienced the death of his mother, I've since learned. I do think that much of this stuff with man-eating trucks and unexplainable witless doom is complete bullshit, but with *The Woman in the Room* King approached the realm of serious literature, and perhaps it is not coincidental that a short film made from this story won an Oscar nomination as best short film of the year in 1984. I have no expectations that King's upcoming movie *Maximum Overdrive* about killer trucks will garner a nomination, or rate one.

As best from *SKELETON CREW* I'd select *Survivor Type,* where King lets loose, and *Mrs. Todd's Shortcut,* King's great loveletter to his wife.

In *Apt Pupil* from *DIFFERENT SEASONS* I find those qualities I'd most expect from a writer interested in both horror literature and what is called mainstream literature, but also a writer capable of appealing to the mass market in America. King features a ghoulish young all-American boy in a small California town, a boy who happens to learn that an old man living nearby is a fugitive Nazi war criminal, a "death doctor" in charge of concentration camps. What else would this boy do than come sucking around, plaguing the German for *details* of the Holocaust?

The plot sounds like a great gimmick for a story, like Bradbury's gimmick for *The Small Assassin*—hey, let's have a *baby* crawl around killing people. I can see how *The Small Assassin* appealed at first to the audience of teenage boys who originally read it in its pulp magazine appearance, and to the succeeding generations of teenage boys who discover it in some printing or another of a Bradbury book or an anthology. Unfortunately, *I* didn't read the story until after I had *had* a baby, and I found it hopelessly stupid—a great *gimmick* for a story, but only a gimmick.

Of course, I see the parallels between King's story of a boy's infatuation with a "real monster" and Peter Bogdanovich's film *Targets* (1968) which stars Boris Karloff in one of his last great roles, as a man who has played movie monsters all his life. The theme of sniper killers in both is obvious too. Many people in America, many people we'd consider all-American—such as King—do *love* monsters. What could be better than to have a monster, a Nazi war criminal, for your *very own*?

In the notes at the end of *SKELETON CREW* King calls *Apt Pupil* "a particularly good example of this disease I have—literary elephantiasis." indicating the story is too long. True, if it had been shorter it would have had more impact strictly as a gimmick story—I think *THINNER* is a great short gimmick story lost in novel-length packaging.

But what King does in *Apt Pupil* is worth the added wordage. He goes beyond the mere idea of the gimmick to establish a mythic picture of the mental decay of the American boy, a boy interested in monsters who in due course of time becomes interested in murder, and the parasitic relationship of the Nazi and the monster fan. It is one of the few King stories in which the material he normally presents as sub-text becomes the *text: we* may become monsters too—*here's* how. It is Stephen King, bestselling horror writer, working with material I think no one else could exploit as well, creating a tale of such large proportions and such resonance that it will defy easy pigeonholing by the academic hordes.

In a word, it is the story where King takes the material which seems most uniquely his own, and makes *literature* out of it.

The more frightened people become about the real world, the easier they are to scare. Sociologists report that people in the cities are hardened to violence. It's possible to get casual about it—to say, "Oh dear, a woman is getting beaten up. What's for dinner?" But the quantum fear grows, and that's why horror films are so popular. People have fears to get rid of.

In *Creepshow* there's a segment in which this guy's overwhelmed by cockroaches. To handle the bugs, we hired the "roach wranglers." They work for the Museum of Natural History in New York, and they're used to handling bugs. We had about 3,000 cockroaches, and at first the roach wranglers were pretty cool. But each day they got a little more freaked out. These bugs were living in big garbage cans and eating dog chow and bananas—a mixture that just reeked. By the end of the film, the wranglers were so scared that if you'd slapped one on the back, he'd have gone straight to heaven.

—*Stephen King*

Stephen King Goes to the Movies

by Chuck Miller

Movies based on the works of Stephen King are an integral part of the King phenomenon. Movies sell books and books sell movies. King's vivid, cinematic style of writing lends itself to adaptation into film. This potential was recognized early in his career by Bill Thompson, his editor at Doubleday. The movies, good, bad or indifferent, are yet another dimension of King's universe.

One: *CARRIE*

CARRIE is Stephen King's miracle. Until this book sold to Doubleday, King and his family lived a hand-to-mouth existence in rural Maine. Teaching high school English classes by day and writing fiction at night, he lived with his wife and three small children in a rented trailer. A few of his stories had seen print but he had authored four unsold novels and he despaired of the life of a frustrated, unpublishable writer. *CARRIE,* his fifth novel, was salvaged from the waste basket by his wife Tabitha, who persuaded King to finish the aborted short story about a troubled adolescent girl with telekinetic powers. It soon became a full-length novel and their lives were changed forever.

The book is written and reads somewhat like a movie script. King has humorously compared its intensity to the B-grade film *The Brain From Planet Arous.* Aimed at teenagers, it contains all the right elements: repressed by her mother and scorned by her peers, an innocent young girl loses her emotional balance. Pushed cruelly over the edge, she unleashes her pyrotechnic revenge upon her persecutors. It's a teenage fantasy of retribution and justice brought to life on the page by Stephen King and on the screen by Brian de Palma and his crew.

Bill Thompson recognized King's storytelling talents and sensed the book's potential. Doubleday bought *CARRIE* for $2500, a respectable price for a first novel in 1974. Its subsequent sale to paperback, to New American Library (NAL), was for a phenomenal $400,000. Considered in the light of *THE EXORCIST* and *THE OTHER* (two contemporary horror novels preceding *CARRIE* which became successful films), *CARRIE* no doubt looked like a good movie prospect to NAL, and their high-stakes gamble paid off royally.

Director Brian de Palma expressed an interest in the book and several studios considered it for production. Film rights were purchased by Twentieth Century-Fox for producer Paul Monash. Six months later, the rights fell into the hands of United Artists, with Monash still on board as producer. After initial reluctance, he accepted de Palma as director and together they went on to produce a winner, a financial and critical success.

From hardcover to paperback to the silver screen,

King's own phenomenal success story begins with *CARRIE.* Each successive King novel would gain him more readers and, subsequently, more movie goers.

In *CARRIE,* King displays many of the themes and concerns that run through his other books—and movies. King very intentionally deals with everyday people whose lives slip over the edge, into the realm of the fantastic.

Carrie, the shy, socially awkward girl, is a member of every high school class that ever was. Margaret White, her mother, the devout fundamental Christian, lives in every American small town. Billy Nolan, the always-in-and-out-of-trouble-maker, and the rich bitch Chris Hargenson are familiar "pop" figures in our high schools, in beach-party movies and in television soaps. *Carrie* lives somewhere between *American Graffiti, Peyton Place,* and *The Bride of Frankenstein.*

King's own stint as a high school teacher (and of course earlier as a student) familiarized him with the characteristics of small-town students and parents. If King speaks with authority in his fiction, it's because he speaks from experience; he deals with what he knows: small towns full of regular Americans, going about their everyday business—until something unusual, often dreadful, changes the world around them.

Sissy Spacek came to the film via her husband Jim Fisk, the film's production designer. She tested for the parts of Sue Snell (Carrie's friend), Chris Hargenson (Carrie's nemesis) and, finally, Carrie White.

The movie opens with a most unusual scene: Carrie White's first menstrual period, which occurs traumatically in the high school's group showers, after girls' gym class. That Carrie should have no idea what's happening to her requires the audience's willing suspension of disbelief.

In for a penny, in for a pound. Soon the audience is asked to believe that Carrie has the power to move objects with some hidden part of her mind. Her mother's oppressive religious beliefs and repressive overprotectiveness seem naturally to be somehow involved in Carrie's mental situation. She's a rather strange girl, and her powers are somehow triggered by the shock of menstruation. Something primordial is going on within, while her mother quotes Old Testament denunciations of evil spirits and the Devil.

In the role of quiet fanatic, Piper Laurie communicates a belief that her own past sins may be transferred to her daughter. While most parents hope their children will avoid their mistakes, Carrie's mother takes this one step further, into the realm of madness.

When Carrie asserts herself and accepts Tommy's invitation to the Prom, her telekinetic power, like a muscle, is strengthened by her resistance to her mother's hysterical pressures. Gradually she learns that her "power" has tremendous force.

The machinations leading to Carrie being showered with pig's blood are common teenage pranks, believably exaggerated. King and de Palma stretch their audience's suspension of disbelief into a universe where bizarre things really happen, a place where people can and do get *hurt.* Intensity, exaggeration and especially malevolence are trademarks of King's prose. Brian de Palma manages to portray the essence of King's novel, a mixture of tension, horror, comedy and innocent delight, with a wonderful lyrical style—and without the misanthropy we'd have gotten from Hitchcock or Polanski.

At the Prom, Carrie revels in the dream-like atmosphere, like Cinderella, marvelling at the magic of her own presence there. She's free (for the moment) from her mother and is happy to be an attractive young woman, accepted by her peers. De Palma's Prom captures the timeless, fairy-tale quality of all Senior Proms. The formal gowns, the first tuxedoes and the surrounding glitter and pageantry magically transform a high school gymnasium into the setting for an American adolescent ritual.

This is Stephen King's backyard. If his books and the movies that grow out of them grip our imaginations more strongly than a visit to an art museum, it's because they speak directly to our secret self, like modern myths. At their most successful, they wake our private, primitive fears.

The story begins and ends in blood. When Carrie is drenched in pig's blood on the stage, the surprised promgoers laugh like unforgiving children. In response, like a dark, avenging angel, Carrie wields her hidden powers with devastating telekinetic force, indiscriminately destroying the people and buildings around her.

Carrie was shot on a fifty-day schedule at a cost of $1.8 million. It garnered two Academy award nominations, for the performances of Sissy Spacek and Piper Laurie.

Two: *'SALEM'S LOT*

On screen, *'Salem's Lot* moves out like a slow train grinding uphill. The landscape's familiar, if you've ever watched the late late show: the small off-track town with lots of dirty laundry, a creepy haunted house brooding on a hill, a couple of kids out walking through the spooky woods at night, a neglected graveyard and a very *bad* smell in the air.

Stephen King himself might have lived there. You get the feeling this could be his home town, where he grew up, where he taught high school English.

King completed *'SALEM'S LOT* just before he got

his first big bucks from the paperback sale of *CARRIE.* Bill Thompson, the man who helped change the shape of America's nightmares, warned him then that he might get typecast. But who would have guessed that King would become a regular brand name, like Kleenex, Karloff and Capone.

However, King's sprawling slapdash novel of vampires ravaging New England wasn't easy to translate onto celluloid. Some of Hollywood's Best took a stab at the screenplay: Stirling *(The Swarm)* Silliphant, Robert *(Alice Doesn't Live Here Anymore)* Getchell, and Larry *(It's Alive)* Cohen. Then Warner Brothers had a corporate brainstorm: why not make a miniseries and run it on TV? Paul Monash, *Carrie*'s producer, scripted something that Warner and Richard Kobritz *('Salem's Lot*'s producer) and King himself all claimed to like, and the film was born.

Kobritz somehow persuaded the studio to take on Tobe *(Texas Chainsaw Massacre)* Hooper as director—not an easy task, because you couldn't have gotten *that* movie on TV with a crowbar. It was far too intentionally sick and gruesome for the prime time crowd. But *Texas Chainsaw* had made a big splash and a lot of money and so Hooper was brought on board.

'Salem's Lot was filmed in eight weeks at summer's end in 1979. It aired first as a four hour miniseries on CBS during the November "sweeps" and was later released in an abridged theatrical version in Europe, and on videocassette in the U.S. and elsewhere. (There are scenes in the later shortened releases not in the original TV version, and vice versa.) The film's strong cast of characters—James Mason, David Soul, Lance Kerwin, Bonnie Bedelia, Ed Flander—play their roles seriously, without a hint of farce or tongue-in-cheek.

Since much of *'Salem's Lot* (the movie) is concerned with mood, it's better viewed from start to finish on videotape than interrupted every twelve minutes on prime-time TV with upbeat ads for cornflakes and cough syrup. It's a vampire movie, after all, and requires believability (King's forte as a fiction writer).

'Salem's Lot makes use of many of the familiar conventions of vampire lore: the Master's coffin, fear of the cross, wooden stakes driven through the heart. Yet both movie and book ignore the vampire's traditional attractive sexuality, which underlays most earlier versions in both media. King's Barlow is a frightful blood fiend; in the movie he is a demon without speech or the appearance of humanity. The vampire's sidekick, Straker, has a more fluent and colorful role in the film, and James Mason makes the most of it, managing to be both dignified and sinister.

Both movie and book leave room for a sequel; both end without the vampire epidemic having been contained. (At one point, *'Salem's Lot* was considered for development as a weekly TV series; to King's relief these plans were dropped.) King has had thoughts about a sequel, wherein Mark, the runaway, receives a long distance phone call from his dead mother. King would also like someday to restore *'SALEM'S LOT* to its longer manuscript form.

Three: *THE SHINING*

THE SHINING was published in hardcover by Doubleday in February, 1977. It was King's third published novel and the third to be adapted to the screen. With *THE SHINING,* King's reputation as a brand name writer of horror fiction became fixed in cement.

The book was written in the Fall of 1974 when King moved his family to Colorado in search of a new homestead. In late September, King and his wife Tabitha found themselves the only guests in a large hotel in Estes Park which was preparing to close for the winter. Feeling this would be the perfect setting for a ghost story, he set aside the mainstream novel he had been working on at the time, a kidnap story loosely based on the Patty Hearst-SLA events. He then decided to go ahead with his "haunted hotel" story.

Bill Thompson at Doubleday was enthusiastic when he saw the manuscript. Doubleday's formidable sub-rights department capitalized on what could now be neatly categorized as a "Stephen King novel," and the ricochet effect of the brand name bestseller began in earnest. *THE SHINING* was chosen as a lead selection for The Literary Guild bookclub. Paperback rights went to New American Library for a large sum of money. And *THE SHINING* was optioned as a movie.

The Producer's Circle Group bought film rights. Stanley Kubrick read the book and became enthusiastic about the cinematic prospects inherent in King's work. He decided *THE SHINING* should be part of his three picture contract with Warner Brothers. Producer's Circle sold the book to Warner Brothers for him and Kubrick gained complete control of *THE SHINING*. Kubrick produced and directed the film, and shared screenwriting credits with Diane Johnson.

The focus of King's novel (Jack Torrance's gradual descent into madness) was altered on screen. In Kubrick and Johnson's screenplay Wendy gradually realizes that her husband was a madman from the beginning.

In the movie, Jack is told by a ghostly denizen of the hotel "You have always been the caretaker." Wendy, and the audience, are frightfully enlightened as to Jack's true state of mind when she leafs through his manuscript, finding page after page filled with the single typewritten sentence: "All work and no play makes Jack a dull boy." After that pivotal scene we can only applaud the madman's eventual demise.

Jack assumes his rightful place in the framed photograph on the wall of the ballroom, appearing in the forefront of the revelers, above the inscription "Overlook Hotel, July 4th Ball, 1921."

Kubrick's *The Shining* intends to be a study in psychological terror, which stands diametrically opposed to King's portrayal of the essence of natural and supernatural evil. King has said *he* would like to remake *THE SHINING* as a different sort of movie, this time with himself as the director.

Four: *CREEPSHOW*

Creepshow is a tip of King's hat to the *E. C.* horror comic books of the 50s. *E.C.* (Entertaining Comics) was the brain child of William Gaines. *E.C.* produced a variety of titles in various genres, but in their horror line they plumbed the depths of terror: *Tales From the Crypt, Vault of Horror, Haunt of Fear.*

Their stories dealt with adultery and betrayal, revenge and poetic justice, always with a humanistic twist. Rotting corpses, disembodied limbs and severed heads were a regular staple. In later years these comics have been appreciated by aficionados for their tight plots and intricate artwork. In the 50s, they raised a furor which extended to the halls of Congress and resulted in the self-governing Comics Code, which thereafter censored such lurid scenes and themes. Today, all that survives of the *E.C.* line is *MAD* magazine. But in various interviews and in his non-fiction book, *DANSE MACABRE,* King recalls the profound effect *E.C.* horror comics had on his imagination as a child.

Pittsburgh-based film director George A. Romero shares King's memories and fondness for *E.C.* horror comics. In conversation one evening over beer, the two decided what they *really* wanted to create was a movie which would scare the audience from start to finish. An anthology format seemed like a good way to achieve this result. They decided to resurrect this stuff *exactly* as it had been and show it on the silver screen. *Creepshow* was born.

We open on a residential Twilight Zone-type town, in a house on "Maple Street," for a brief intro skit with Tommy *(The Fog)* Atkins and Joe *(Son of Tabby)* King. The kid mouths off, gets smacked, his comics get trashed and then we shift to the first of five vignettes that do their best to be both juvenile and frightening. In an 8-million dollar PG sort of way.

Since these guys love comic books, they hope you'll like them too, in the guise of clever effects: gimmicky graphics, like splash pages dissolving into live action; freeze frame finales graduating into comic panels (created for versimilitude by Jack Kamen, one of the *E.C.* originals); flash-back scenes framed in ornate borders; bright orange action-highlight lighting, and so on.

In "Father's Day" we're served up the standard back-from-the-grave-to-do-you-in Gothic yarn. Grandad Nathan has his cake and eats it too.

In the next segment, "The Lonesome Death of Jordy Verrill," we get Stephen King cast (some say typecast) as a proverbial hayseed from rural Maine. King was instructed by Romero to play it broad as a freeway, and he does just that. One night a meteor plunks down in Steve's back farmyard. He cracks it open and dreams of selling it to the local college. Some slime drains out and splashes on his hand. Next day he's got green gunk growing on his fingers, face and nether regions.

Is this the greening of a horror writer? "Stephen King turns into a daffodil," claims special-effects man Tom Savini.

Next we come to "Something to Tide You Over,"

which takes a hard look at the consequences of infidelity. Ted Danson has been diddling with millionaire-video-nut Leslie Nielsen's wife. After Nielsen films his revenge against the pair, they return from a watery grave in true comic book fashion, to revisit Nielsen's own style of homicide upon him.

Next up is "The Crate," another nasty tale about avoiding alimony, with Adrienne Barbeau as The Shrew who Meets the Tasmanian Devil.

In the final segment, "They're Creeping Up On You," antiseptic skinflint E. G. Marshall gets his from a thousand giant cockroaches. Welcome to E. G.'s sterile, germ-free motel, where the roaches check in but *don't* check out. The denouement is every inner-city dweller's nightmare.

Then back to Maple Street. We find Joe King up in his room, sticking pins into a voodoo doll bought from an ad in one of the comics, while downstairs in the kitchen dad's having seizures. Fortunately, nobody ever died from reading a comic book, or watching a movie. Did they?

Five: *CUJO*

Cujo's big and he's turning bad, but rabies takes a few days to really get cooking. While Cujo's getting ugly and learning to slink around—all of which is against his better nature—back in town there's some hanky-panky going on.

Mom's fooling around with the handyman. Dad's ad agency is going belly up because America's kids are regurgitating his client's cereal. Young Tad, their son, is having trouble sleeping 'cause there's something lurking in his closet.

Out on the farm, Mrs. Cambers wins the lottery and skips off with her boy Brett. Her husband Joe takes the opportunity to hoist a few beers with his buddy Gary down the road. Finally Cujo's had enough. He finishes off Gary, then Joe. Then Mom heads out to the Cambers' farm for some quick car repairs and when she gets there her car won't start. Next thing you know Cujo's crawling all over the hood, ripping up the windshield wipers.

After a couple days trapped in a Pinto, things aren't looking good for Mom and the kid. Dad's still out of town on business, the battery's dead, and the mailman's not delivering. Mom makes a break for the house and up pops Cujo, looking like the return of *Jaws*. Mom stabs the dog and plugs him with a .38 Special. Dad manages to show up before the credits roll.

CUJO appeared in hardcover in August, 1981 from the Viking Press. *Newsweek* felt the book was very obviously written for the screen, but King denies this. Nevertheless, he subsequently wrote the screenplay. Taft International purchased film rights the same year. King's screenplay was revised by Barbara Turner (as Lauren Currier) and by Don Carlos Dunaway. King received no screen credit, due to a decision of the Screen Writers Guild which he does not contest.

Lewis Teague *(Cat's Eye, The Lady in Red)* directed and Daniel H. Blatt and Robert Singer produced the movie. Although set in New England, the film was shot in Northern California, on a five-million-dollar budget.

Six: *THE DEAD ZONE*

THE DEAD ZONE is a key departure in King's writing. The book was published in August 1979 by Viking and it solidified King as an automatic bestseller in hardcover. His published books to this date include

CARRIE, 'SALEM'S LOT, THE SHINING (purely horrorific novels), *NIGHT SHIFT,* a collection of horror stories, and *THE STAND,* an epic fantasy. *THE DEAD ZONE,* a book more science fiction than horror, displays mature themes. It delves into the ambiguous nature of good and evil and moral responsibility and reflects the social angst of the Seventies.

As a movie, *The Dead Zone* echoes these same themes. *The Dead Zone* was targeted for a broad, mainstream audience, rather than simply promoted as a horror/thriller film. This was a real problem for a movie directed by David Cronenberg, based on a novel by Stephen King, released on October 21 for Halloween.

For Stephen King, *THE DEAD ZONE* is a newsreel of the entire decade of the Seventies. Involved in a traffic accident, Johnny Smith spends five years in a coma and awakens to a different world. His legs have been damaged, his mind has developed abnormal prescient powers and his girlfriend has married another man. Johnny cannot return to his daily activities as a school teacher. The crucial element is chance: King's central symbol in this novel is the wheel of fortune at a small town street fair. Johnny Smith is everyman, forced to take action against a future which he cannot effectively control.

In the film, screenplay writer Jeffrey Boam gives us moral, decent people who have enormous responsibilities thrust upon them. The film was originally to be made by Lorimar, with Boam's screenplay, Stanley Donen (*Singing in the Rain, Charade, Saturn 3*) directing, and Sidney Pollack (*Tootsie*) producing. Lorimar, faced with the commercial failures of *Cruising* and *Fastwalking* among others, closed down their feature film division. *The Dead Zone* went into a limbo of its own for a year or so. It was then picked up by Dino

DeLaurentiis, who returned to the source and asked King to write a screenplay.

King's script followed the structure of his novel closely: it was brutal, with a strong focus on Frank Dodd, the Castle Rock Killer. Next, DeLaurentiis commissioned a script from a Russian filmmaker, Andrei Konchalavsky. This version, which failed to capture the nuance of American setting, was translated from Russian into English into Italian before finally being turned down.

Debra Hill was brought in as producer. Hill worked with John Carpenter on three chapters of *Halloween,* and with DeLaurentiis on *Halloween II* and *III.* They returned to Jeffrey Boam's version. When David Cronenberg was selected as director in the summer of 1982, Cronenberg, Hill and Boam secluded themselves in a Toronto hotel room for three days and came out with an acceptable script.

In the final version, King's novel of the parallel stories of Johnny Smith and Greg Stillson becomes John Smith's story. The beginning is concerned with Smith's accident and his awakening from a five year coma into a different world. The middle portion deals with Johnny's increasing awareness of the responsibilities connected to his precognitive power. The final part gives us the confrontation between good and evil, John Smith and Greg Stillson.

John Smith makes the moral decision to accept his burden. He takes on the mantle of the most feared monster of modern times (since November 22, 1963): the lone sniper.

The Dead Zone takes place in a mythical, Rockwellian New England town. It was filmed outside of Toronto in January, 1983, which pleased Canadian Cronenberg who lives there. It also made the producer Debra Hill happy. She was able to save 20% of the film's seven-million-dollar budget on the Canadian exchange rates.

Seven: *CHRISTINE*

The novel *CHRISTINE* was finished in manuscript form in the summer of 1982. Stephen King sold the hardcover publication rights for a much publicized advance payment of $1.00 when he could have asked for, and received, several million. There were several reasons for this precedent-setting move. It left the publisher with money on hand that could now go toward developing the work of new authors. It also simplified a lot of publisher mumbo-jumbo otherwise known as royalty statements. His book would now earn and pay full royalty from the day the first copy was sold.

In the matter of selling film rights, however, King has found it best to take as much money as possible up front. Movie options are not always exercised. The best laid plans of mice and men often go awry, especially in Hollywood. It is important for an author not to tie up his valuable film property unless there is money on the line. And finally, whoever invests a lot of money is going to want to complete the film.

Before the hardcover hit the stands in Spring 1983, producer Richard Kobritz had a finished screenplay in hand. Ever since their work together on the TV movie *'Salem's Lot,* King had regularly sent his manuscripts to Kobritz in advance of publication. Kobritz felt *CHRISTINE* had it all: teenagers, rock and roll, and America's love affair with the automobile.

Kobritz chose John Carpenter to direct *Christine.* He had hired Carpenter in 1977 when he was known only for his early genre films *Dark Star* and *Assault On Precinct 13*, to direct the TV movie *Someone Is Watching Me.* (Carpenter's subsequent films, *Hallow-*

een, The Fog, and *Escape From New York,* made money and everyone was happy. But his remake of *The Thing* did so poorly at the box office that Universal Pictures, which had reportedly arranged with Carpenter to work on *Firestarter,* handed that project to another director.)

Carpenter chose Bill Phillips to pen the screenplay for *Christine,* which was finished in January 1983, a few months before the first edition of the hardcover was published by Viking Press. Filming began in late April, just after the book hit the bestseller charts. With a projected budget of $10 million, Carpenter wanted to shoot the film within a 30 mile radius of Los Angeles. The movie was shot in five weeks and *Christine* was ready for a Christmas 1983 release.

In less than a year, four King movies hit the screen: *Cujo, The Dead Zone, Christine,* and *Firestarter.* This caused a lot of problems for the folks at New American Library, King's paperback publishers. Suddenly they had a lot to do: a movie tie-in edition for *CUJO,* a movie tie-in for *THE DEAD ZONE,* and they arranged with Viking to publish the paperback of *CHRISTINE* some months ahead of schedule. So in the space of a few weeks the regular paperback of *CHRISTINE* on the stands was followed closely by another with a movie tie-in cover. Doesn't publishing sound like fun?

Christine the movie is the story of a boy and his car, or rather a car and her boy. It opens in Detroit in 1957, as a brand new 1958 Plymouth Fury rolls off the assembly line, two-tone red and white. One auto worker gets his fingers smashed by the hood. Another drops his cigar ash on the front seat—bye, bye, he's found dead at the end of the shift. (The shop steward is mystified; there's nothing about this in the union's contract.)

Thus begins Christine's long history of malevolent interaction with her owners. Arnie Cunningham, obsessed with the car, is transformed from a nerd with glasses to a nerd without glasses. He picks up a girlfriend, Leigh, and drops off an old friend, Dennis. And yet the film and the book both succeed in overcoming their ridiculous premise: THE REVENGE OF MY MOTHER, THE CAR.

The demon-machine is not a new idea; King employed the theme previously to good effect in two stories from his *NIGHT SHIFT* collection. *The Mangler* first published in *Cavalier* in 1972, concerns a haunted folding machine. *Trucks,* also published in *Cavalier* in 1973, is about the revolt of the flatbeds, pickups and eighteen wheelers. In the past decade, the theme also appeared in several movies. The 1974 TV movie *Killdozer,* based on a story by Theodore Sturgeon, is about a construction crew attacked by their own heavy equipment. *The Car,* a 1977 film starring James Brolin, has a sinister auto terrorizing a small community.

Surprisingly, the *concept* of Christine succeeds in both mediums. Once again King has captured the *Happy Days* flavor of middle America. The book and the film draw their power from this source, The movie, as *American Graffiti Gone Awry,* is a simple story of teenaged revenge and retribution. It forgoes the nastier implications of evil inherent in King's novel. In the book, the nature of the evil of Christine is left ambiguous: is the car itself evil, or is it possessed by the evil spirit of its first owner, Roland LeBay? The movie establishes in the first scene that it was evil the day it rolled off the assembly line. Bad to the bone, it corrupts its owners to its malevolent will.

In the end, Arnie goes down with his car and Dennis and Leigh stand by as Christine is reduced to a compressed block of scrap metal. But as the film wraps, the metal in the block begins to shift slightly, to the strains of "Bad to the Bone."

The book and the film are filled with rock and roll music, and Christine herself will only play R&B from the late 50s and early 60s. The film's original music was composed by John Carpenter in association with Allen Howarth.

According to Kobritz, the cast and crew, to a person, referred to the car as "Christine" or "her," always in feminine terms. King has said the '58 Fury represented to him a 50s car with no mystique: as opposed to a Thunderbird, '57 Chevy or Ford Galaxy it captures the spirit (or ghost) of its age.

Actually, 18 different Furies had to be located for use in the film. From January to April, 1983 the hunt for Furies raged, with ads in major newspapers, and owners traced through car clubs and State Departments of Motor Vehicles, and a nationwide junkyard hotline. Some of the 18 cars were bought just for parts, with 14 different cars used up during the filming.

All of these assorted vehicles were made the same blazing two-tone red and white, crowned with chrome. The producers kept a body shop going full time during production, repairing damaged cars and working on the junkers. When the film was finished, there were two cars left complete. These were later used in publicity for the movie.

Eight: *CHILDREN OF THE CORN*

Children of the Corn is a 12,000-word short story first published in *Penthouse* in 1977 and collected in *NIGHT SHIFT* the following year.

Filmplan of Canada and United Artists both expressed an early interest in filming the story. A Maine-based documentary maker, Harry Wiland, had hopes of making it his feature film directorial debut, but the arranged financing through Home Box Office and 20th Century-Fox collapsed when they backed out of the project. *Children of the Corn* was then picked up by Hal Roach Studios. George (*Force: Five*) Goldsmith worked on several rewrites of King's script for the film. New World, Hal Roach Studios and Goldsmith came to terms and preproduction began.

The film's director, Fritz Kiersch, began his career in commercials. He and Terrance Kirby had created their own production partnership about 2 years before they began working on *Children of the Corn.* They became involved with Donald Borchers of New World (this is after Roger Corman's departure from New World) and learned that the new owners shared Corman's philosophy of giving young guys a chance. So Kiersch became the director of *Children of the Corn* and Terrance Kirby co-produced the film with Donald Borchers.

Shortly after turning 32, Kiersch set off for location to begin production. *Children of the Corn* was filmed in Iowa in less than a month. Time was a crucial factor: as the end of summer grew near, the color of the corn began to change from green to gold. The movie was produced for $3 million.

King's story returns to his familiar locale: a small isolated town taken over by an insidious supernatural force. In this case, the force originates from a corn deity, "He Who Walks Behind The Rows." Through Isaac and his henchman Malachi, the corn god directs the children of the town to murder their elders (anyone past the age of 18). The isolated village as setting is a time honored tradition in horror movies and books: Shirley Jackson's *The Lottery*, Ira Levin's *THE STEPFORD WIVES,* and Thomas Tryon's *HARVEST*

HOME employ the different versions of this setting to good effect.

King, as always, writes most powerfully from his own experience. Here again King is concerned with common human emotions carried one step beyond. Children often harbor hatred towards their parents at one time or another, only King's children of the corn bring out the butcher knives for real. (Likewise, a parent's fear of his or her own children is not uncommon. Ray Bradbury successfully explored this feeling in *The Small Assassin,* as did William Peter Blatty in *THE EXORCIST.*)

The movie opens in the Midwest town of Gatlin. On Sunday morning, following church services (where the sermon is "Corn, Drought and The Lord"), families adjourn to the local restaurant for their Sunday meal. Young Malachi and friends lock the doors and begin their bloody work in a ruthless, calculated manner. Job, a small boy, watches his father murdered before his eyes. He and his sister Sarah form an alliance against the repressive commands of Isaac which are implemented by the sadistic Malachi.

Meanwhile, a medical student named Burt and his girlfriend Vicky stumble into town, having gone out of their way despite the cautionary warning of a mechanic: "Gatlin got religion. They don't cotton to outsiders. And they probably don't have a phone there either."

Eventually, they free the children of the corn from the evil dominance of Isaac, exorcise "He Who Walks Behind the Rows," and escape. Vicki declares at the end of the film, "Let's get the hell out of here." Most of us wanted to do that at the film's beginning. With its random direction and makeshift story line, the movie violates our suspension of disbelief early on. There is never a real concern for developing believable characters. Instead of horror, we are left with sudden shocks, a splattering of blood and a bemused sympathy for the cast.

Nine: *FIRESTARTER*

FIRESTARTER was published in September 1980 in hardcover by Viking Press. In some respects, with *FIRESTARTER,* King is reworking themes he first presented in *CARRIE.*

Despite a major creative innovation—George C. Scott—the film has problems. David Keith's an ex-acid-head hippie who finds his wife stuffed in a closet with most of her fingernails missing and figures out he's in trouble. Then he and his daughter Drew (*E. T.*) Barrymore spend a lot of time running from Secret Service types, till at last there's no place left to run.

Firestarter has one of those simplistic, broad-stroked scripts, full of clear cut good guys and bad guys, that are usually enjoyable (to those of us who don't like existential French comedies with subtitles). As typified by the Western, they tend to work on your subconscious *directly,* without interference from the higher centers. Pauline Kael objects to this sort of film, but you don't have to *think* while you're watching, and that's not all bad. The best of this type can sometimes even achieve mythic dimensions—especially when Clint Eastwood stars.

But not this time. Not even with George C. Scott playing both Rainbird the Psychotic American Viet Nam Vet and John the Friendly Orderly. He sports a milky glass eyeball while he courts young Drew, and who can blame him if he hams up his lines: "She's very beautiful, she's very young. Yet inside her is the power of the gods."

Martin Sheen, boss of the Shop, plays Scott's straight

man. They keep busy teaching Drew to melt concrete blocks and burn up blocks of ice.

Sheen dies, Keith dies, Scott dies and some serious pyromania follows. We finally get to *see* some of the mass-destruction which King does so well in print. The incendiary special effects aren't bad—fire balls, fire bombs, fire rockets, exploding jeeps, exploding houses, exploding trees, exploding helicopters, and guys in asbestos suits yelling "Take cover, take cover!"—but as usual, the book is better. Maybe because King's heart is really in it; he *believes* in this kind of stuff. And maybe because (to justify the budget), the final fiery scenes go on for such a long, long time.

FIRESTARTER film rights were bought in 1980 by Dodi Fayed, the Egyptian producer, for $1 million. These were sold to Dino DeLaurentiis, who then sold his interest to Universal Pictures and stayed on as the executive producer.

The film was shot at the DeLaurentiis facilities in Wilmington, North Carolina, September through November, 1983, at a cost of $15 million. An early version of the script was written by Bill Phillips (who went on to do the screenplay for *Christine)*. A new *Firestarter* script was written by Stanley (*Eye of the Needle*) Mann. Mann's script follows the book of *FIRE STARTER* closely. King himself made suggestions, many of which were incorporated. Mark Lester directed the film.

Ten: *CAT'S EYE*

Several years ago, the British producer Milton Subotsky bought six of the *NIGHT SHIFT* stories for a two-movie deal. King was offered the chance to direct as well as write the screenplays. But, at the time, he had his own fears about wasting other people's money.

Subotsky never exercised his options, and with King's acquiescence, he began selling off these rights to Dino DeLaurentiis. King worked up an additional story idea into a screenplay about a little girl and her cat. With this, DeLaurentiis found the linking device to tie the tales together: a cat.

The cat meanders in and out of the three stories, which are peppered with King in-jokes: a character named Carrie, a dog that looks like Cujo, a car like Christine.

"Quitters, Inc." is the nightmare of anyone who has ever tried to quit smoking cigarettes. Especially if you happen to be the spouse.

"The Ledge" takes a darkly humorous look at making and paying off bets. A twist of infidelity is added to activate the tale.

"The General" is the original script in this stew, developed with Drew Barrymore in mind. A heroic cat, called General, valiantly battles a horrific troll living in the wall of the little girl's bedroom.

Carlo Rambaldi (*E. T.* and *Dune*), supplied the special effects for the troll, along with Jeff Jarvis who worked on *Firestarter* and *Poltergeist*. Besides the regular sets, sets built eight times normal size were used, for a small person in a creature suit. (These king-sized sets made an entry in *THE GUINNESS BOOK OF WORLD RECORDS* for largest bed and pillows.) Karl Miller, who worked with the director on *Cujo*, trained the dozen or so different cats who were "General" on screen.

Lewis Teague (*Cujo, Fighting Back*) directed. For *Cat's Eye* he was able to extensively prepare for the film. He worked closely with King and DeLaurentiis at the newly finished Wilmington, North Carolina studio.

Cat's Eye never quite finds its niche. Despite attempts at cohesion, it retains the look of an anthology film. The humor, while not as broad or low-brow as the jokes in *Creepshow,* doesn't come across on the big screen. Terror is never truly realized in the script. Called a humorous suspense thriller, the film's attempt to reach the PG-13 *Gremlins* audience falls short. It's never quite humorous, suspenseful or thrilling.

Eleven: *SILVER BULLET*

Silver Bullet is the story of a disabled boy confined to a wheelchair (called The Silver Bullet in the movie) who becomes increasingly aware that the terror menacing his town of Tarker's Mills is a werewolf. The story runs from May to a chilling climax on Halloween night.

The basis for the movie is *CYCLE OF THE WEREWOLF,* which appeared in hardcover as an expensive limited edition from Land of Enchantment in 1983.The book was heavily illustrated by Berni Wrightson, who illustrated the book version of *CREEPSHOW*; it sold quickly and was re-issued as a trade paperback by NAL in 1985.

The story was optioned by Dino DeLaurentiis and filmed at his Wilmington, North Carolina facility. It marks Dan Attias' first feature film directorial debut. Martha (*Cat's Eye*) Schumaker is the producer. Carlo Rambaldi worked on the werewolf costumes and Michael McCracken, Sr. accomplished the make-up effects. King wrote the screenplay.

As a novelette *CYCLE OF THE WEREWOLF* is episodic, contrived to conform to certain holidays in each month of the year. As a screenplay, *Silver Bullet* is well-plotted and excellently paced. Its fine characterization allows it to achieve maximum effectiveness as a horror film.

With *Silver Bullet,* King has fulfilled all the promises, promotional hype and hyperbole which surrounded his earlier movies. ("The ultimate in terror from the master of the macabre, Stephen King . . .", etc.) The effect of the horror in the earlier films is less than overwhelming. This is not so with *Silver Bullet.* In this movie King delivers on screen the full dimension of his horror fiction, which is extensive. The man can write horror dramatically and effectively, but this has rarely been translated onto film.

Silver Bullet displays the best of King's considerable storytelling talents. The suspense is magnificently achieved. The blue collar humor strikes just the right note. The horror is realized without gimmicks, director's tricks, or over-use of gore. (The gore that does appear is the result, not the source of the horror.) With this film King has captured the frightening feeling of facing the unknown. In *Silver Bullet* the diabolical unknown is personified in living color.

The characters are well-drawn and completely believable. These are people you can meet on any street, in any barroom, in any American town: the vigilante hunters, the small-town sheriff, the man whose boy is murdered by the Beast are characters we know and care about.

Marty (Corey Haim) is the disabled boy who stands between the Beast and the ruin of his hometown. Marty's sister, Jane (Megan Follows) stays by his side to fight the werewolf. Their often drunk, happy-go-lucky Uncle Red (Gary Busey) comes to believe their incredible story of the werewolf with one eye. The werewolf, Reverend Lowe (Everett McGill), is himself tortured by nightmares and convinced that all things are the Will of God.

Director Dan Attias shows considerable talent, creating just the correct mood for each scene. He moves King's screenplay along with a confident and able hand. This is a happy marriage of talents. Screenwriter, actors and director combine their abilities to create a first-class horror movie. *Silver Bullet* is not *THE HARDY BOYS MEET REVEREND WEREWOLF*, but it is a howling good time.

Twelve: *THE NIGHT SHIFT COLLECTION*

Two student films based on short stories from King's *NIGHT SHIFT* collection were packaged together in 1985 for the burgeoning videocassette market. Billed as *The Night Shift Collection*, copies are currently distributed by Native Son International.

Part one, *The Woman in the Room*, is a 1983 30-minute film produced by Gregory Melton and directed by Frank Darbont. Michael Cornelison plays John, Dee Croxton plays his mother and Brian Libby is the prisoner. King has called *The Woman in the Room* the best short film ever made from his work.

The movie deals with an intense subject, for anyone who has ever experienced an infirmed loved one's suffering. In this case the woman in the room, John's mother, is dying of abdominal cancer. She is in a state of constant pain and her anguish is shared by her son, who visits her daily at the hospital. His false cheer and her maternal reassurance do not mask the truth which is known by both of them: she will suffer painfully until she dies.

John is an attorney representing a convicted killer facing the death penalty. After a conversation with this man John resolves to end his mother's suffering.

With her full consent, he feeds her Darvons until the bottle is empty. He carefully removes all traces of his fingerprints and she clutches the bottle in her hand. "I think I will sleep now, John." She dies in her sleep as John leaves the room and the film ends.

The horror of both the film and the story arises from their all too real circumstances. This film evokes deep memories of fear and pain in anyone who has watched helplessly as someone they love suffers before death comes. For King this is a personal story, drawn from his own experience: his mother died shortly before he achieved the huge success he now enjoys.

In part two, *The Boogey Man,* Lester Billings returns home one night, singing to himself, pleasantly drunk. In the bathroom he discovers the slain body of his little girl. The police are called and he is considered a suspect in the murder. We learn that his older boy died under mysterious circumstances, called a crib death, several months earlier.

Lester visits a psychiatrist and his story of the Boogey Man unravels. His older boy and little girl were reluctant to sleep in one room of their home. They feared the Boogey Man would come out of the closet to get them. They were right.

Lester's wife Rita is subsequently committed to an institution. He lies awake nights guarding his last child, a toddler named Andy. Some weeks later he wakes up hearing the child's cries for help. Lester enters the child's bedroom but refuses to open the closet, despite some very strange things going on in there. He abandons the little boy to whatever lurks in the dark and runs from the room terrified.

Later, he is leaving the psychiatrist's office. He stops to make another appointment with the secretary. A note on her desk states she'll return shortly. Lester goes back to the empty inner office. He opens the closet door to find the doctor inside: "If you believe in something strong enough, maybe it becomes real." As Lester screams the doctor sheds his human skin to become The Boogey Man.

The Boogey Man's contrived storyline works better in print than on film. Transferred to the screen it conjures memories of a Fifties' Marvel comic written by Stan Lee and drawn by Steve Ditko. The director's subject matter limits him to a telegraphed one-punch effect.

Nonetheless, *The Boogey Man* won an award at the New York University Film Festival. The 1982 film was the project of Jeffery C. Schiro, then a student at NYU Film School, who produced, directed, edited and wrote the screenplay. Michael Reid plays Lester Billings, Bert Linder is the psychiatrist Dr. Harper.

Thirteen: *Things to Come*

There's not likely to be an end any day soon to movies based upon the works of Stephen King, since a number of published works, unpublished novels, and original screenplays are available for cinematic adaptations.

King continues to work with George Romero on a variety of projects. Because of the financial success of *Creepshow* (which was moderate for a major studio, but major for Romero's modest, Pittsburgh-based Laurel Productions), there is already a finished script on hand for *Creepshow II.* King has taken a less active role. The script is based on his short stories, but was written by Romero.

As with the first *Creepshow,* this movie purports to help establish a track record for Laurel Productions in order to tie down the distribution and financial backing needed for their on-going project *The Stand.* For

The Stand adaptation, King himself has written several screenplays, including a two-part version, in an effort to compress the complex 823 page novel into a workable script.

In the meantime, Romero's Laurel Productions has produced a weekly syndicated TV series *Tales of the Darkside.* One of King's short stories *The Word Processor of the Gods,* first published in *Playboy* in January 1983, was filmed for the series with a script by Michael McDowell.

King turned down a cool $1 million for film rights to *PET SEMATARY* and instead sold the option to George Romero in exchange for a token advance and creative and financial interest.

The stories from *NIGHT SHIFT* have yet to be fully developed. Various anthology movies have been planned and are still in flux. At one time, there was to be a 20th Century-Fox and NBC TV movie based on three of the stories.

Over the last few years, King assembled another story collection, *SKELETON CREW,* which was published in Summer 1985 by Viking-Penguin. *SKELETON CREW* will no doubt prove to be a treasure trove of movie options. One of the stories, *Gramma,* is slated for the CBS anthology series *The Twilight Zone,* with teleplay by Harlan Ellison.

King's short novel *The Mist,* originally published in the massive anthology of horror stories *DARK FORCES,* has been adapted to an 80 minute audioplay. There are also plans to film this story of a technological nightmare unleashing a vast array of predatory monsters in a small town in Maine.

DIFFERENT SEASONS, published in hardcover by Viking in 1982, contains four short novels. One of these, *The Body,* the tale of a rite of passage for four young boys, contains some of King's most powerful mainstream writing to date. *The Body* is currently filming in Oregon under the direction of Rob Reiner.

Also available is King's surreal, episodic work, *THE DARK TOWER: The Gunslinger.* Set in a timeless realm where magic and reality meet, this ongoing epic shares with Clint Eastwood's *High Plains Drifter* and *A Fistful of Dollars* all the elements of the phantasmagorical morality play.

Although plans to develop *'Salem's Lot* into a weekly TV series were dropped, there is room for a sequel, which King fully intends to write some day: according to King, Ben and Mark (and Father Callahan who escaped town in the book) will be called back to 'Salem's Lot, knowing full well what horrors await them there.

King's personal appearances on the screen continue with interviews and talk show appearances on television. He can even be seen on an American Express Card commercial.

King has taken his first shot as director, for the DeLaurentiis production of his *NIGHT SHIFT* short story, *Trucks.* The movie, tentatively entitled *Maximum Overdrive,* was filmed at the Wilmington studios from a screenplay by King.

King's major published work in 1984 was a massive collaboration with friend Peter Straub, *THE TALISMAN.* Straub is the author of several bestselling horror novels, including *GHOST STORY* and *JULIA,* both made into films.

THE TALISMAN, published by Viking-Penguin, is the result of several years' work. Film rights to the book were purchased before publication by the phenomenally successful producer-director Steven Spielberg.

Over the past six years, five novels by "Richard Bachman" were published by Signet/NAL: *RAGE, THE LONG WALK, ROAD WORK, THE RUN-*

NING MAN and *THINNER.* Before it was revealed that Bachman was King, several of the Bachman novels were already under film option. As of this writing, *The Running Man* is scheduled to be filmed in Canada in 1986 with Arnold Schwarzenegger as the lead.

Believe it or not, a deal to develop a musical version of *CARRIE* has been signed between composer Michael Gore (*Fame*), screenwriter Lawrence D. Cohen (*Carrie, Ghost Story*) and 20th Century-Fox. The big-budget musical will have lyrics supplied by Dean Pitchford.

For the future, King has several more novels waiting in the wings which will no doubt find a home on the screen, though King maintains that his written words are the beginning and the end of his work.

As a kid I was afraid of all the things that children are always afraid of. Ghosts. Boogies. You name it.

I was afraid of the dark. I liked to go to monster movies, but after the monster movie was over and I was *alone*, I'd think: what if that thing comes and gets me?

I had a big imagination. When you're a kid, you're not in control of that. It's like giving a little kid a great big V-8 automobile and saying, now drive this.

—*Stephen King*

King as a Writer for Children

by Ben P. Indick

Children's literature, into which the ubiquitous and irrepressible Stephen King has now ventured with *THE EYES OF THE DRAGON*, is perhaps as old as the art of story-telling itself. One can readily imagine the wide eyes and open mouths when children once listened to tales told round fires, and later to Homeric histories and the doings of those dread but human gods who crowded his pantheon. Still later, they "listened to the lays of minstrels and joined in the refrains of ballads . . . stood absorbed before those vivid pictorial dramas of action and color which we call the Mystery, Miracle and the Morality plays."[1]

Modern writing for children has numerous subdivisions—for differences in age, style, content, purpose, etc. In the early centuries of the printed book, however, with literacy limited even among adults, and books being very rare, those children who had been taught to read first fed their imagination on adult fare.

Such a book as John Bunyan's *PILGRIM'S PROGRESS* (1676–8) was a sermon in the form of an allegory, the message of an earnest Puritan anxious to demonstrate the dangers and pitfalls of life. It was, however, a colorful and multicharactered adventure story as well, with positive appeal to young minds. A generation later Daniel DeFoe would enchant them as he did their elders in his odyssey of the heroic and solitary Robinson Crusoe (1719). At the same time, Jonathan Swift was preparing his scathing satire *GULLIVER'S TRAVELS INTO SEVERAL REMOTE NATIONS OF THE WORLD* (1726). Of those "remote nations" only Lilliput would attract children, but its appeal was lasting.

It is quite ironic that these masterpieces would eventually be regarded primarily as literature for children. In the absence of any other fictional matter, these books, rich in elements appealing to active imaginations, were taken to their hearts, and, abridged, adapted and bowdlerized, remained there. A contemporary adult, reading the originals, will be perhaps surprised to note they still retain vitality and liveliness. It indicates that the unsophisticated child mind nevertheless discerns that which is honest and capable of fulfilling its needs, a truism to be kept in mind by all potential writers for children.

When reading matter designed specifically for children began to appear in the latter half of the 18th century, it was usually in the form of tracts and didactic works, praising conformity, satisfaction with one's station in life and the accepted morality, though the adventurous child might find reading pleasures elsewhere, in works reflecting the Romanticism which was sweeping art, poetry, drama and fiction. Those 18th century moppets capable of reading might even manage to purloin one of the newly popular Gothic romances, steeped in outrageous and fanciful melodrama. These were surely preferable to dry tracts and sermons relieved by little poems.

A positive change for the better was the work of Charles and Mary Lamb, who retold Shakespeare (1807) and Homer's *ODYSSEY* (1808), in stories written intentionally for children. Walter Scott's novels, beginning to appear soon thereafter, while not slanted for young readers, were probably composed with them in mind as well. The same is true of James Fenimore Cooper and Washington Irving. Cooper in particular achieved worldwide popularity with his robust tales of pioneers and Indians, as exotic then as extraterrestrials in our own time. Richard Henry Dana's *TWO YEARS BEFORE THE MAST* (1840) fueled dreamers of maritime adventure, and Nathaniel Hawthorne, following the lead of the Lambs, offered a vivid and idiosyncratic retelling of Grecian legend in his *THE WONDER BOOK* (1852) and *TANGLEWOOD TALES* (1853).

Verse, because it offered the hypnotic pleasures of rhythm and rhyme, as well as readily grasped images, would always satisfy young minds, even when the intent was pietistic and moralistic. But as early as 1822, Clement Moore produced "A Visit From St. Nicholas," whose sole purpose was to delight its readers. In 1846 Edward Lear's *BOOK OF NONSENSE* appeared, with all the fun of easy jingles and the fantasy of preposterous creatures.

Fairy tales, that perfect medium for the child, reached print in France (1698) in the work of Charles Perrault. They were soon translated and were probably the first fairy tales to appear in England.[2] Not only those immortals . . . Cinderella, Red Riding Hood, the Sleeping Beauty and Puss in Boots . . . but Mother Goose herself appeared (on the title page of the French edition), in the role of story-teller. She would later achieve real status in England, in jingles whose innocuous-seeming allegory cloaked other less obvious meanings.

The tales of the Grimm Brothers, carefully collected from folk tales, appeared in Germany in 1812–14 and in England several years later. Hans Christian Andersen's fairy tales, mostly creations from his own imagination, came out initially as incidental works, from 1835 on; they were translated into English in 1846. The genre would soon be permanently mined by other writers, including John Ruskin's *THE KING OF THE GOLDEN RIVER* (1851), W. M. Thackeray's *THE ROSE AND THE RING* (1855), Charles Kingsley's *THE WATER-BABIES* (1863) and Charles Dickens' *THE MAGIC FISHBONE* (1868).

The medieval impression left by most early fairy tales was so strong that when L. Frank Baum published *THE WONDERFUL WIZARD OF OZ* (1900) he took pains in his introduction to point out that he had eliminated "the stereotyped genie, dwarf and fairy." However, his "modernized fairy tale" might not have come about without the appearance in 1864 of a work whose sole intention was to entertain an audience of several little girls, a cleric's book without moral preachments, Lewis Carroll's *ALICE'S ADVENTURES IN WONDERLAND*. It was perhaps the first true children's book, but was loved as well by adults for its genial satire. Charles Dodgson, sometimes annoyed by its success, carefully kept his own persona apart from his pseudonym, but the success of the book spurred writing for children in all fields: fantasy, always a staple, in George MacDonald's *AT THE BACK OF THE NORTH WIND* (1871); patriotic realism in Edward Everett Hales' *THE MAN WITHOUT A COUNTRY* (1863); domestic, if sentimental realism, in Louisa May Alcott's *LITTLE WOMEN* (1867); science fiction in Jules Vernes' *20,000 LEAGUES UNDER THE SEA* (1869); American nostalgia in Mark Twain's *THE ADVENTURES OF TOM SAWYER* (1871), whose hero makes a brief appearance in the more complex *THE ADVENTURES OF HUCKLEBERRY FINN* (1884). And, at the same time, the popular "dime novels" with their varied fare for older readers (which would later be represented for children by such popular genre series as Frank Merriwell, Horatio Alger, Tom Swift, The Hardy Boys and Nancy Drew).

Illustrations were often a part of children's books, but the picture book for very young children, usually with simple verse or prose to be read aloud, was developed with great beauty in the 19th century by Walter Crane, Randolph Caldecott and Kate Greenaway, and became a tradition which continued in the Peter Rabbit books of Beatrix Potter, the enduring *MILLIONS OF CATS* of Wanda Gag (1928), the books of Maurice Sendak and at last the "I-Can-Read" picture books for beginning readers, initiated by the inimitable Dr. Seuss and his *THE CAT IN THE HAT* (1957).

So cursory an overview omits numerous names, but the growing popularity of literature for children resulted in 20th century specialization. Not only "easy readers," but books for advancing readers such as Madeline L'Engle's science fiction novel *A WRINKLE IN TIME* (1963), books for teen-age fantasy devotees such as Lloyd Alexander's *THE BLACK CAULDRON* (1965), the frequently controversial books of Judy Blume such as *TIGER EYES* (1981), and Robert Cormier's *I AM THE CHEESE* (1978)—books whose social and sexual content is germane to the consciousness of the young reader growing into an adult world.

A commonplace in books for children has been the

presence of young heroes and heroines: Mother Goose's Jack and Jill, the Grimms' Hansel and Gretel, MacDonald's Diamond, Stevenson's Jim Hawkins, Baum's Dorothy, Milne's Christopher Robin and more. Their presence is not mandatory and does not necessarily indicate that a book will be satisfactory for young readers, nor must all children's books have them; numerous fairy tales are peopled with adults alone, and many stories have animal characters. Sometimes a book may confuse potential readers by virtue of its characters: *WATERSHIP DOWN* by Richard Adams (1972) is concerned with hares and other animals, a superb adult book appearing as a children's fantasy.

The books of Stephen King are filled with child characters, a necessary part of his milieu. King's forte is credibility, with home, urban and suburban scenes, the familiar trademarks of the commercial arena, all readily identified by his readers with their own lives. As a father and former teacher, King's frame of reality demands the presence of young people. *CARRIE, THE SHINING, THE DEAD ZONE* and *FIRESTARTER* all feature children of extraordinary psychokinetic abilities; *'SALEM'S LOT, The Mist, CUJO, CHRISTINE, DIFFERENT SEASONS* and *PET SEMETARY* all contain more ordinary children and teenagers. The books are intended for an adult audience, although their popularity has extended as well to numerous teenaged readers. Not until *THE EYES OF THE DRAGON* (1984) did King specifically designate one of his works as a book for children. It was not, however, the first. In *THE TALISMAN* (1984) there was already the seed.

THE TALISMAN

THE TALISMAN is a collaboration with King's fellow-master of the supernatural and the weird, Peter Straub. Like King, Straub's writings have had young children in their casts, from the weird revenants of *JULIA* (1975) to the pubescent teenagers who provided the violent prelude and the ghostly vengeance of the climax in *IF YOU COULD SEE ME NOW* (1977). In his *SHADOWLAND* (1980) Straub concentrated on young protagonists in opposition to his villainous adult magician; not a children's book, it nevertheless has episodes involving the Brothers Grimm and the sharply delineated black and white world of the fairy tale.

THE TALISMAN goes even more directly into the imagination of an actively dreaming child, considered metaphorically: the many adventures of the young protagonist are seen wholly through *his* eyes, taking place not only in his (our) world but in a thoroughly realized alternative world. In both worlds it is adults who are his enemies. The dream of such a child is to endure and triumph in a great quest, against all the trials with which an inimical world confronts him. There are antecedents to this in classic novels, to which the authors are indebted.

Not a prototype by any means, but bearing certain common elements is Walter Scott's 1825 novel of the identical title, *THE TALISMAN.* Here is a characteristic Scott tapestry of an exotic past, in the time of the Crusades, with Britain's King Richard the Lion-Hearted and his opponent Saladin of the Saracens. Sir Kenneth, a knight in attendance on Richard, is sent on a mission by the ailing king. One result of his efforts is the discovery of a Moslem physician who is able to fashion from a talisman a potion that cures Richard. If this is reminiscent of Jack Sawyer's mission through two worlds to find the talisman which will cure his desperately sick mother, one may add as well that in a sense two worlds also meet in the Scott novel, that of the Christians and the other of Islam. Scott's story goes on into a love story and a battle with a resultant agreement between the opposing forces, but at the end the young hero is given the talisman as a wedding gift. Although it still effects some cures, it is no longer as potent as it had been. Similarly, the fabulous globe of King and Straub weakens, and, after its final magic has been performed, vanishes. One need hardly posit a purposeful influence, but it would appear possible that the colorful adventure by Scott, once read in many schools, may have left its imprint on the minds of either or both of the authors as young readers.

More direct is the relationship in inspiration and form to Mark Twain, to whom the authors make no attempt to disguise their debt. Indeed, the book is prefixed with a quotation from *THE ADVENTURES OF HUCKLEBERRY FINN*, and concluded with lines from *THE ADVENTURES OF TOM SAWYER*, although it is the former which contributes the basic form of the novel. Thus, while it is in no way a paraphrase of Twain's classic, it rather deliberately encourages comparison.

The hero's name is Jack Sawyer, and his age is 12, close to that of Huck. Jack has a single parent, his sick mother; Huck has, for a time, his father, a hopeless alcoholic. Jack, like Huck, is forced by circumstances on a journey. Each is befriended by a kindly, faithful black man. Huck's Jim is a slave; Jack's Speedy is no slave and is much older than Jim. He recognizes in Jack a "little travelin' man," but does not accompany him. To an extent, Jim's role, even in their mutual affection, is taken by Wolf, Jack's friend—not a white man either—from the Territories, the alternate world. Both lads have goals: Jack's is his quest for the healing talisman, while Huck and Jim seek escape from pursuit and slavery. Huck's various adventures on the Mississippi are mirrored in the very different series of episodes Jack encounters en route to his undefined West.

While *THE TALISMAN* is not intended as a young person's book *per se,* no insightful young reader would fail to understand the import of Jack's terrifying adventures: the need for a job to gain funds; schools which are the extreme extensions of the worst dream a young person might have of such institutions; adult figures who are hostile and do not comprehend the world and the needs of youth. Such a reader would easily empathize with Jack's exertions and reactions. Jack, like Huck, is always an honest appraiser, of the situation and of his own capabilities.

King and Straub tend to draw in bold colors. They offer their hero the option, for a time, of easy exits from his problems; when that option is gone, Jack can be as ingenious as Huck. Twain is less accommodating with such devices, and is less prone to the depiction of utter villainy, which is part of the machinery of a fantastic quest. Even a fateful blood feud is viewed with understanding by Twain, and he offers a humorous side-trip along his river-road with his 19th century actor-vagabonds, the Dauphin and Duke. King and Straub, faithful to their own time, offer Jack a road map through the real and the fanciful, spotting it with place and product names, as well as a familiar scatology and contemporary images, as when the Talisman "sent back a thick ribbon of light like a deathray in a space movie."

The debt to Twain is one of love and respect. The basic style of the novel, a *quest,* originates in broader traditions, which have graced some of the finest books for young readers. The quest novel has its own special parameters. An ordinary novel might be one in which the lives of the characters intertwine, in which ambitions are expressed, realized or lost, and in which developing characterization and turns of the plot determine the outcome, which may be inevitable or unexpected. The quest is more like a path to a goal stated early and thereafter pursued around whatever number of incidental episodes the novel can sustain. Such episodes may be complete stories in themselves, but they nevertheless remain little detours along the preordained path, and eventaully the purpose of the quest must be confronted. Since the intention of the hero is evident so early, growth through characterization is necessarily limited.

An ancient prototype is King Polydectes' assignment of Perseus to bring back the head of the Gorgon; before the task is completed many unrelated adventures occur. In Mallory, Arthur's knights exhaust themselves in their fruitless pursuit of the Grail but create a lasting variation to the genre. A beautiful and neglected modern juvenile quest fantasy is Walter de la Mare's *THE THREE MULLA-MULGARS* (1919), in which his three brave and pathetic monkeys, bearing their own talisman, the Wonderstone, engage in a long and perilous journey to discover the royal mulla-mulgar monkey Kingdom of Assasimmon.

In 1937 the most famous of modern quest novels commenced with Bilbo Baggins and a band of Dwarves seeking a dragon's hoard, and concluded some years later in a quest to destroy Evil, in J. R. R. Tolkien's *THE HOBBIT* and its successor, *THE LORD OF THE RINGS*. Tolkien's books have inspired innumerable others, including the Terry Brooks Shannara series and the David Eddings Belgariad. Its echoes would also frame King's epic quest novel *THE STAND*.

In *THE TALISMAN*, the authors have utilized the idea of the quest as the underlying thread along which are strung a series of adventures, the quest itself being the mysterious and powerful object which alone can save the lives of the mirror-image women of the two worlds, Jack's mother Lily, and Laura DeLoessian, Queen of the Territories. Ironically, although neither *THE TALISMAN* nor *THE LORD OF THE RINGS* is intended for children, basic human elements in each will attract young readers. Tolkien appeals not because he has young people as major characters, which he does not, but because there are surrogates in the presence of his hobbits; their naivete and sense of wonder are those of bright children: thrust into a new world alternately beautiful and terrifying, they pull imaginative young minds along with a fantasy born in fairy tales. King and Straub require no surrogates: Jack, and, later, his friend Richard Sloat, are young people, and, if their adventures tend more toward suspenseful horror and terror, at heart they are extensions, as stated above, of the reality young readers understand.

As a quest novel, however, *THE TALISMAN* owes little in plot or content to Tolkien. Unlike the latter's potent Ring which the antagonists both desire, and which is present at all times, the Talisman only makes its appearance at the climax. Like Frodo, Jack is tempted by the innate power of the object, endangering the entire quest. Jack is able to conquer his weakness, and has the inner strength to surrender voluntarily, if briefly, the Talisman to Richard; Frodo, at the moment of decision, cannot bring himself to give up the Ring, and is saved only by the intervention of Smeagol.

There is an interesting corollary to both books in

the earlier de la Mare Mulla-Mulgar novel. The monkey Nod, like Frodo and Jack, must bear the Wonderstone on his journey. Cold and hungry, he encounters the beautiful Water-maiden, eternally sad in her loneliness. She begs him to allow her to hold the stone—"I think I should never be sad again." He has been forbidden to relinquish it, but faced with her loveliness, he cannot refuse. Taking it, she vanishes beneath the surface of her lake, and he is forlorn. After several wretched days in which his labors all appear to have been in vain, she reappears and returns his Wonderstone, asking only "that when you and your brothers come at last to the Kingdom of Assasimmon and the Valleys of Tishnar, you will not forget me."

It is a moment of great poignancy, especially when read aloud for children, fully the emotive equal of Jack and Frodo's experiences. To the child, who will endow great importance to even an insignificant-seeming object, there is no difficulty in understanding the significance of such a Ring, Wonderstone or Talisman. There is, however, one element required for the children's book in which *THE TALISMAN*, however exciting, satiric and even at times brilliant, is uninterested; this is the story-teller's love for children and for their eager reactions. It is an impulse which is at the heart of Stephen King's first true book for children.

THE EYES OF THE DRAGON

It is interesting that some of the finest children's literature originated as tales *told* by loving adults to children. Clement Moore wrote his poem for his own children, and it was first published without his knowledge.[3] Lewis Carroll wrote down Alice's adventures, which he had first simply made up for his boating friends, in hand-manuscript as a gift for a real little girl, Alice Liddell. Robert Louis Stevenson created *TREASURE ISLAND* for his stepson. Beatrix Potter's beloved rabbit originated in a letter to the oldest child of her former governess. Kenneth Grahame's *THE WIND IN THE WILLOWS* began as nightly bedtime stories and continued later in letters to his son.

Hans Christian Andersen once wrote: "The story-teller's voice must be heard in the style. This means the writing must be as near as possible to speech. The tale may be for children, but it must be understood by adults as well."[4] Thus no matter what the nature of the fantasy, the child will require logic, honest characters and credibility. If the story-teller has his own children as a first audience, his words must also be true to their conception of him. In King's case, this means, as a beginning, a fantastic work, and, furthermore, action, physicality, even references to matters rarely found, or, in the past, even deemed proper in a children's book. Children are a discerning audience, and will reject preachments and condescension; if the book seems honest to them, it will be no less honest for adults. This was the author's ambition, and was so stated in the initial advertisement for the novel, "that comparative rarity: a children's novel for all ages."[5]

King once played a game of preparing little manuscripts for his children, in which all could take part. This same presence of the father who enjoys sharing his children's imagination is transformed into that of story-teller for a mass audience in *THE EYES OF THE DRAGON*. (Since at the time of this writing, the novel has appeared only in a very limited edition,[6] the entire story will not be revealed here; the pleasure of discovering it is reserved for the reader until the book is published in a trade edition in 1986. However, it will be discussed in general terms for its contributions to the field of children's literature.)

The book, not coincidentally, is dedicated to Peter Straub's son Ben and to King's daughter Naomi, whose names are appended to important characters, a hallmark of a story intimate both to the narrator and his particular audience. (King has written elsewhere that the novel began as a story for his daughter, "who likes fantasy fiction but cares not at all for tales of horror.")[7] The simple plot may be described in one sentence: a prince is unjustly accused of regicide and must seek, against great odds, freedom and victory. This is a staple of legend, realized here through thorough characterizations, realistic scenes, suspense, ingenuity, and, perhaps above all, human understanding.

Although placed in a medieval setting, *THE EYES OF THE DRAGON* is modern in the unromanticized modesty of its protagonists. The king, Roland, is "neither the best nor the worst ever to rule the land," and is, the author must admit, perhaps even as kings go, "mediocre." Thinking is hard work for him: "When he thought deeply, his nose got stuffed up." Yet, he is lovable and all too comprehensible to any child-reader exasperated by a sometimes incompetent father. Modern as well is the book's frank, unabashed approach to sex, a baby in its mother's belly, an aging man's "flaccid penis" in the presence of his naive young bride. Such socially embarrassing practices as nose-picking, flatulence and bodily relief, all described with graphic humor, are not exercises in vulgarity, but part of the growing insight of a voyeuristic son who sees a man where he had previously seen only a symbol. Such frank descriptions and vocabulary have nothing to do with prudery.

As in many a fairy tale, there is a good son and a bad. If the former needs no apologies, King is able to make the latter understandable, and to that degree sympathetic. On one occasion, forgetting his most princely older son for a moment, the king impulsively embraces his less likeable, less intelligent, less handsome younger son. "Thomas never forgot that day—the bright sunshine, the damp, slightly moldy odor of the moat water, the warmth of his father's arms, the scratchiness of his beard." It is, however, an isolated moment, and the boy's bitterness returns when, in pique, he injures and then kills a helpless old dog. Readers young and old will understand what lay behind such cruelty: "He was often a confused boy, often a sadly unlucky boy, but I stick to what I said, he was never a bad boy, not really."

King enjoys the story-teller's role, often dropping asides to the reader, sometimes as a caution to consider the possible consequences of an action; "I leave it to you to decide" he will say. At times, he is even a companion to the reader; describing a maze of corridors, King writes: "You would have become lost very soon, and I probably would have gotten lost myself before long, but Thomas knew this way as well as you know your way through your own bedroom in the dark."

Although uncommon in twentieth-century literature, this familiar, almost intimate tone was popular with 18th century novelists such as Henry Fielding and Tobias Smollett, and was adopted by C. S. Lewis in his popular Narnia fantasies for children. Thus, in the third volume, *THE VOYAGE OF THE 'DAWN TREADER'*, Lewis writes: "There was a boy named Eustace Clarence Scrubb, and he almost deserved it . . . I can't tell you how his friends spoke to him, for he had none . . ." Lewis, books offer many adventures, but the tone is paternal, harmless even in moments of potential peril, and pointedly moralistic. Young listeners enjoy the extravagances; older readers may find the work somewhat precious.

In his story-teller's role, King is fascinated by all of his characters, including the villain, and after all, what would a fairy tale be without a mouth-wateringly bad villain? In the author's capacious bag of nasties, he has never done better than Randall Flagg, the Dark Man of *THE STAND,* who was evil merely by his own presence, his mystery, purpose and ruthless ambition. It is no small marvel that the evil magician in *THE EYES OF THE DRAGON* is none other than a character named—Flagg! His character is much altered, by no means the *other* Flagg, and yet, intrinsically, he is the same. It is as if King were cautioning that, after all, Evil is by any name or manifestation—Evil. The use of this medieval Flagg as evil personified in modern context is a master's stroke.

Fantasy per se is not truly the author's prime interest in this novel, and is the domain of the wicked Flagg alone, thereby causing his power to appear all the more dangerous and powerful. The young reader will concentrate his fear and realize that only courage and ingenuity, qualities which do not require sorcery, can save Peter, the hero. The unexpected appearance of a dragon, a fabled creature even in the era of the story, is wonderfully abrupt and quickly told, but to the characters, the memory of that encounter is never forgotten. Dragons, the reader realizes, are, like magic, unique. This dragon will play no culminating role as did Bilbo's Smaug, but it has its very special place in a story which is more concerned with honesty and knavery.

There are moments in all of King's novels when he pauses from his headlong pace and his tendency to shock. It may be in reaction to a glut of excess, or the need of a breather between the pendulum swings from real to unreal. At such times he may comment on human beings. In *CARRIE*, the tone is sardonic, as extracts are quoted from books written in some future time about the benighted girl. In *THE DEAD ZONE* the narrative expresses bitterness at Fate, which has made a normal life impossible for the unassuming hero. In King's outright horror books, he may take a moment to emphasize the destructive effects on human psyches involved.

In a novel of heroic legend, however, such as *THE DARK TOWER*, there is a more cautious, more deliberate style as demanded by the form of epic literature; such narrative pauses are longer and are sometimes reinforced by vague references to the past. In *THE EYES OF THE DRAGON*, King's intention to write for a young audience, his highly evident narrative presence, and the mythical framework of the story itself, all combine to produce the sense of a more measured manner of tale-telling.

It is a happy consequence, for it gives King a greater freedom. He can allow himself the luxury of wise observation, which is appreciated by the adult reader and understood as well by the child.

"No one ever forgets a toy that made them supremely happy as a child," he writes in this regard, "even if that toy is replaced by one like it that is much nicer." And again, in *THE EYES OF THE DRAGON*, when one character manages to be given credit for something in which he had taken no part, he merely "smiled and said nothing." To achieve greatness, King indicates, "Sometimes all you had to do was look wise and keep your mouth shut." At one point he writes: "Guilt is like a sore, endlessly fascinating, and the guilty party feels compelled to examine it and pick at it, so that it never really heals." (Obviously, tellers of tales for children are well aware of the propensities of children for repeated examination of such sores. In his *THE VOYAGE OF THE 'DAWN TREADER'*, Lewis' Eustace, having been transformed into a dragon, is restored to his normal self by pulling off the dragon's skin. He comments: "You know, if you've ever picked the scab off a sore place, it hurts like billy-oh, but it *is* such fun to see it coming away.")

At times, King's ruminations, those of a reflective adult explaining, not talking down to the young reader, achieve a melodious beauty of metaphor: "A dust of years drew over the bright pleasures of childhood and they were forgotten. . . . Now let many years pass, all in a twinkling—one of the great things about tales is how fast time may pass when not much of note is happening. . . . What is history except a grand sort of tale where passing centuries are substituted for passing years?"

Yet he can be easily colloquial as well: "We will have to speak more of him later, but let it go for now." And, when one of the boys has made a gift which is ignored by its recipient, he feels the gift is "pukey"—as he is quite literally about to be himself.

Nonetheless, there is a brooding menace and a foreboding sense of drama to be played out. Foreshadowing, a technique used in King's earliest books, is well employed here, as we learn very quickly that the young hero will face disgrace, but neither the manner nor the time in which it will come.

King, ever the lover of literary allusions, cannot resist a direct reference to one of the most well-known creations of his illustrious forebear, H. P. Lovecraft. (For an admirer of the Gentleman from Providence, it was a delight to discover this quite appropriately used. The reader is welcome to discover it as one of the charms of the novel.)

Less obvious, but perhaps distilled from memories

of Mallory and T. H. White, are scenes of the conception of Roland's two sons. The first has the impetuosity and exultation of Uther Pendragon's consummation of his love for Igraine; the second has echoes of the uncertainty but the inevitability of Arthur's seduction of his half-sister. The conclusion of the second book of White's tetralogy *THE ONCE AND FUTURE KING* is a climactic moment in the Arthurian story, for the naive young king, tired and lulled by a "love-philtre," is unable to resist Morgause. "It is impossible to explain how these things happen," White writes, perhaps because Arthur "had never known a mother of his own, so that the role of mother love took him between wind and water." In King's novel, old Roland is unable to rouse himself to the act of love and requires an aphrodisiac. Like White, King cannot find reasons for the sudden emotions which that night caused Flagg to prepare an especially strong potion. Speaking of Flagg, King writes: "Perhaps it was something in the wind that urged him to do it." For Arthur, the consequence is a son who will be his murderer; for Roland, it is the unhappy Thomas, who will witness his murder.

In the end, the unusually chaste story-teller who has been carefully and lovingly measuring his words must be faithful to himself and the writer we have known. A character sees in an uneasy dream "streams of fresh blood washing in bright, accusing threads between the cobblestones and running down the gutter in rivulets." In a smashing and breathless climax there are echoes of the frenzy of *THE SHINING* and the great evil symbol of *THE STAND*.

For the prolific King, who was impelled to write this tale for his children, as a labor of love (which in its initial limited edition is a beautifully printed treasure), the result is a story to stand with the great fantasy adventures for young readers, Walter de la Mare's

THE THREE MULLA-MULGARS, Ursula LeGuin's *EARTHSEA* trilogy, Lloyd Alexander's *PRYDAIN,* Susan Cooper's *THE DARK IS RISING* and J. R. R. Tolkien's quest of the immortal Fellowship.

1. Cornelia Meigs, Anne Thaxter Eaton, Elizabeth Nesbitt, Ruth Hill Viguers, *A CRITICAL HISTORY OF CHILDREN'S LITERATURE* (New York: The Macmillan Co., 1953) p. 20. This is a splendid, encyclopedic survey of the field from its beginnings.

2. Ibid. p. 113.

3. Ibid. p. 163.

4. Isabelle Jan, *ON CHILDREN'S LITERATURE* (New York: Schocken Books, 1974) p. 46.

5. *The Magazine of Fantasy and Science Fiction,* Nov. 1984, p. 3.

6. *THE EYES OF THE DRAGON* was pre-sold and published in 1984, by Philtrum Press, Bangor, Maine, in an edition of 1250 copies, illustrated by Kenneth R. Linkhauser.

7. *Castle Rock,* June 1985, "The Politics of Limited Editions," p. 4. For information about this monthly newsletter for Stephen King fans write: Castle Rock, Box 8183, Bangor, ME 04401.

The thing that haunts me is, I know there have been a lot of really terrible writers who thought they were good writers. The worst was Jacqueline Susann; that woman thought she was William Faulkner . . . And there are a lot of other writers the same way. So I try to be hard on myself, to maintain some perspective on my own work.

—Stephen King

The Mind's a Monkey: Character and Psychology in Stephen King's Recent Fiction

by Bernadette Lynn Bosky

> " 'The mind is a monkey,' Robert Stone's protagonist muses in *DOG SOLDIERS*, and he is so right."
>
> —*Stephen King*

Asked what he thought was the most important element of writing horror, Stephen King replied, "Character. You have to love the people in the story, because there is no horror without love and without feeling." Much horror in "supermarket novels" fails, he said, because "you don't believe the people, and therefore you don't believe the horror, and you're not scared."[1] King's greatest success is in this area where so many fail; his talent for the depiction of his characters, coupled with affection for them and an endless desire to understand their natures and motives, may be his greatest strength as a writer.

It is certainly his most remarked-upon strength. Many

of the essays in the ground-breaking collection *FEAR ITSELF* examine King's ability to depict real social and psychological concerns. Don Herron even suggests that King's success is due to his depiction of ordinary people and settings, not the supernatural content of his work,[2] while Fritz Leiber argues that in *THE DEAD ZONE* King's "ground[ing] the psychic phenomena in the physical," in a physically and psychologically realistic world, makes the otherwise incredible element more believable.[3]

Elsewhere, attention has been focused on King's building of credibility with realistic minutiae—his work "filled," as Alan Ryan puts it, "with carefully chosen and fully imagined details"[4]—from the habits of small-town life to seemingly omnipresent brand-names. In his writing, King is encyclopedic. He is like Fran Goldsmith in *THE STAND*, recording all the details of contemporary American life from the sublime to the ridiculous, or like those 19th century novelists drawn to both social realism and *copia* such as Theodore Dreiser (whom King has admired and compared to Charles Dickens). King may well be read in universities next century for the reasons that Dreiser continues to be read now.

King's documentary approach, however, is not the reason for his overwhelming popularity, nor does it explain the deep emotional response so many have to his writing. No one can dispute King's ability to stir the reader, one of the most basic goals of fiction. One reason for this success is the development of character in King's writing, a matter more of *why* people do things, than what they do or how it is described.

In a way unusual among contemporary writers, many of King's characters are slightly idealized and romanticized, although still quite believable. Deborah Notkin noted, "[King] does not, of course, paint a rosy picture of a loving and flawless human race; he simply focuses, again and again, on people . . . who behave slightly better than we expect."[5] As King said of his own characters, "They seem like people you would *like* to know or even people you *do* know." Certainly those memorable characters and moments attract one to King's fiction: Irv Manders in *FIRESTARTER* standing up to the Shop because of his principles and disinterested affection; Howard Cottrell and the other Denver residents aiding Dick Hallorann on his terrifying errand of mercy in *THE SHINING;* Dave Drayton's love for his son Bill in *The Mist,* or Dennis Guilder's genuine appreciation of and friendship shared with Arnie Cunningham in *CHRISTINE.*

But perhaps another appeal of King's fiction is less apparent, though stronger. Why do readers like King's characters so much when the personalities depicted are unappealing? Harold Lauder, cherishing his hatred and alienation in *THE STAND,* attracts the reader at least as much as Dennis Guilder does, even if the attraction is mixed with repulsion. In some ways, Jack Torrance is at least as sympathetic a character as Dave Drayton. Certainly, characters who, as Peter Straub puts it, "examine their world in a way that's plausible and acceptable"[6] are attractive, no matter what their specific personalities. In King's fiction, however, it goes beyond that. The way in which any author's characters react—their basic psychological structure, apart from specific actions—demonstrates a view of human nature and implies a view of the universe. In King's fiction, these views express basically optimistic and attractive premises, no matter how bleakly individual characters or plots may develop.

This premise remains remarkably consistent throughout King's career, and is evident in *CUJO* and later works. Great emphasis is placed on humanity's ability to choose, even in his more naturalistic works like *CUJO*. No matter what choice an individual in the story may make—even that of Harold Lauder or Jack Torrance—a world of meaningful choice is affirmed. The mind-view King presents supports several popular romantic notions, including the use of common intuition, in a quite credible, integral manner. The supernatural presence of prophetic dreams and "feelings" implies forces beyond the material that many people now would like to believe in but may not be able to—except within the boundaries of fiction.

This last premise is perhaps the most obvious. In an interview, King paraphrased Stanley Kubrick: ". . . it doesn't matter whether the supernatural forces are good or evil; all that matters is that they exist. It means that after this life, there's *more*."[7] In *The Mist,* the narrator says of the popularity of supernatural fiction, ". . . when the machines fail . . . , when the technologies fail, when the conventional religious systems fail, people have got to have something. Even a zombie lurching through the night can seem pretty cheerful compared to the existential comedy/horror of the ozone layer dissolving under the combined assault of a million fluorocarbon spray cans of deodorant." The various hunches, feelings, encounters, dreams, and visions in King's fiction affirm that more sophisticated (and generally more reliable) modes of perception are available to us than those we normally use, and that there are perhaps entire spiritual realms of existence besides. The existence of precognition and telepathy implies a more substantively ordered, connected and purposeful universe than modern science can concede.

In King's fiction, natural human intuition is almost always correct and its results are often positive if followed—which it rarely is by the adult characters.

Bad results from acting on one's feelings usually indicate supernatural "poisoning"; Jud Crandall tells Louis Creed in *PET SEMATARY* that the influence of the burial ground can be like heroin to dope addicts, "poisoning their bodies and poisoning their thinking." This frightening supernatural intervention has the paradoxically positive result of broadening human ability while restricting human responsibility for failure: when acting on intuition goes wrong, it is the fault of malefic "outside" influences. Many of King's characters consistently refuse to trust their inner hunches, but there is usually at least one character in each story who does follow intuition, often with heroic results and probable, satisfying resolution.

Sometimes those who follow their intuition will fail. Vic Trenton speeds out to Camber's farm in *CUJO*, spurred by the literal vision of a red-eyed (Cujo-like) monster in Tad's closet, but arrives too late to save Tad. Rachel Creed, in *PET SEMATARY*, races back to Maine from Chicago (in some ways reminiscent of Hallorann's race to the Overlook in *THE SHINING)* because of her feelings about her daughter's prophetic nightmares, arriving too late to stop her husband in his "wild work," and just in time to be killed herself. But these are exceptions. Moreover, King has said that he originally intended for the child to be saved in *CUJO* (as happens in the movie); and *PET SEMATARY'S* Rachel would probably have been able to prevent what occurred had it not been for supernatural interference. For instance, Rachel fears the battery cable inexplicably came loose "just long enough for . . . something irrevocable to happen," and she is right. However, even if the action is futile, the reader respects the character's right perception and is uplifted by their willingness to act on intuition, despite the psychological unease and physical difficulties involved.

More often the action is not futile. In *The Breathing Method,* the doctor is unable to save his pregnant patient despite his willingness to believe a "precognitive interlude" that announces her doom. Yet he is able to deliver her child safely because on a hunch, and very much against his usual practice, he packed his forceps that night. Dennis Guilder's efforts in *CHRISTINE* can't save Arnie's life, but because he and Leigh accepted the incredible and acted, they saved his soul. Later, at the moment Dennis later finds out Arnie died, he has a vision, unusually mild and wistful for King:

> "Then Arnie was there, and of course that *had* to be a dream.
>
> *Thanks, man,* he said, and I noticed with something like terror that the left lens of his glasses was shattered. His face was okay, but that broken lens. *Thanks. You did okay. I feel better now. I think things are going to be okay now.*
>
> *No sweat, Arnie,* I said—or tried to say—but he was gone."

There is tragedy here, but there is also nobility, and the implication that even in the face of overpowering evil something good and positive in the human spirit will be saved.

As these examples show, the supernatural perceptions and incidents also serve as a vehicle for one of King's major literary strengths: showing basically good people genuinely caring about each other. In many of King's stories, psychic rapport is an extension of love, especially familial love. Although telepathy as a "wild talent" exists apart from affection in King's fiction (as in *THE DEAD ZONE* or *FIRESTARTER),* the psychic abilities in his fiction from *CUJO* on are enhanced by affection, and presented as a normal dimension of the human mind. Hallorann tells Danny in *THE SHINING*, "I think all mothers shine a little, you know, at least until their kids grow up enough to watch out for themselves." In *The Mist*, Dave Drayton's hunches are consistently and specifically protective of his wife and his son. He feels "for no concrete reason" that his wife should join him in his trip into town, and after he has failed to convince her, feels "another flash of unease" when he thinks of her at home alone. He is successful in preventing his son from venturing out to watch the mist, also for "no concrete reason." Characters in the novels do have intuitions about acquaintances, such as Dennis Guilder's feeling in *CHRISTINE* that George LeBay had not told him everything about Ronald LeBay, but much more often the intuitions concern those they love.

Prophetic dreaming is another factor that becomes more pronounced in King's later work. *The Monkey*, for example, presents a vivid vision of Hal's mother's death. "The boys were never told any of this," it is explained, "but Hal knew it anyway. He dreamed it again and again . . ." The fear Charity Camber feels at her son Brett's sleepwalking, including the pronouncement "Cujo isn't hungry no more, no more," is primarily why she returns to Maine early. Dennis Guilder has two waking visions and three dreams that indicate to him each danger before it affects him personally: that Christine has a dangerous attraction; that the car can renew itself; that it will kill anyone who interferes; that LeBay himself has begun possessing both the car and Arnie; and that an obsession with his football will prevent Dennis from coming between Arnie and Christine. As the events develop, Dennis repeatedly sees the similarities to his dreams and is made uncomfortable by them. It is partly because of such a similarity that Dennis speaks with George LeBay, providing the key knowledge of his automotive opponent. There is no doubt that Dennis has such dreams because of his affection for Arnie.

Dreams and intuitions based on ties of familial love form an inspiring but ultimately weak and ineffective counterpoint to the influence of the Wendigo-blighted burial ground in *PET SEMATARY*. Ellie Creed consistently dreams the horrible events—her cat Church's death, Gage's removal from his coffin, and his homicidal return—in time to prevent at least some of them if there had not been interference. The reactions of other characters in the novel to these dreams can be emotionally cheering for the reader, even if disaster is not entirely averted. During the opening of Part Two the design of the novel is stated: "horror spawns horror, one coincidental evil begets another, often more deliberate evil, until finally blackness seems to cover everything"; the horror spirals outward, like the Pet Sematary's graves and the burying ground beyond it. But a more subtle effect is that familial concern and intuition likewise seem to spiral out. Rachel's love for Ellie combines with her own misgivings to create a touching solidarity:

> "It's very important, isn't it?"
> Ellie nodded.
> "Honey, I believe that it is. But you could help me if you could tell me more. Is it just the dream?"
> "No," Ellie said. "It's . . . it's everything now. It's running all through me now. Can't you feel it, Mommy? Something like a—"
> "Something like a wind."
> Ellie sighed shakily,

Just as Ellie and Rachel reinforce each others' intuitive awareness, Rachel's mother is brought, albeit more reluctantly, to side with Rachel, supporting her rapid return to Maine: "I've begun to feel nervous, too. I'll feel better if I know Louis is all right."

Another source of warning in *PET SEMATARY* is Victor Pascow, the jogger who dies in Dr. Louis Creed's office. Unlike the warm and human insight presented by his family, Pascow's aid is little less frightening than the forces he warns against. When Pascow appears to warn Creed against going beyond the Pet Sematary, "There was a look on his face which Louis at first mistook for compassion. It wasn't really compassion at all; only a dreadful kind of patience." Pascow has his message to pass on, not even as a friend but as an emissary of some unknown and apparently impotent force. This aspect of *PET SEMATARY* is unique among King's books, as the entire novel is uniquely bleak, surpassing even the atypically grim *CUJO*. Generally, the prophecies in King's fiction present an optimistic view of human affection and abilities.

The major limitation of the characters' prophecies and hunches is that they are so easy to disregard, in the immediacy of his characters' actions and concerns. King develops this credibly, based on sound psychologizing. Although readers obviously like the supernatural aspects of King's fiction, the characters almost uniformly find the inexplicable experiences inherently terrifying, apart from the message conveyed. There are some notable exceptions to this.

As Douglas Winter has noted in *THE ART OF DARKNESS*, his book about King, children in King's fiction are much more apt to accept such experiences. "Childhood itself is a myth for most of us," King states in *DANSE MACABRE*. "We think we remember what happened to us when we were kids, but we don't. The reason is simple: we were crazy then. Looking back into this well of insanity as adults . . . we attempt to make sense of things that make no sense . . . and remember motivations which simply don't exist." Children do not resist their impressions partly because they have not learned adult standards of sanity and already exist in a shocking and primal world that adults can barely recall or comprehend. It is a sad irony, exampled in books like *THE SHINING, CUJO*, and *PET SEMATARY*, that children, who often understand the intrinsics of evil best, have the least power to change it.

Some of King's most admirable protagonists, like Dr. McCarron in *The Breathing Method* or Dennis and Leigh in *CHRISTINE,* are wary of the experiences but rarely if ever resist them. Mostly, however, a supernatural experience is met at least initially with attempts to rationalize or simply ignore it. The only adult exception to this is an otherwise unsympathetic character, Will Darnell in *CHRISTINE.* "In a very real sense," Darnell muses, "there was no supernatural, no abnormal. What happened, happened and that was the end." Perhaps because Darnell is a single-mindedly practical man, he accepts the truth about Christine with an ease both admirable—although unfortunate for him—and perhaps unique in King's fiction.

Of course, characters who have accepted the supernatural as commonplace or inescapable fact do fear how others might react to any acknowledgement on their part. As George LeBay says in *CHRISTINE* about his hesitation about speaking of his brother, "There is only so much a person can say in defense of one's beliefs, because the irrational . . . it creeps in." This sometimes makes the job of confronting supernatural evil even more difficult, since intuition can form the basis of one's own action but may not necessarily be sufficient to convince another, as when Dave

Drayton fails to convince his wife to seek the safety of the town in *The Mist.* In other instances, however, explaining oneself is not a problem, because of the intuition many of King's most sympathetic characters seem to share. When *CHRISTINE*'s Dennis Guilder asks Michael Cunningham to tell him whenever Arnie leaves town, he is asked the reason. "I'd as soon not go into that," he replies. "It's complicated and it would . . . well, it would sound crazy." Nonetheless, Michael's own suspicions prompt him to agree without question. The characters in *CHRISTINE* have unusual success convincing others to follow their hunches, while in *CUJO* and *The Mist* selling intuitive judgements proves more difficult.

But often in King's fiction the hardest person to convince of the reality of supernatural experiences and the validity of their insight is oneself. Repeatedly, disasters occur or are barely avoided because of self-denials and rationalizations. One of King's strengths, setting him apart from lesser horror writers, is that this is not just a stylistic or plot convenience—if the character's premonitions of doom were acted on, there might not be much story to tell—but rather, is based on a consistent understanding of how people think. In normal human emotions and thought and in supernatural experiences, the ability of the mind to reject is at least as important as its ability to perceive. As Larry Underwood thinks in *THE STAND*, "Thank God for tunnel vision. . . . Thank God for selective perception. Because without it, we might as well all be in a Lovecraft story."

This view of "extra-normal understanding" as being dangerous in itself characterizes many outstanding horror writers. H. P. Lovecraft begins his story, *The Call of Cthulhu*, "The most merciful thing in the world, I think, is the inability of the human mind to correlate all its contents. We live on a placid island of ignorance, and it was not meant that we should voyage far." King himself has mentioned being impressed by Arthur Machen's statement, ". . . that true evil is when a rose begins to sing. I'm not sure I understand perfectly what he meant, but the feeling of the statement is so clear!"

Unlike Lovecraft or even Machen, King is less concerned with overtly metaphysical speculation than with the effect of emotion on human actions. His passages on why his characters react as they do to the supernormal are not as philosophically rationalized as Lovecraft's, but they are more emotionally effective. One of his most extended discussions, in *The Mist*, specifically refers to the statement by Machen:

> I realized with fresh horror that new doors of perception were opening up inside. New? Not so. Old doors of perception. The perception of a child who has not yet learned to protect itself by developing the tunnel vision that keeps out ninety percent of the universe. . . . Terror is the widening of perspective and perception. The horror was in knowing I was swimming down to a place most of us leave when we get out of diapers. . . . When rationality begins to break down, the circuits of the human brain can overload. . . . the dead walk and talk; a rose begins to sing.

The psychological basis King provides is convincing: human beings derive a sense of security from thinking that experience follows certain knowable scientific rules, and many supernatural experiences threaten that premise. Louis Creed thinks of the visitation by Pascow as, "the irrational that refuses to be broken down into the normal causes and effects that run the Western world."

Because of this, King's characters fear supernatural experience more as a cause of insanity than as its symptom. Dennis Guilder, after his ride with phantoms inside Christine, and Louis Creed, after the dying Pascow spoke to him about the Pet Sematary, both feared insanity, yet they were eager to explain away their experiences as hallucinations. The significance of a world vastly different than the one they took for granted might actually drive them mad; better to believe in temporary hallucination than to discover that their familiar, ordered world is a self-made illusion.

For the most part, King presents his characters' behavior without providing this explicit reasoning. (This is a technique King also uses well in presenting the horrors themselves, as Peter Straub points out: in *'SALEM'S LOT*, for instance, the menace of modern-day vampires may seem incredible, but "the characters feel so strongly that their emotion comes out toward the reader," making the reader believe the situation.[8])

King's characters' reactions cover a revealing range of human nature. One response is a simple and total rejection of the threatening situation. A more common one is temporary denial—not the suppression of a thought, but pushing it away. In other instances, a character will rationalize until the experience becomes manageable, achieving the effect by changing the facts of the experience or by finding a less threatening explanation of the facts.

The alienness that makes these experiences threatening also makes them easier to dismiss. In *PET SEMATARY*, Creed speculates that the mind simply cannot accept something like a UFO sighting or a horrible apparition: "There was a giggling fit or a crying fit . . . and since it was its own inviolable self and would not break down, you simply passed terror intact, like a kidney stone." In King's fiction, this tendency is dangerous primarily because it prevents action; in fact, Creed "passing terror intact" after Pascow's dying words and post-mortem visitation makes it easier for the spirit of the burying ground to gain control. Although the consequences of passive inaction surpass the psychological consequences of repression, this latter phenomenon is mentioned, quite powerfully, in *CHRISTINE*:

> "I think that everybody has a backhoe in his or her head, and at moments of stress or trouble you can fire it up and simply push everything into a great big slit-trench in the floor of your conscious mind. Get rid of it. Bury it. Except that that slit-trench goes down into the subconscious and sometimes, in dreams, the bodies stir and walk."

Brent Norton, in *The Mist*, presents the most extreme case of denial in King's recent fiction. Because, as the narrator speculates, "Norton's sanity hinged on not being convinced," he dismisses the warnings of huge creatures outside the supermarket as a "joke," "a lie," and "lunacy." Norton eventually walks into the deadly mist, because he believes that is what his professed arguments demand of him. "I think, deep down, that he knew what was going to happen to him," Drayton says. "I think that the logic he had paid lip service to all his life turned on him at the end like a tiger that has gone bad and mean."

This act of total repression is less common in King's fiction than is a continual pushing away and setting aside of some intrusive idea or intuition, both more credible and more dramatic than total dismissal. Dennis says of his dwelling on a dream of Christine, "I shook the thought off." Hal Shelburn in *The Monkey*, shocked by the reappearance of the malevolent wind-up toy after thirty years, tries with even less success: *"I won't think about that.* But now of course it was all he *could* think about." Sometimes, the denial is overcome by the character's own better sense, as Donna Trenton often overcomes her own dangerous denials in *CUJO.* When she felt Cujo was "psyching out" her weaknesses with more than canine ability, "She tried to reject the thought as soon as it occurred to her, and then stopped trying. Things had become too desperate now to indulge in the luxury of lying to herself."

In *PET SEMATARY*, Louis Creed consistently refuses to consider anything disturbing, especially the increasing evidence that the power of the burial ground is exerting control over him. Rachel tells Louis that the truck driver who ran over Gage, "said that when he got to Ludlow, he just felt like putting the pedal to the metal. He said he didn't even know why." While Rachel does not know why either, Louis does, but he "thrust these thoughts away" rather than admit it to himself. His reaction to the ease of getting Rachel and Ellie out of town so he can revive Gage is similar: *"It's almost magic,* Louis thought . . . and Jud's voice responded promptly, *It's been full of power before, and I'm ascared. Oh, get fucked,* he told Jud's voice rudely." Louis is described as "a man with no deep religious training, no bent toward the superstitious or the occult. He was ill prepared for this . . . whatever it was." That refers not only to Pascow's dying words, but also to the process of obsession throughout the novel. Louis' materialistic training and willingness to dismiss the supernatural aid and abet the spirit controlling the horrors in his life.

An even more common way for King's characters to react to the inexplicable is by reforming the experience to fit their worldviews. King knows how fragile and unreliable the human memory is. As the narrator points out in *The Monkey*, "with an old, old memory like this one, you had to be careful not to believe too much. Old memories could lie." This human mental process, perhaps inevitable as the years pass, is an immediate deliberate defensive response to supernatural terror. "But already his mind seemed to be wrapping those few moments in a protective film," King writes of Creed after Pascow's death, "sculpting, changing, disconnecting." Dennis Guilder speculates in *CHRISTINE*, "I think one of the reasons there is so little convincing evidence of psychic phenomena is that the mind goes to work and restructures the evidence. A little stacking is better than a lot of insanity."

When the evidence of the unnatural is too obvious to be changed by memory, logic will often find rationalizing, nonsupernatural explanations. Many of King's characters, especially the young professional men, are intelligent and reasonable, but their reasoning powers can function as a two-edged knife. When Stephanie Drayton in *The Mist* becomes concerned with the gathering fog, David explains the phenomenon to her in scientific terms that are both quite reasonable and quite erroneous. Although Stephanie is not totally convinced, this may contribute to her later decision to stay at home despite David's entreaties to come into the town. In *CUJO*, the same reasoning ability that helps Vic Trenton save his business and deduce his wife and son's probable location produces perfectly good reasons to dismiss his own prophetic dream and intuitions of trouble:

> As he lay down he glanced at the telephone and felt a sudden irrational urge to call home. Irrational? That was putting it mildly. It was ten minutes to two in the morning. He would not only wake her up, he would probably scare the living hell out of her in the

bargain. You didn't interpret dreams literally, everyone knew that. When both your marriage and your business seemed in danger of running off the rails at the same time, it wasn't really surprising that your mind pulled a few unsettling head games, was it?

Vic does not phone then, forgets the dream, and neglects to call later during the day. This incident—like that of Charity Camber overcoming her unease about Brett's sleepwalking and likewise not calling home about Cujo—shows how impotent intuition can be if not acted on quickly.

PET SEMATARY is a symphony of these rationalizations: of explanations of events, of motivations, of possible consequences. When Louis has his first intuition of disaster, holding Gage on the stairs, he accounts for it "physiologically and psychologically," as the doctor that he is. Later, he can no longer ignore what is going on, as when the cat returns from the dead and even Louis sees that it is impossible that the cat was only stunned, although he briefly tries to believe that. But when Creed cannot avoid belief that some supernatural force is at work, he still, tragically, avoids acknowledging the nature or malevolent extent of that force. Sometimes, as with his misgivings about digging up Gage, he simply "pushed the voice aside."

Most often, Creed's mind will seize on any rationalization that keeps him from accessing his true situation. When Jud Crandall offers the explanation that he took Creed to bury Church so that Ellie would see "sometimes dead is better" and accept the inescapability of death, Creed seizes on it too quickly. "He felt better now. He had an explanation. It was diffuse, it relied more upon the logic of the nerve endings than the logic of the rational mind, but under the circumstances he found he could accept that. And it meant he could forget the expression he thought he had seen on Jud's face briefly last night—that dark, capering glee." Even when Jud immediately cries and admits to his own rationalizing, Creed clings to that explanation, and uses it himself shortly thereafter. The rationalizations grow more and more shoddy as the the burial ground increases its hold on Creed, until they are finally a parody of rational thought. After he has seen the Wendigo on the trip to bury Gage, Creed "gibbered to himself, *it may still come out all right; there is no gain without risk, perhaps no risk without love,*" and falsely assures himself that he can stop Gage *"if something happens . . . something bad. . . .* His thoughts dissolved into the droning mutter of prayer even as his hands groped for a pick."

Another reason for the emotional appeal of King's fiction is, as Deborah Notkin states about *'SALEM'S LOT*, "King emphasizes the often-overlooked benefits of living through the worst of situations. . . . King holds out hope that if fear doesn't kill you, it leaves you with something invaluable you could not otherwise attain."[9] Parallel to Louis' descent is a touching ascent for Rachel. This is left implicit in *PET SEMATARY*, perhaps because her death is almost unbearable as it is, but the progress in her ability to accept death and the responsibility for dealing with its consequences is praiseworthy. Originally obsessed with denying death, she comes to accept that she no longer has the luxury of denying anything, no matter how frightening. Although she tries to explain Ellie's dream of Pascow in terms of subliminal memory, which she had learned about in psychology class, she finally will not allow herself that escape. "But this isn't psych class . . . ," she tells herself. "Something is dreadfully wrong here and you know it—you feel it." Her return to Maine, given what she suspects and how she feels about death, is a heroic but little-celebrated strike against "Oz the Gweat and Tewwible," so long feared by Rachel.

Many characters would like to deny their intuitions because of the actions such knowledge would demand of them, but King's more sympathetic characters often overcome this by honesty and responsibility. Dennis says of the "logic" of dismissing his impressions of Christine as hallucination, "It ignored the hard facts, but it was comfortable. To believe such a thing would allow Leigh and me to pursue our ordinary lives. . . ." When Donna Trenton, in her natural but still macabre imprisonment inside her own car, tries to justify staying in the car, "Reluctantly, her mind told her that was a deadly-false bit of reasoning." When Donna realistically assesses herself and the situation, she finds even more convincing reasons why she must act with definite purpose, and soon.

Stephen King has been accused by some reviewers of being anti-rational, but this label is not accurate. King's outlook is both optimistic and romantic, especially in the accuracy of intuition among the good of heart, but he is both more realistic and complex than some would give him credit for. First of all, intuition is not presented as infallible, just generally reliable. The false alarms are realistic and make the real preternatural insights more credible in their context. When Vic Trenton announces his intent to return to Maine, his partner says, "Jesus, it feels wrong. It feels all wrong," displaying conflicting intuitions believably like life. Moreover, vivid visions of disaster that do not come true provide first a jolt and then dynamic relief, like a cat scaring the heroine in a monster movie. Two examples of this are Drayton's image of his son and wife killed by flying glass during the storm that begins *The*

Mist (the picture-window does break, but much later, when they are downstairs) and Hal's image of being attacked in *The Monkey.*

These false intuitions may forestall the presumption of anti-rationality or oversimplification on King's part. Irrational impulses in King's fiction come from some combination of three sources: right intuition, possibly supernatural and often linked to affection; unjustified conclusions, often the result of concern, anger, or some other deep emotion; and supernatural obsession, inspired by something like Christine or the burial ground beyond the Pet Sematary. King's characters must make decisions while undergoing these feelings, often with very little justification for doing so. Logic is of little help, since it can prove any desired conclusion, but this does not mean one may abandon it. Many times in King's stories, logic is essential in saving people from the major trap which accompanies emotional intuition: obsession.

The personalities seen in King's fiction walk a dangerous tightrope between dismissal of and obsession with the irrational; and if logic and denial too often prevent action based on valid hunches, they also may function as safeguards in avoiding emotional imbalance. Also, just as the premonitions King's characters have about loved ones are an amplification of normal human insight, obsessions in his fiction may have supernatural instigation, but they are always outgrowths of the protagonist's own obsessive personality.

King's best fiction follows Peter Straub's dictum that in good horror "the bad stuff, the evil, just doesn't come out of the blue, as something invented; it should come from the characters themselves . . . if the evil that's out there is some echo or reflection of the people who have to fight it, then it does have weight."[10] This characteristic, more often true of King's novels than of his shorter works, explains why *THE SHINING* and *PET SEMATARY* are more effective than *The Mist* or *The Monkey*, in which the inner and outer manifestations are too sketchily integrated. King's recent short story collection, *SKELETON CREW*, contains a number of stories that deal with the obsessive state of mind. *Paranoid: A Chant* is a strong presentation of a purely internally-caused psychological state, while *Beachworld* and *The Raft* show, more clumsily in the former case and more effectively in the latter, hypnotic obsession by an exterior force. None of these stories is as effective as the confusion of interior and exterior causes and effects that the characters confront in *The Ballad of the Flexible Bullet.* Other stories, like *Nona* and *Uncle Otto's Truck*, also examine obsession to greater or lesser degree.

In most of King's fiction, the part of the mind that leads toward sanity and integrity (in the literal sense of wholeness) and the part of the mind that leads toward obsession and dissolution are separate and in constant battle, but they indubitably spring from the same grounds. Supernatural intervention may aid one side or the other—particularly malefic forces influence the latter—but this can only occur because the character possesses those tendencies and yields the corresponding influences. In King's novels, all human beings have that dark side, but his darkly obsessed protagonists are more susceptible to it because of psychological flaws: Carrie White and Arnie Cunningham, the outcasts; Dr. Louis Creed, whose profession and temperament make him too willing to manipulate life and death without awe of their mysteries; Jack Torrance, who, as Deborah Notkin points out, fools himself regarding his mental stability and might still have undergone "deterioration, loss of self-control and eventual destruction" because of his own history and weaknesses, even if the Overlook did not interfere.[11]

King's non-fiction study, *DANSE MACABRE*, analyzes supernatural horror's treatment of this psychological duality, especially seen in works such as Robert Louis Stevenson's *DR. JEKYLL AND MR. HYDE.* "[W]hat we're talking about here, at its most basic level," King states, "is the old conflict between id and superego, the free will to do evil or deny it." King also presents this in Friedrich Nietzsche's "mythic terms" of a "split between the Apollonian (the creature of intellect, morality, and nobility, 'always treading the upward path') and the Dionysian (god of physical gratification; the get-down-and-boogie side of human nature)." King states later in *DANSE MACABRE* that some books, like Shirley Jackson's *THE HAUNTING OF HILL HOUSE* or Peter Straub's *GHOST STORY*, combine external evil with this inner struggle, and "it is exactly this blurring about where the evil is coming from that differentiates the good or merely effective from the great."

Douglas Winter's statement to the contrary, *CHRISTINE* is noteworthy among King's novels for *least* showing this menace as "internal evil: the upsurge of the animal, the repressed unconscious, the monster from the id . . ."[12] Rather, *CHRISTINE* presents another kind of terror: once LeBay dies, Arnie Cunningham's state is not obsession but outright possession. As a result, Arnie's reaction is slightly different from those of King's other characters. He does not deny the facts and rarely rationalizes regarding their significance; often he accepts the situation intellectually, but feels none of the usual emotions.

The result is as frightening as the more common response, but in an entirely different way: the reaction of Jack Torrance or Louis Creed is terrifying because it is so universally human, while that of Arnie is terrifying as a sign that he is helplessly becoming completely alien. The reader feels that helplessness and is shocked by the alienness, as after Arnie realizes that he has lied to Leigh and is overcome by guilt:

> He stood on the walk, looking at his stalled car . . . and suddenly he hated it. It had done something to him, he wasn't sure what. Something.
>
> . . . He opened the driver's side door, slipped behind the wheel, and pulled the door shut again. He closed his eyes. Peace flowed over him and things seemed to come back together. He had lied to her, yes, but it was a little lie. A mostly unimportant lie. No—a *completely* unimportant lie.

Arnie then notices that the leather key ring he had gotten from Ronald LeBay is renewing itself, "But, like the lie, that was really unimportant. Sitting inside the metal shell of Christine's body, he felt quite strongly that was true. He *knew* it. Quite unimportant, all of it." This ability to accept the *outre* without being at least tempted to rationalize or dismiss is unusual and scary.

Arnie's possession after LeBay's death would be impossible, however, were it not for his attraction to Christine earlier. Arnie's feelings of great potential hidden by ugliness, of being unappreciated and socially excluded, pave the way for his seduction by Christine. LeBay's endless vendetta against the "shitters," matches Arnie's own anger against the "fucking sons of bitches" who keep him down and, as the chapter with Arnie's outburst is titled, "Outside."

Two of the most stunning scenes of "the free will to do evil or deny it" in King's fiction have little or nothing to do with the supernatural. Harold Lauder's acceptance of all-consuming hatred in *THE STAND* and Vic Trenton's rejection of anger and hurt in *CUJO* form a pair of scenes showing that no matter how much or little control we have over situations, we always choose whether or not to control our emotional reactions to these situations.

In the drawing up of sides between good and evil in *THE STAND*, Harold Lauder begins on the side of the angels and ends up on the side of the Walkin' Dude. Like Milton's Satan or the characters in a Charles Williams novel, Harold makes ongoing choices: the possibility of turning away from evil is present at each step, although each denial does make choosing the good more difficult next time. One such nexus occurs when Harold finds Fran Goldsmith's diary and reads what she has written about him and her love affair with Stu Redman:

> As he trained [the flashlight] beam on the front cover . . . there was a moment of sanity, For a moment part of his mind cried out *Harold! Stop!* so strongly that he was shaken to his heels. And stop he almost did. For just a moment it seemed *possible* to stop, to put the diary back where he had found it, to give her up, to let them go their own way before something irrevocable happened. For that moment it seemed he could put the bitter drink away, pour it out of the cup, and refill it with whatever there was for him in this world. *Give it over, Harold,* the sane voice begged, but maybe it was already too late. . . . He turned to the first page, trained his flashlight on the words, and began to read.

Harold's thought "maybe it was already too late"—like the constant protestations of Marlowe's Doctor Faustus that his damnation is irrevocable or Jack Torrance's belief that "He had not done things; things had been done to him"—seems to be simply an excuse for his decision and subsequent behavior. In fact, Harold "contemplated jettisoning the hate" after reading the diary as well.

King gives two convincing, and frightening, reasons for Harold's choosing the pathway of hate. First, Harold has too much of an investment in his past self to see the self-destructiveness and even factual inaccuracy of that identity. *THE STAND* is romantic and pro-pastoral, but the opposite of nostalgic: the good characters and their settlement embody acceptance of the advantages and demands of new beginnings, while the bad characters and their settlement cling to the old ways unquestioningly, despite their destructiveness. Harold cherishes the hatred in him after reading the diary, making the same mistake:

> In that hour or instant, he became aware that he could simply *accept what was,* and that knowledge both exhilarated and terrified him. For that space of time he knew he could turn himself into a new person, a fresh Harold Lauder cloned from the old one by the sharp intervening knife of the superflu epidemic. . . . And he himself, when faced with the knowledge that he was free to *accept what was,* had, of his own free will, rejected the new opportunity. To seize it would have been to murder himself. The ghost of every humiliation he had ever suffered cried out against it. His murdered dreams and ambitions came back to eldritch life and asked if he could forget them so easily.

Of course, murdering his old self is precisely what he should do. Harold will not let himself realize that his rejection of hope and change also murders his new, better self before it is born.

Louis Creed faces a similar cusp in *PET SEMATARY*, and decides similarly, with tragic results. When Louis talks on the phone to Rachel's father, "an idea suddenly occurred to him. It was crazy and attractive in its very sanity. He would let bygones be bygones . . . and he would let Gage lie in his Pleasantview grave . . . . Perhaps it would be like starting over again." He tells himself that he cannot because it would be "the same as murdering his son" or "killing him a second time"; when "a voice inside him tried to argue that this was not so" he "shut the voice up briskly." Arnie Cunningham also feels the possibility of starting over, when he leaves town for Darnell and LeBay stays back with Christine, and he also denies it. "Far in the back of his mind—hardly even acknowledged, but there," Arnie wonders "how things would be different if he . . . kept on going. If he just left the entire depressing mess behind." His immediate answer is, "But of course he wouldn't. Leaving Christine after he had put so much into her was of course impossible."

Repeatedly, King's characters demonstrate the dangers of throwing emotional and behavioral good money after bad. This attachment to the past makes those characters even more susceptible to the influence and effects of obsession, since they are unwilling to admit their errors and correct their behavior.

In *DANSE MACABRE*, King discusses Miss Foley, trapped in the evil carnival's mirror-maze in Ray Bradbury's *SOMETHING WICKED THIS WAY COMES*. "In terms of the new American Gothic," King states, "we can see that the mirror-maze is the catch-trap, the place where too much self-examination and morbid introspection persuades Miss Foley to step over the line into abnormality." This narcissism, which King discusses elsewhere in *DANSE MACABRE*, is the second reason why Harold Lauder chooses as he does. His own hate-filled journal, perhaps originally intended to discharge that hate, actually reinforces it. "What about the equation inside his own skull? The relativity of Harold. The speed of blight. Oh, he could fill twice as many pages as he had already written about that," King writes, "becoming more obscure, more arcane, until he finally became lost in the clockwork of himself and still nowhere near the mainspring at all. He was perhaps . . . raping himself. Was that it? It was close, anyway. An obscene and ongoing act of buggery." His narcissistic obsession with digging deeper into his own sickness is a process of morbid self-involvement disguised as self-understanding.

This scene from *THE STAND* is one of King's most psychologically tragic, a self-chosen damnation perhaps unequalled until *PET SEMATARY*. In *CUJO*, one of King's most pessimistic books in terms of events, there is a parallel and opposite scene in which Vic Trenton chooses sanity and forgiveness. After Vic receives a note from Steve Kemp, anonymously revealing an affair with Vic's wife, he consistently struggles against the demands of what he knows to be an irrational and hurtful part of himself.

Trenton receives the letter at work. After "[a] part of him had realized that it would be dangerous for him to go home now," he deliberately chooses a quiet place with good associations—a duck pond in Deering Oaks Park—and thinks about his situation. At each point, "the angry, hurt part" of his mind bows "grudgingly" to Trenton's awareness that hurting his wife, physically or through their son, will accomplish nothing. He is even able to question his own motives and reject them if they are unworthy: ". . . although he didn't want to ask it, there was another question:

Exactly why did he want to take Tad and go, without even hearing her side of the story?" His answer is that he had known this was the way to hurt Donna, "But did he want to turn his son into the emotional equivalent of a crowbar, or a sledgehammer? He thought not." Finally, he is able to deduce logically that the letter must be from a frustrated suitor, which means Donna ended the affair on her own. He is still left "wonder[ing] what the hell he was going to do," but he has avoided the rage that might have caused something he would later regret.

This process of emotional control and redemption, displayed for the reader, is in part a result of Vic's honesty with himself. The sad irony of Harold's journal is that it never really sought explanations for "the equation inside his own skull," which would have required the sort of painful questions of motive and effects that Vic asks himself but Harold obscures. It is also a result of Vic's ability and willingness to reject troublesome thoughts.

King realistically presents his characters with the choice of which interior voice to follow and which to silence. The tragedy of *PET SEMATARY* is that Louis Creed begins to follow his intuitions only when he should begin to doubt them. His premonition regarding Gage and his visitation from Pascow are dismissed because they do not fit into his materialistic worldview. After Church's undeniable return from the grave, Creed is vulnerable to the voice of corruption, speaking through Jud Crandall:

> You're a good man, Louis, but you ask too many questions. Sometimes people have to do things that just seem right. That seem right in their hearts, I mean. And if they do those things and then end up not feeling right . . . they think they made a mistake.

> . . . . What they don't think is that maybe they should be questioning those feelings of doubt before they question their own hearts. . . . And the things that are in a man's heart—it doesn't do him much good to talk about those things, does it? . . . Don't question, Louis. Accept what's done and follow your heart.

Both voices, of course, are "in the heart," in that each represents part of the mind, just as Vic Trenton acknowledged the "hurt part" and the reasonable parts of his mind. Jud's advice implies that the doubts are less naturally a part of Creed than his ability to accept Church's return as beneficial—actually, the reverse is true—and suggests that Creed not discuss the matter with anyone else. This cuts Louis off from his inner promptings to the contrary and assists the burial ground's siren voice.

As a result, all the human strengths that save Vic Trenton from being consumed by anger at Donna's affair, that help Donna survive her ordeal in the Pinto, and that lead Rachel to admit her intuitions and return to Maine—all these strengths aid Louis Creed in damning himself. Logic, which helps Vic avoid a destructive path, helps Creed cling to his. When Creed assures himself that Church's resurrection is satisfactory, and so Gage's will be, he thinks the comparison "made a balance of logic which was hard to deny." Having rationalized himself into the decision, only the careful, logical, pursuit of it keeps him going: "His plan kept unreeling in his mind. He looked at it from all angles, poked it, prodded it, looked for holes or soft places. And he felt that in truth he was walking along a narrow beam over a gulf of insanity. . . . He walked the balance beam of rationality; he studied his plan." Breaking into Pleasantview to dig up his son, Creed applies honest and logical consideration to reaching his goal. But he will not or cannot give equal consideration to the consequences of his choosing it.

Donna and Vic Trenton, on the other hand, not only repeatedly can tell "correct" impulses from rationalization and dangerous obsession, but have the will and ability to follow the first and disregard the others. Many critics have insisted that *CUJO* is a purely naturalistic novel. Douglas Winter, for instance, says that the horror in *CUJO* is "entirely predestinate," and offers as evidence the novel's penultimate paragraph—for Cujo, "Free will was not a factor."[13] Actually, the novel's implied philosophy blends free will and determinism, possibility and limitation, not always consistently but generally convincingly. It is true that Donna has little control over her exterior situation, and Cujo has none over his. However, the novel affirms the existence of choice on a subtle but very important level: the characters generally have control over their *reactions* to events, especially over their emotional states. Thus, the pessimism regarding the events of the book is mitigated by an optimism regarding human psychology and its ability to preserve our emotional well-being under the most trying circumstances.

For instance, Donna makes one of the few decisions open to her—whether, or when, to leave the car and face Cujo—on the basis of a correct blend of logic and intuition. By both his immediate treatment of the scene and Vic's reasoning afterwards, King implies that her decision was, at least, the best one open to her. Certainly, as Rachel Creed did regarding Ellie's dream of Pascow, Donna overcomes rationalizations she would like to believe, and honestly faces the truth. "Better to wait, wait for a better chance . . . ." she thinks. "But she didn't dare let the *idee* become *fixe*. There wasn't going to be a better chance than this one. . . . It had to be true; all logic declared it to be true." She manages her Pinto microcosm as well as she can, conserving what food they have and helping Tad as much as possible. While Donna's failure in her tasks despite her right choice is tragic, there is a certain relief that, unlike so many characters, from Jack Torrance to Louis Creed, she has the strength and courage to make that choice at all. While *CUJO* certainly does have more elements of naturalism than other fiction by King, it also has a romantic faith in human spirit that links it to King's other works.

Denial is often not only beneficial, but necessary—because, unlike Louis Creed, Donna and Vic Trenton choose the right things to deny. Through the contrast between Steve Kemp's reaction to the end of his affair with Donna and Vic's reaction to finding out that it had happened, King shows his characters' ability to choose internal reactions, if not necessarily external events. First, while Trenton faces his own motives and choices with difficult honesty, Kemp instead rationalizes:

> Had the retribution been too heavy for the offense? So she didn't want to make it with him anymore, so what? He had trashed most of the goddam house. Did that, maybe, say something unpleasant about where his head was at?
>
> He began to work on these questions a little at a time, the way most people do, running an objective set of facts through a bath of various chemicals which, when taken together, make up the complex human perceptual mechanism known as subjectivity. . . . he tore down what had happened and then carefully rebuilt it—redrew it in his mind—until both the facts and his perception of the facts jibed in a way he could live with.

While the imagery supports a naturalistic stance, Kemp does choose to immerse his thoughts in that chemical bath, a choice others reject.

King's presentation of Vic Trenton is even less naturalistic than his presentation of Kemp. Vic, like the characters in King's other recent books, chooses among conflicting perspectives; unlike Louis Creed, he chooses correctly. When Vic is overcome by the idea that Donna's not answering the phone means she has run off with Kemp, he resists that "strange and jealous part of his mind" first with logic and then, when that side of him has "an answer for everything," with a simple act of will: "Forget logic. She had told him it was over, and he had believed her. He believed her now." Vic also realizes the dangers of morbid self-examination, and avoids it as Harold Lauder does not. When he decides that his marriage is basically sound, he thinks, "There had to be some careful thought—but perhaps not too much at once. Things had a way of magnifying themselves."

Donna Trenton presents an even stronger, almost heroic, example of following only the right intuitions. She confronts her threatening circumstances enough to respond to them appropriately, but refuses to dwell on fears. When Cujo disappears into the garage and eats from the trough of food Joe Camber had poured out for him, Donna begins to suspect that the dog is eating the bodies of other victims. After logic cannot disprove the idea, she pulls herself out of that thought by sheer will, repressing the image of death and consequent nausea, "because she could be very determined." "*Stop,*" she tells herself. ". . . *Think about anything. Think about tomorrow. Think about being safe.*" When fear reoccurs, she simply "slammed a door shut somewhere in her mind."

Throughout King's fiction from *CUJO* on, one force

that helps defeat obsession is affection or responsibility for another, especially familial love. In *The Mist*, Drayton says of his confrontation with the "spiders" outside the supermarket, "I felt my mind trying to tear completely loose from its moorings. I believe now that it was only the thought of Billy that allowed me to keep any semblance of sanity." When Vic Trenton considers taking Tad and leaving Donna forever, feelings of responsibility and affection for his partner, and his partner's "wife and two kids," help keep him from rash action.

Jud Crandall—arguing as Creed's true friend rather than from domination by the spirit of the burial ground—implies that Creed's hope for giving up his dangerous plans lies in caring for his family. He says, in telling Creed about Bill Baterman's revival of his son Timmy,

> Missus Baterman was dead ten years then, along with the second child she tried to bring into the world, and that had a lot to do with what happened. A second child might have helped to ease the pain, don't you think? A second child might have reminded old Bill that there's others that feel the pain and have to helped through. I guess in that way you're luckier—having another child and all, I mean. A child and a wife who are both alive and well.

It is part of the grim design of *PET SEMATARY* that consistently, and despite the urgings of those around him, Creed cannot take this implied advice, largely because of his past trafficking with the burial ground.

It should be clear that a major strength of King's supernatural fiction is its roots in a credible and appealing view of human psychology. In fact, although King's strongest work depends on the meeting of human psychology and supernatural forces, the three non-supernatural novellas in *DIFFERENT SEASONS* show that his affection for his characters and desire to understand their motives also serve him creditably when no preternatural force is present in the story. *Rita Hayworth and Shawshank Redemption* and *Apt Pupil*, especially, form a matched set comparable to Harold Lauder's acceptance of irrational hatred in *THE STAND* and Vic Trenton's rejection of it in *CUJO*.

Andy Dufresne, in *Rita Hayworth and Shawshank Redemption*—like Richard Pine in *Survivor Type* or Donna Trenton—is persistent and determined. He has mastered all parts of his mind; he escapes prison and finds a new life through the kind of luck that favors the prepared mind. The kind of person who feels "there's no harm in hoping for the best as long as you prepare for the worst," he takes up rockhammering to stay sane and finds it provides a chance for physical as well as psychological well-being.

Todd Bowden, in *Apt Pupil*, is as persistent and determined as Dufresne, but his weaknesses allow his obsession to dominate and finally destroy him. Like Dufresne's, Todd's personality helps create its own luck, since without his discovery of and relationship with Dussander, Todd's "GREAT INTEREST" could not have taken the deadly direction it did. In Todd's case, his fascination with the Nazi death-camps helps him recognize an elderly neighbor as a Nazi officer in hiding, and his persistence in detective work forces the man to admit his identity. Moreover, like Harold Lauder, Todd Bowden's descent is further fueled by sick sexual fantasies that feed his obsessions.

King's overall approach to character, vital to both his fantastic fiction and his occasional non-fantastic works, is based in credible psychologizing that also reaffirms notions his readers believe or would like to believe: the importance of choice, the existence of the supernatural, the power of love. He presents a romantic but not simplistic view of the mind, which includes the value of both irrational and logical reaction, although it points out the limitations of each. As King's characters make their choices and try to maintain the delicate balance of mind the human condition calls for, the reader feels affection for them and gains understanding of them.

The reader can also gain understanding *through* them. Ultimately, we read fiction to understand ourselves. Stephen King, in the conclusion to *DANSE MACABRE*, mentions a poem by James Dickey, which he calls "a metaphor for the life of a rational being, who must grapple as best he/she can with the fact of his/her mortality." King continues,

> We fall from womb to tomb, from one blackness to another, remembering little of the one and knowing nothing of the other . . . except through faith. That we retain our sanity in the face of these simple yet blinding mysteries is nearly divine. That we may turn the powerful intuition of our imagination upon them and regard them in this glass of dreams—that we may, however timidly, place our hands within the hole which opens at the center of the column of truth—that is . . .
>
> . . . well, it's magic, isn't it?

One reason for Stephen King's overwhelming popularity as a writer is that the magic mirror of his fiction shows us an image of ourselves and our world that we want to believe, and find we can believe—at least for as long as we join him in his books.

1. Charles Platt, "Stephen King" (Interview), *DREAM MAKERS VOLUME II* (New York: Berkley Books, 1983), p. 297.
2. Don Herron, "Horror Springs in the Fiction of Stephen King," *FEAR ITSELF: THE HORROR FICTION OF STEPHEN KING* (San Francisco, California and Columbia, Pennsylvania: Underwood-Miller, 1982), pp. 57–82.
3. Fritz Leiber, "Horror Hits a High," *FEAR ITSELF: THE HORROR FICTION OF STEPHEN KING*, p. 89.
4. Alan Ryan, "The Marsten House in *'Salem's Lot,*" *FEAR ITSELF: THE HORROR FICTION OF STEPHEN KING*, p. 171.
5. Deborah L. Notkin, "Stephen King: Horror and Humanity for Our Time," *FEAR ITSELF: THE HORROR FICTION OF STEPHEN KING*, p. 132.
6. Paul Gagne, "An Interview with Peter Straub," *American Fantasy.*
7. Charles L. Grant, "TZ Interview: Stephen King," *The Twilight Zone Magazine,* April 1981, p. 23.
8. Gagne, Straub Interview, p. 21–22: also Jay Gregory, "TZ Interview: Peter Straub," *The Twilight Zone Magazine,* May 1981. p. 8.
9. Notkin, p. 134.
10. Gregory, Straub Interview
11. Notkin, p. 135.
12. Douglas E. Winter, *THE ART OF DARKNESS* (New York and Scarborough, Ontario: New American Library, 1984), p. 123.
13. Ibid. p. 97.

You learn just to exist with your fears. Which is what we do as grownups: we have a much smaller circle of fears because we block the rest of them out, very efficiently. Part of growing up is that systematic quenching of one's imagination.

—*Stephen King*

King's Characters: The Main(e) Heat

by Thomas F. Monteleone

What's the secret of Stephen King's enormous success?

There have been a lot of theories and postulations put to that question, some of which will be found in other chapters in this book, but for my money, I go with this one: people like, buy, and read Stephen King's books because they are filled with great characters.

The Main Heat. That title came from a friend. I started thinking about the phrase and began to realize how appropriate it is. If you take away the interesting, well-drawn characters in King's novels and stories, you have some pretty ordinary tales. I mean, who could imagine a book about *vampires*—one of the oldest horror clichés in the genre—becoming a runaway bestseller?

Since *'SALEM'S LOT*, you don't have to imagine it. And the book was such a hit because of the way

King jumped into the town with both feet and dragged all the very real people out for us to meet. Sure there were stereotypes among them, but there were others who simply rang true, whom we will always remember.

But I don't want to limit my discussion to just one book; I used *'SALEM'S LOT* just to illustrate my initial contention—people like to read Stephen King because he writes about people we know. They are real; they are *familiar*. They are not removed from the normal hum-drum of our everyday world—they are *part* of it. His characters make us smile and they make us sad because they have the same likes and dislikes, the same fantasies and fears that the rest of us have. When you read a Stephen King novel or a story you realize very quickly that *everything* he writes—plot, theme, idea, resolution—springs from the characters he creates. When you're introduced to one of his characters, whether he's a spear-carrier or a protagonist, you can bet even before you've picked up much of the plot, that you'll know about that fellow's distrust of politicians, or his stamp-collecting hobby, or his passion for the Red Sox, or even his irritating habit of belching in public.

In *FEAR ITSELF*, a book about Stephen King, Don Herron highlights this quality of King's work when he writes that "King is a capable author who writes clearly and mostly uses as characters "ordinary" people—couples with children, small town cops, teenagers—while most horror fiction writers have followed Poe into a literary style so exotic and opulent that the average reader seldom lasts more than a few pages. Until recently, characters in horror fiction all seemed to be pale-blooded librarians cataloging the occult or aged recluses living alone in crumbling mansions filled with sarcophagi, tomb rubbings, and rats."

King seems to have changed all that.

Readers can easily identify with the personality traits King colors into his characters. He has an eye for the little things, the details which are capable of defining people in a few deft, familiar strokes. Even King's secondary or minor characters are depicted with attentive, almost loving, care. Watson, the Overlook handyman in *THE SHINING,* laughs at college educations, hates homosexuals, and has the memorable habit of blowing his nose into a brightly colored bandanna and thrusting it into a pocket "after a short peek into it to see if he had gotten anything interesting." George Meara, the mailman in *CUJO* maintains a running dialogue with himself as he delivers the day's post. A large part of his conversation is a humorous fascination with his own flatulence. Dud Rogers, the "dump custodian" in *Jerusalem's Lot*, liked to shoot rats with .22 caliber hollow-point shells, while fantasizing that he was actually shooting various townspeople. *THE STAND*'s Tom Cullen had the endearing habit of saying that "M-O-O-N" spelled whatever particular word he was presently fixating upon. (I remember waiting for Cullen to finally mention the moon, and spell it correctly. . . .) And of course there was Wolf, Jack Sawyer's faithful companion in *THE TALISMAN*, who punctuated many of his sentences with the wondrous cry of "Wolf!" King believes you can tell a lot about a man by naming the kinds of cigarette he smokes. And he's right—you can.

Another aspect of King's characterizations which jumps off the page is his use of natural, often colloquial, sometimes even crude, dialogue. One of the older axioms of good writing says that realistic, effective dialogue can help create believable characters. The people in Stephen King's stories talk the way *we* talk. They do *not* speak like many fictional characters—literate and grammatically correct, but sounding very phony because of their authors' slavish obeisance to an English textbook. King's folks are definitely different. "His characters swear," writes Don Herron. "They excrete. They often act crudely, grossly. The hot-rodder Billy Nolan in *Carrie* is described as having the 'unfailing ability to pinpoint the vulgar.' King has this ability in spades, and uses it often. It is a kind of honesty, and I suspect it is one of his greatest commercial assets."

Now, I don't know about you, but as I read between the lines of that quote, I get the feeling that Herron is praising with faint damns, or maybe vice-versa. In *FEAR ITSELF*, Herron's main complaint with King seems to be that he is a "popularizer" of horror fiction, that he is (Oh God! No!) a "commercial" writer.

[I have news for Herron: we're *all* commercial writers—it's just that some of us aren't as commercial (successful?) as others.]

Herron implies that there is something inherently *wrong* with being "commercial," and he or anyone else who assumes that position is forgetting something very important. Throughout literary history, the writers we revere today often were uniformly popular and "commercial" in their own time. We honor their work today because it has proven to be an honest, valid reflection of the times in which it was written.

Only a fool would say that King's work is not a wonderfully realistic representation of contemporary America. If Stephen King is pinpointing the vulgar, then it is only because there is much in our modern society that is indeed vulgar.

I think we all realize this, even if only on a subconscious level, and King certainly knows it as well. His characters are a product of their environment, and of King's. They are an odd collection of elements: cable TV, K-Marts, life insurance, health spas, McDonald's restaurants, a mania to buy a new car just because the calendar had molted off twelve pages, and a thousand other seemingly unrelated items.

Though King's characters are recognizable, his protagonists are not usually created according to the several unwritten, "commercial," rules of thumb. Sometimes they are fairly young (in their thirties or forties), but they can also be teenagers (such as in *CARRIE* or *CHRISTINE)* or even children (as in *FIRESTARTER* and *THE SHINING)*. Sometimes they are well-educated and sometimes not, but they are usually well-read. Sometimes they are employed in professions rather than merely jobs—writers, advertising executives, commercial artists, etc., but they can also be like Stu Redman of *THE STAND*—an honest, hard-working blue-collar.

King's adult protagonists are very much a part of the American suburban landscape. They *are* like the rest of us, and even perhaps a bit like King himself. Characters like David Drayton in *The Mist*, Andy McGee of *FIRESTARTER*, Vic Trenton of *CUJO*, and Louis Creed of *PET SEMATARY* are all hard-working family-men with middle-to-upper-middle class homes, values and desires. They are content with their jobs, in love with their wives, adoring of their children—when tragedy strikes and they are forced into the strange country of King's imagination.

Even though the adult protagonists like John Smith of *THE DEAD ZONE*, Ben Mears of *'SALEM'S LOT*, and Jack Torrance of *THE SHINING* are prevented from leading normal, "suburban" lives because of intervening problems (such as Smith's accident and coma, or Torrance's alcoholism), the reader is still presented with adult characters who at least *aspire* to a kind of middle-class normalcy with which we can all identify.

And this is one of the major reasons why so many people like to read a book by Stephen King: there's going to be somebody in there who thinks and acts *just like they do.* We all have the same dreams and fears as King's adult protagonists. We all worry about the rent or the mortgage, our wives and husbands cheating on us, getting that promotion, losing the job, hearing some creep break into the house at three a.m., having Mongoloid children, the list goes on and on . . . and King's characters feel the *same* way. They know what they want, they know what they need to do to keep the wolves from their doors, and they are pragmatically going about the business of getting it done.

Until the Boogeyman comes.

And when He does come, King has his hard-working family-men do their best to protect Mom, the Kids, and Country. I say this not in a pejorative sense, but in King's own vernacular style. When the Boogeyman comes, we see people *very much like ourselves* reacting and acting in ways we would like to, if the chips were suddenly down.

But there is another class of protagonist which King handles with perhaps more skill than any writer of fiction—in or out of the fantasy/horror genre—working in America today. I am referring to The Kids. The child characters in King's work are a special group indeed, because he lets us get inside their heads and read their thoughts, feel their emotional responses to the world outside, and most importantly, share in the fears which are so unique to non-adults.

Included in this group, even though they are not children *per se,* are the teenagers Carrie White of *CARRIE*, and Arnie Cunningham of *CHRISTINE* and Dennis Guilder, *CHRISTINE*'s narrator. King has an acute memory for what it was, and still is, like to come of age in the bizarre technicolor atmosphere of the typical American high school. His teenaged characters are very much aware of themselves and how they do, or do not, "fit into" the mini-society of high school. I think King's readers appreciate this. His realistic portrayals of the rigors of adolescent social life ring so true, and push so many memory-lane buttons, that King's audience can only nod its collective head and say: "Yeah, that's the way it was, all right. . . ."

When we see the world through the eyes of a Carrie White or an Arnie Cunningham, we are suddenly aware of how terribly cruel and heartless adolescent life can be: the callous denial of friendship and companionship often brought on by real or imagined differences that will seem so trivial in adulthood. Letting us inside the heads of the ugly ducklings is effective, to be sure, but King takes things one step farther. He allows us to share in the satisfaction of striking back, the inevitable *revenge* which comes gushing out in response to the pain and punishment endured by his sympathetic protagonists. Within the reader, this catharsis may evoke past injustices that still cry out to be avenged, further enhancing strong identification with King's characters. This primal, loss-of-innocence kind of vengeance has a timeless, almost classic appeal, especially when its landscape is defined by the boundaries of the American high school and populated by the archetypal figures of every high school class in the country.

We all remember the nerd in class who was a pariah and an outcast. He was either ourself, or he was somebody we were damned glad not to be. We may even have helped to torment this poor kid, or we may have just watched from the sidelines. King was once there too, he remembers, and he uses that familiar image of the awkward, misunderstood, usually sensitive adolescent to portray the pain and emotional chaos of coming of age in America. We all remember that process and when we find the author re-affirming the fears and frustrations we felt back then, in novels such as *CARRIE* and *CHRISTINE*, we can't help but like and empathize with this writer.

Douglas Winter, in his fine, cleverly-titled book, *STEPHEN KING: THE ART OF DARKNESS*, supports this contention: "That journey, the coming of age, is an important underpinning of all of King's novels, and in *CARRIE*, we see glimpses of the true danger that King perceives along its path."

The true danger. What Winter alludes to here is the act of growing up, of losing the magic and the innocence of childhood. That means not just growing up, but growing old. And growing old means, ultimately, death. All of King's characters are preoccupied with this concern, at first subconsciously, then something in the narrative brings it all back home, makes them aware of their own mortality. Like that dream which Dennis Guilder has at the end of *CHRISTINE*: it's not just about the possibility of the car coming back, it's also about the *inevitability* of the death which awaits us all.

As fascinating and compelling as King's dead-on evocations of adolescence might be, I think his most intriguing characters are his pre-pubescent ones—the *real* Kids like Charlie McGee of *FIRESTARTER* and Tad Trenton in *CUJO*, Danny Torrance in *THE SHINING* and Mark Petrie of *'SALEM'S LOT*, and even Todd Bowden in *Apt Pupil.*

The only modern American horror writer other than Stephen King who seems capable of recreating his distinct memories of childhood and the fantasy-world of children is Ray Bradbury. But where Bradbury's view of children and their world is often distorted through a saccharine, nostalgic lens, King's view is a hard-edged rendering of the shadowy, horrific, and often monstrous *weltanschauung* of the child. One of my favorite passages from *'SALEM'S LOT* illustrates this point beautifully:

> Before drifting away entirely, he found himself reflecting—not for the first time—on the peculiarity of adults. They took laxatives, liquor, or sleeping pills to drive away their terrors so that sleep would come, and their terrors were so tame and domestic: the job, the money, what the teacher will think if I can't get Jennie nicer clothes, does my wife still love me, who are my friends. They were pallid compared to the fears every child lies cheek and jowl with in his dark bed, with no one to confess to in hope of perfect understanding but another child. There is no group therapy or psychiatry or community social services for the child who must cope with the thing under the bed or in the cellar every night, the thing which leers and capers just beyond the point where vision will reach. The same lonely battle must be fought night after night and the only cure is the eventual ossification of the imaginary faculties, and this is called adulthood.

And that, my friends, I call a fine piece of writing. And a fine piece of insight into what it's like to be a kid. I think we all know, and we all remember, but it's this kind of writing by King which makes the reader aware all over again.

Knowing and remembering is not the same as *feeling* it all over again, and that feeling is the special gift King gives his readers. We're reading along and suddenly we're inside the mind of little Tad Trenton, and goddammit, there *is* something in that closet that's going to come out and get us! But it doesn't have to be a monster in the closet. For some of us it was a clawlike hand reaching out from under our beds, or maybe a giant eyeball at the bedroom window, or maybe the picture of a clown on the bedroom wall that seemed to change into a hideous creature when the light grew dim and shadowy and the angle from our beds was a little askew.

The exact incident or bug-bears that might have lurked in our own personal childhoods doesn't matter. The important point is that there *were* special things which terrified us as kids, and that's why King's so effective when he's writing about that special time in all of our lives.

Death, to a child, is a difficult concept to grasp. When Uncle Sal dies, parents have a hard time explaining it to their children. Yet most kids have their own perception of the process, which makes perfect sense to them. Perfect sense in *their* world of night terrors—where every imaginable kind of grotesquerie is *real* on its own terms. Death, writes King, "is when the monsters get you."

This naturalistic explanation of the child's mind is an elegant insight on King's part. Such a simple and yet profound observation. In his recent film screenplay, *Cat's Eye,* King returns to this theme with magical results. In the third episode, Drew Barrymore discovers an evil little troll living in her bedroom wall. It is *real.* And yet her parents, because they have lost their power to think beyond the simple, mundane reality of suburbia, cannot accept what they are eventually forced to confront.

Through his Kids, King gives back that power, that sense of wonder, to his adult readership.

* * *

There is one aspect of King's Kids which sticks in the craw of some critics and readers: except when they're being scared, the Kids don't act like *kids*. I've heard it said that King's children think and react like adults, that they seem far too wise for their years, and they are, as if by definition, not very likeable for those very reasons.

There is, perhaps, something to this line of criticism when you think about how sophisticated *THE SHINING'S* Danny Torrance seems to be. He is totally aware of his father's drinking problem and the resultant domestic hassles it creates with Mom. Danny seems to just *understand* the world very well for a five-year old—at least better than *I* did when I was the same age. There is the tendency to explain this away by mentioning Danny's power, his "shine," and I guess having that kind of powerful psychic ability would give one a different view of things right from the start. The same criticism has been levelled at Charlie McGee in *FIRESTARTER* because she acts like a little woman instead of a little girl. At some points in the novel, when she consoles and advises her father, there seems to be a total role-reversal taking place.

For the sake of argument, the cause of literary criticism, and just for fun, I spent a few days asking acquaintances, friends, and even relatives what they thought of King's Kids. One thing I heard over and over was that kids are just a lot more sophisticated these days.

How true. How damned true.

Kids are under a constant information blitz from radio, TV, and computers. The liberated attitudes of modern parents have abolished the old saying "children are to be seen and not heard." Kids today can't help but be smarter, more aware, and more sophisticated. I've noticed it in my own son, Brandon, and

I'm sure King has, as a writer, observed his own children carefully. The point is, the child characters in King's books are effective and believable because they have not yet lost their sense of wonder, or their fear of the monsters. Readers intuitively realize this and immediately identify with the Kids. We all remember the world when it was filled with magic and wonder and terror; and for most of us it was a damned exciting time to be alive.

King's fiction returns to this theme again and again. In fact, he does a beautiful job of laying bare his feelings on the subject in the final pages of *DANSE MACABRE* when he writes:

> Children see everything, consider everything; the typical expression of the baby which is full, dry, and awake is a wide-eyed goggle at everything. Hello, pleased to meet you, freaked to be here . . . Children believe in Santa Claus. It's no big deal; just a piece of stored information. They likewise believe in the boogeyman, the Trix Rabbit, McDonaldland. . . all these things are taken as a matter of course.

But things, unfortunately, do not stay that way:

> The changes come gradually, as logic and rationalism assert themselves. The child begins to wonder how Santa can be at the Value House, on a downtown corner ringing a bell over a Salvation Army pot, and up at the North Pole generaling his troop of elves all at the same time. The child maybe realizes that although he stepped on a hell of a lot of cracks, his or her mother's back is yet all right. Age begins to settle into that child's face. "Don't be a baby!" he or she is told impatiently, "Your head is

always in the clouds!" And the kicker, of course: "Aren't you ever going to *grow up*?"

And you get the distinct impression that King believes growing up is not such a great idea.

Now it's coming clear, isn't it? King writes so effectively about Kids because he has retained the memories and the sense of wonder. He knows that this ability is the key to making it all work as a fantasist and a teller of scary stories. Listen:

> The job of the fantasy writer, or the horror writer, is to bust the walls of that tunnel vision (of the average adult) wide for a little while; to provide a single powerful spectacle for the third eye (of the imagination). The job of the fantasy-horror writer is to make you, for a little while, a child again.

That spells it out as plainly as possible. When you consider this central purpose in King's work and you think about his characters, you can see the mechanism at work. Kids or not, all of King's protagonists have retained a respect for the mysterious, and a knowledge that, yes, there still *is* some magic left in the world—even if sometimes it's "bad" magic. Even Father Callahan, when he grappled with Barlowe in *'SALEM'S LOT*, had not totally lost the imaginative gift—for one brief instant he saw the vampire as his personal childhood boogeyman "Mr. Flip," and he was more terrified than ever.

King's characters are a fascinating bunch. They are the stuff of fear and dreams, the raw elements which animate his stories—the main heat indeed. They are prosaic and familiar, molded by the mundane middle-class society in which they toil. They are sensitive adolescents trapped in bizarre rites of passage, unable to fully understand the power which threatens to overwhelm them. They are adults who have forgotten the ways of the child; they are kids who already have the wisdom of adults. To paraphrase Pogo: "We have seen the characters, and they is us."

In some ways, I feel like a Welsh sin-eater. Do you know about them? They'd come around when somebody was dying and the family would put a lot of food on the table. The sin-eater would sit down and eat every bite of it all by himself.

In doing so, he was supposed to symbolically take the sins of that person on himself and then the person could die and go to heaven. Of course the sin-eater would go to hell at the end of his life, because by then his soul would be black with all the sins he'd eaten.

My soul must be very black, indeed.

—Stephen King

The Skull Beneath the Skin

by Tim Underwood

. . . pulp fiction, with its five-and-dime myths, can take a stronger hold on people's imagination than art, because it doesn't affect the conscious imagination, the way a great novel does, but the private, hidden imagination, the primitive fantasy life—and with an immediacy that leaves no room for thought.
—*Pauline Kael*

If you want to talk to the learned, talk to the vulgar.
—*Leibniz*

Stephen King's enormous talent expresses itself through vulgar sensibilities. His common touch takes him places greater writers seldom go—inside the cabs of ten-wheel diesels, onto secretaries' desk-tops, inside the boss's briefcase, on the Greyhound bus, on planes and trains, in every walk of life. These days his books are *everywhere*.

But there's a downside to this ubiquity: because King is so contemporary and fashionable in his concerns, his work probably won't last. He may still be read in twenty years, but not with the enthusiasm that he is today. Stories like *The Raft* or *The Mist* may have the power to disturb, but their effects are ephemeral. Neither story resonates in the mind like W.W. Jacob's *The Monkey's Paw,* Edgar Allan Poe's *The Premature Burial*, J. Sheridan Le Fanu's *Green Tea*, Algernon Blackwood's *August Heat*, Shirley Jackson's *The Lottery*, or even Oscar Wilde's *The Picture of Dorian Gray*. King may well know obscurity in his own lifetime as have many famous writers, such as Joseph Hergeshimer, the towering bestseller of sixty years ago who, almost overnight, was deserted and forgotten by his readers.

I don't think this fate will surprise Stephen King—he has always been his own best interpreter, promoter and apologist. He and his literary agent, Kirby McCauley, brilliantly orchestrated every aspect of his explosive career. In five years they transformed a successful young writer into the fastest selling fiction author in America.

That this metamorphosis could not have occurred without a sophisticated game plan and a lot of work away from the typewriter is a subject for another book. Instead, let's look at *The Body*, one of King's lighter works, and *PET SEMATARY*, one of his darkest.

I. The Body: King as Court Jester

King's early novels are filled with rage and nastiness. But in *The Body* he manages an awkward embrace of what he found so repulsive in much of his earlier work: humanity. Unlike those earlier *horror* novels, *The Body* presents us with evil in just one dimension: man's inhumanity to man. If there's not much of the supernatural occurring in the story it's because King no doubt feels the material is strong and effective enough to stand on its own. *The Body* is an offbeat look at Growing Up in Rural America—an experience which distorts and spoils the lives of innocent children. Stephen King obviously shares with '50s author Grace Metelious some very negative feelings about life in small town America, but he can't help but find some laughter there.

The Body is laced with a wild gallows humor which at times approaches celebratory glee. Its underside-of-the-rock attitudes and madcap delivery invite comparison with Terry Southern's wonderful story-collection *RED DIRT MARIJUANA*. Like Southern, King laughs loudest when he's in pain.

Tobias Wolff wrote that in every good writer is the willingness to say that unspeakable thing which everyone else in the house is too polite to mention. King himself is not inclined to shy away from speaking of cruelty or insanity or even excrement if it might enhance his story's impact or make a good joke. In fact, King's willingness to broach the unspeakable and break taboos is more like a compulsive eagerness. To some extent this is literary *machismo* on King's part, a kind of oneupmanship and deliberate attempt to shock. Fortunately, behind this facade seems to be a caring human being.

It's worth remembering that elsewhere in our literature that's not always the case. For sheer, heartfelt brutality on the printed page, poet Charles Bukowski has no equal. For putting his readers inside unbalanced demented minds, there was none better than Jim Thompson, whose novel *POP. 1280* recently gave birth to the misanthropic persona of columnist Joe

Bob Briggs. Though they're both effective writers, neither Bukowski nor Thompson loves his characters or means well by them. On the other hand, King appears genuinely concerned for the welfare of others. His readers know it, and this accounts for a large measure of his popularity.

The Body is actually a gargantuan short story, in which King takes his usual shotgun approach to writing: he blasts away with all he's got, good, bad and ugly. The storyline jumps forward, back and sideways—not always with success, but it's nice to see him experiment and take chances. Knowing his readers will probably follow him anywhere, he meanders off into recollections of a hilariously pathetic pie-eating contest. He also shoehorns in an interesting passion play involving the narrator now grown up, which is promising but distracting.

King seems reluctant to censor his own creative outpouring for fear he'll leave out something vital. But the truth is that his real talents have little to do with literary discrimination. He's not primarily concerned with the higher centers of the brain; his aim is visceral. For maximum emotional impact, to give his fans the most for their money, King has gradually disciplined his runaway narrative momentum and honed his sense of timing. In response to strokes from the critics, he's also recently shown a great infatuation with pop-culture artifacts. And whatever he does on the page, he does in excess.

The Body is about life's casualties, in this case a young boy named Gordie and his friends, circa 1960. These kids are preteen survivors from a fall of innocence. The title's dead body is just the story's catalyst, something to initiate a Huck Finn odyssey into the woods surrounding a small New England town.

Before the kids can grow up and control their own lives, their youth is ruined. This apparently for King is part and parcel of the human condition. He offers no solutions or alternatives to this sad situation, just a few laughs along the way. But despite its black humor, *The Body* is painful to experience precisely *because* it implies that a better world is or was somehow possible for these children.

It's a bittersweet reminder of what it was like to grow up in a small town in 1960. The boys belong to an informal club whose members kill summertime in a treehouse in Castle Rock, Maine. They communicate through posturing. They're very much aware of their shortcomings and they confront each other in aggressive banter. Like that of most young males, their talk is concerned with overcoming fear and cultivating strength. They speak a hip language and profess a devil-may-care attitude in the face of the small-town life surrounding them—which is presented as empty, hypocritical and mean.

The story's prologue tosses out what is intended to be a startling vision of a dead human being: "I wake up from dreams where the hail falls upon his open eyes." This unnecessary red herring, possibly dropped in because King is not quite confident that the kids' narrative will hold our interest, is followed by some maudlin sentiment about hiding away our "secret heart." The *real* story opens with a measured pace in the kids' treehouse, where we meet the boys and hear a bit about their background. It's mostly bad news. Teddy's dad disfigured him by burning his ears on the stove, Chris' alcoholic father beats him severely, and so on. The off-stage adults function as models of weakness, foolishness and failure.

It's a dark view of modern society—Charles Dickens on a very rainy day. But unlike Dickens, King is not attempting to initiate social reform. He's merely telling a story he hopes will entertain. That's too bad, because Dickens used the popularity of his writing, politically, to make England a better place for the lower classes to live.

Terrible events have already misshapen these youngsters—accidents, deaths of loved ones, betrayal at the hands of adults—but they're still eager to learn about the world around them, and to prove themselves capable of mastering it. In a macabre echo of Mark Twain, when the kids hear of a fresh corpse out in the woods, they set out to find it. Since it's out there they have to witness it together. (King probably writes of horrors for the same reason—to share them with others.)

The surrounding scenery, as the boys practice growing up, is affectionately littered with images of repair and rural life among decay, a Rockwell portrait gone to seed. The story's narrative voice careens back and forth between ironic Raymond Chandler and jive Terry Southern. For instance, their clubhouse screen door:

> It was flyproof but really rusty—I mean that that rust was *extreme*. No matter what time you looked out that door, it looked like sunset.

King provides a strong dose of Modern Male Adolescence: peer group pressure, contempt for all adults (especially relatives), buried affections, sexual prudery and ignorance, fascination with death and dying. These typical young Americans play cards, tell dirty jokes and wise off as much as possible:

> "Screw," I said, and picked up a *Master Detective* to read while they played the hand out. I turned to

"He Stomped the Pretty Co-Ed to Death in a Stalled Elevator" and got right into it. . . .

Teddy was shuffling the cards in his clumsy way and I was just getting to the gooshy part of the murder story, where this deranged sailor was doing the Bristol Stomp all over this girl from Bryn Mawr because he couldn't stand being in closed-in places, when we heard someone coming fast up the ladder nailed to the side of the elm. A fist rapped on the door. . . .

Teddy reached for the top card on the pile of Bikes. Chris reached for the Winstons on the ledge behind him. I bent over to pick up my detective magazine.

Vern Tessio said, "You guys want to go see a dead body?"

Like George Lucas' poignant and comically romantic *American Graffiti, The Body* is a slice of American life filled with pre-teen rituals and rites of passage. It's a compassionate celebration of sorts, too, which allows its characters to come to grips with the world around them. In *The Body* (and his subsequent novel *CHRISTINE*), King gives us both morbid humor and madcap lament. Vern, one of the gang, has learned the body's location from his brother Billy, who runs with an older crowd:

Charlie and Billy went with a couple of scags named Marie Dougherty and Beverly Thomas; you never saw such gross-looking broads outside of a carnival show—pimples, moustaches, the whole works. Sometimes the four of them would boost a car from a Lewiston parking lot and go out into the country with two or three bottles of Wild Irish Rose wine and a six-pack of ginger ale. . . . Cheap thrills in a monkey house, as Chris sometimes said. They'd never been caught at it, but Vern kept hoping. He really dug the idea of visiting Billy on Sundays at the reformatory.

Their quest for the undiscovered body is a hesitant half-step toward manhood. The kids sense this is a Big Opportunity. They may get a chance to look death in the face, but the subsequent horror offered for a finale comes almost as an afterthought. This is really a story about Gordie's buddies, about nostalgia and camaraderie:

"Go on. Gordie," Chris said. "We'll wait over by the tracks."

"You guys better not go without me," I said.

Vern laughed. "Going without you'd be like going with Slitz instead of Budweiser's, Gordie."

"Ah, shut up."

They chanted together: "I don't shut up, I *grow* up. And when I look at you I *throw* up."

"Then your mother goes around the corner and licks it up," I said, and hauled ass out of there, giving them the finger over my shoulder as I went. I never had friends later on like the ones I had when I was twelve. Jesus, did you?

King, who likes to describe himself as the literary equivalent of a Big Mac and fries, is well aware of his limitations as a stylist. It's not immortal prose, but few American writers today seem to be enjoying their own fiction as much as Stephen King, which may explain *Newsweek* magazine's recent statement that King's books were easy to describe but difficult to imitate.

II. PET SEMATARY: Dr. King hangs out his shingle

Like many of King's novels, *PET SEMATARY* deals directly with death. King takes his readers on a dark journey to air out their secret fears and confront their own mortality. The road is paved with homilies, humor and horror.

PET SEMATARY is also the monstrous come true. It's not the best written or constructed of King's novels—apparently he dusted off and rewrote an early manuscript. The story jerks and starts here and there, it lacks that seamless feeling of being written in one dead heat that is so typical of King. King is a modern medicine man, and this book shows how thoroughly he understands his role as a literary exorcist.

PET SEMATARY drags out the grisly stuff Americans like to hide from. We meet the Grim Reaper in many ugly guises: maimings and disfigurements, messy highway deaths, bad deaths from cancer, sudden deaths of loved ones. There's not much concern with beauty in any of King's works, it doesn't seem to inspire him.

Louis and Rachel Creed, two of the book's central characters, are a young married couple from Maine, with a preschool daughter and son. After moving out to the country, they come across an animal graveyard used by local children.

> Some of the graves were marked with flowers, some fresh, most old, not a few almost totally decomposed. Over half of the painted and penciled inscriptions that Louis tried to read had faded away to partial or total illegibility. Others bore no discernible mark at all, and Louis guessed that the writing on these might have been done with chalk or crayon.

"*Mom!*" Ellie yelled. "Here's a goldfishie! Come and see!"

"I'll pass," Rachel said, and Louis glanced at her. She was standing by herself, outside the outermost circle, looking more uncomfortable than ever. . . . She had never been easy around the appearances of death. . . .

Later Louis and his older neighbor Jud come back. Most of the grave-markers for the children's pets appear to be wooden, but one has been painstakingly carved in stone: HANNAH THE BEST DOG THAT EVER LIVED 1929–1939.

Although the sandstone was relatively soft—and as a result the inscription was now little more than a ghost—Louis found it hard to conceive of the hours some child must have spent impressing those nine words on the stone. The commitment of love and grief seemed to him staggering. . . .

In most of King's work love and grief are inseparably mingled. The mixture certainly saturates and animates *PET SEMATARY*. When Louis' daughter Ellie subsequently learns her cat Church will grow old and die in a few years, death becomes personal. She takes her anger to her father, who is both bemused and distressed.

"Honey," he said, "if it was up to me, I'd let Church live to be a hundred. But I don't make the rules."

"Who does?" she asked, and then, with infinite scorn: "God, I suppose."

Louis stifled an urge to laugh. It was too serious.

"God or Somebody," he said. "Clocks run down—that's all I know. There are no guarantees, babe."

"I don't want Church to be like all those dead pets!" she burst out, suddenly tearful and furious. "I don't want Church to ever be dead! He's my cat! He's not God's cat! Let God have His own cat! Let God have all the damn cats He wants, and kill them all! Church is *mine*!"

There were footsteps across the kitchen, and Rachel looked in, startled. Ellie was now weeping against Louis' chest. The horror had been articulated; it was out; its face had been drawn and could be regarded. Now, even if it could not be changed, it could at least be wept over.

King's most significant function as a contemporary writer and an explanation of his current popularity can be seen right there. Dr. King the Exorcist articulates and externalizes his readers' *private* horrors. He draws their faces, real and imaginary. King's books are tools for catharsis: at the very least they help his readers let off steam. And he obviously relishes the role of spoiler and revels in crude behavior on the page. (This is most evident in his short story collections. As a literary bull in the china shop, King not only breaks the glassware to get your attention, he defecates on the floor.)

PET SEMATARY is also a book in which King relates, through his characters, some of his own feelings towards death—that's the impression given by the intensely personal quality of the narrative. Although parts of *PET SEMATARY feel* autobiographical, whether they recapitulate King's own life and views is probably beside the point. The story's main accomplishment is that it provides an emotional sounding board for King's many followers, a way to feel bad for a while, a way to express fear and such painful emotions as grief, which are not easily vented in American society.

Louis Creed's cousin was crushed to death when Louis was twelve. At the time his mother dealt with the sudden tragedy through prayer:

> . . . it was the praying that finally brought it home to him; if his mother was praying for Ruthie Hodge's *soul*, then it meant that her *body* was gone. Before his closed eyes rose a terrible image of Ruthie coming to his thirteenth birthday party with her decaying eyeballs hanging on her cheeks and blue mold growing in her red hair, and this image provoked not just sickening horror but an awful doomed love.

Once King has established his favorite *mise en scène*—fear, death and loathing—the supernatural is sure to follow. When Louis Creed, a practicing M.D., confronts the dying victim of a messy accident, King paints a clear picture:

> One collarbone jutted from his swelled and twisted right shoulder. From his head, blood and a yellow, pussy fluid seeped sluggishly into the carpet.

In all of King's books, during moments of dreadful narrative intensity, reality, as we know it, shifts. The safe world where terrible things do not happen to *us* dissolves and vanishes like the Emperor's new clothes—as if our everyday vision of an amicable environment is merely a cloak which can be torn aside. This instant of dark epiphany is also a kind of paranoid affirmation for King: there really *is* a boogyman and he's out there waiting for you.

When King rends the curtain and the supernatural intrudes, it is most often a place of dread, full of demons and evil spirits. There may be goodness Up There somewhere, but it rarely manifests itself for Stephen King. *PET SEMATARY*'s message is almost entirely of malevolence and despair. The dying man's broken face twists into an awful grin. Spirits speak through his mouth. In a moment of terror and horror they call to Louis by name.

The malignant supernatural realm enters into Louis' life and alters his reality, but not as a trial to test his faith or an ordeal he must undergo for his soul's purification. It comes to do him harm. For King, *all* contacts with the spiritual dimension are fraught with danger. He never tires of reminding himself and his readers of this. Any of his characters left alive after such collisions are invariably soiled or damaged, physically, mentally and emotionally. King's concerns may be spiritual in nature, but they are far from the shelter of the Christian Church.

Nor, as befits an author born and bred in Maine, is there even a whiff in King's writings of California's current holistic attitudes and approaches toward modern living. His characters don't seek emotional support and well-being through any kind of therapy. They're not out to raise their own or each other's consciousness. There is no recognition of physical and mental health as goals to strive toward. King's characters are mostly just trying to pay the rent and make it through the night.

Louis Creed's wife Rachel witnessed her sister's death from spinal meningitis as a child ("She was in the back bedroom like a dirty secret. . . . The room always smelled of piss and her drugs"). This experience left Rachel a little unbalanced. Louis tries his best to help her come to grips with painful memories and overwhelming grief, which have been long suppressed and left dormant and festering. With great effort, she manages to face the knowledge that her sister's grotesque death had made her glad.

> Louis Creed was no psychiatrist, but he knew there are rusty, half-buried things in the terrain of any life and that human beings seem compelled to go back to these things and pull at them, even though they cut. Tonight Rachel had pulled almost all of it out, like some grotesque and stinking rotten tooth, its crown black, its nerves infected, its roots fetid. . . . That she had been able to remove as much as she had was well nigh incredible. . . . He felt like cheering.

But though Louis helps Rachel deal with *her* buried fears, he nurses and clings to phobias of his own. Like King himself, Louis is the victim of a morbid imagination. Unsettled aspects of his own psyche trouble Louis' sleep and spoil his relations with his wife:

> "Let's go to bed," he said, turning off the lights. He and Rachel went up the stairs together. Louis put his arm around her waist and loved her the best he could . . . but even as he entered into her, hard and erect, he was listening to the winterwhine outside the frost-traced windows. . . . The soil of a man's heart is stonier, he thought, and the wind sang its bitter black song, and not so many miles distant, Norma Crandall, who had once knitted his daughter and son matching caps, lay in her steel American Eternal coffin on a stone slab in a Mount Hope crypt; by now the white cotton the mortician would have used to stuff her cheeks would be turning black.

Whether Stephen King actually shares these feelings

is no matter. They work here as a literary device, casting Louis Creed in a tragic light. He is in all respects an isolated man, awaiting an evil destiny he cannot avoid. Lacking inner strength, without emotional support or any kind of faith to sustain him, Louis' grief will finally unhinge his mind. Responsibility for the disaster in store for Louis may be laid fairly at his own doorstep, but King has created a character with whom it is easy to identify and sympathize, a basically good man in a bad situation.

There is little joy and laughter in King's novels. Happiness is always brief and must be snatched in stolen moments. Grief is an unavoidable, inevitable condition, born out of love in a world of victims. He who laughs, as Brecht puts it, has not heard the bad news. King works hard at establishing and maintaining this underpinning. It's part of everything he writes. In *DANSE MACABRE,* his most important book, where he speaks not only as an author but as a man, he stakes further claim to the rectitude of this view as he contrasts the "unreality" of television to the "reality" in the world around us:

> Mass starvation is a way of life in Biafra; in Cambodia, dying children are shitting out their own collapsed intestines; in the Middle East a kind of messianic madness is in danger of swallowing up all rationality; and here at home we sit mesmerized by Richard Dawson on *Family Feud* and watch Buddy Ebsen as Barnaby Jones.

Louis partakes of this reality when he witnesses his son's death on the highway. It's a tragedy for which he is not responsible. (Had he been negligent it would have been a different story altogether, but King keeps these situations pure. He is creating psychodrama, not intellectual dilemmas.) Louis then turns to supernatural help to reclaim his child from the dead. He visits the backwoods territory beyond the Pet Sematary where lurks an ancient animalistic evil, an entity somehow connected to pagan burial grounds. King's kingdom of fear is too terrible to admit the likelihood of a kindly Christian God. The abominations that go bump in the night preclude any meaningful relationship with a deity.

> . . . Let there be God, let there be Sunday morning, let there be smiling Episcopalian ministers in shining white surplices . . . but let there not be these dark and draggling horrors on the nightside of the universe.

While King the witch-doctor provides a world filled with undeserved and sudden horrors, mocking any joy that might be found in love and beauty, he seems both enamored and entrapped by his own vision of the skull beneath the skin:

> That it was lurking even here, in a place dedicated to such innocent pleasures, could not be denied; some grinning man buying film along Main Street could clutch his chest as the heart attack struck . . . a teenage girl as pretty as a Norman Rockwell cover would suddenly collapse in a flopping epileptic fit, loafers rattling out a jagged back beat on the cement as the signals in her brain suddenly jammed up. There was sunstroke and heatstroke and brainstroke, and perhaps at the end of some sultry summer Orlando afternoon there might even be a stroke of lightning. . . . He was waiting to choke you on a marble, to smother you with a dry-cleaning bag. . . . There was death in a quarter bag of peanuts, an aspirated piece of steak, the next

> pack of cigarettes. He was around all the time, he monitored all the checkpoints between the mortal and the eternal. . . . He was in the water you drank, the food you ate.

King's medicinal properties may be debatable, but his wound-up sensational style of storytelling commands attention, even in a culture dominated by film and television.

In one of her essays, critic Pauline Kael refers to the inexplicable delight that children get out of terrifying stories that give them bad dreams. That same vivid, thoughtless, adolescent intensity in King's work is the major reason for his phenomenal success.

About the Authors

Stephen King is the world's bestselling author of horror fiction.

Andrew M. Greeley, a Roman Catholic priest, is a professor of sociology, a syndicated newspaper columnist and the author of books on theology and education. He has also written bestselling popular fiction. Two recent works are the novel *God Game* and his autobiography, *Confessions of a Parish Priest.*

Robert Bloch, author of *Psycho* and one of the Grand Masters of horror fiction, has been an active writer since 1935. He has written short stories, novels, articles, essays, verse, magazine columns, teleplays and screenplays. He swears he will not stop "until somebody drives a stake through my heart."

Bill Thompson is Executive Editor of Prentice Hall

Press in New York. He has worked with Stephen King on seven books, including the nonfiction *Danse Macabre.* He has also edited the books of Charles Berlitz, Peter Straub, Elmore Leonard and Richard Nixon; and coauthored the definitive book *Croquet.* He and his wife, Andrea, and their daughter, Emily, live in New York City.

Ramsey Campbell is the most awarded horror writer of modern times. His many chilling novels include *Obsession, Incarnate* and *The Face That Must Die*. Mr. Campbell lives in England.

Whitley Strieber is the author of *The Wolfen, The Hunger* (both also appeared as films) and a number of other horror novels. He also coauthored *Warday*, a novel set five years after a nuclear war. His most recent work is *Nature's End*, a novel about the future of the world's environment.

Leslie Fiedler is currently Samuel Clemens Professor at New York State University at Buffalo. A science fiction novel and an anthology of science fiction are among his thirty published books. A distinguished critic, Mr. Fiedler helped spearhead the current wave of academic interest in American fantasy and horror fiction.

Clive Barker is the author of six volumes of acclaimed short horror fiction, *Books of Blood.* He is also an illustrator and playwright; his work for the stage includes *The History of the Devil, Frankenstein in Love* and *The Secret Life of Cartoons.* Mr. Barker's most recent novel is *The Damnation Game.* He lives in North London.

Harlan Ellison has been called "one of the great living American short story writers" by the *Washington Post.* He has won the Hugo Award more than seven times, the Nebula Award three times, the Edgar Allan Poe Award of the Mystery Writers of America, the George Melies fantasy film award twice, and the Silver Pen for Journalism by P.E.N. His recent publications include two books of essays, *Sleepless Nights in the Procrustean Bed* and *An Edge In My Voice* and an anthology, *Media: Harlan's World.* Mr. Ellison lives in Los Angeles.

Michael McDowell is the author of the popular "Black Water" series of horror novels. His work in the film media includes the televised version of Stephen King's *Typewriter of the Gods.* Mr. McDowell's most recent novels are *Toplin* and *Jack and Susan in 1953.* He lives in Massachusetts.

William F. Nolan is twice winner of the Edgar Allan Poe Special Award from the Mystery Writers of America. His work has appeared in 125 anthologies and in over 200 magazines and newspapers around the world. Among his forty-four books is the bestselling *Logan's Run.* His writing for television includes a film of the return of Jack the Ripper, *Bridge Across Time.* He lives with his wife, Kam, near Los Angeles.

Stephen F. Brown has been writing reviews of science fiction and fantasy for many years. His reviews and columns have appeared in *Science Fiction Review, Heavy Metal,* the *Washington Post* and myriad other publications. He is currently working as an assistant editor of a new science fiction magazine, *Stardate.* Mr. Brown has been a Washington, D.C. bookseller for the past eight years.

Don Herron, founder of The Maltese Falcon Society, originated the *Dashiell Hammet Tour* in San Francisco, now a popular tourist excursion in that city. In 1985, City Lights Books published his comprehensive literary tour guide to northern California, *The Literary World of San Francisco and Its Environs.* Mr. Herron recently edited *The Dark Barbarian,* a critical anthology about Robert E. Howard. He is a frequent contributor to books and periodicals about modern horror and fantasy fiction.

Ben P. Indick has published commentaries on the writings of Ray Bradbury, L. Frank Baum, Robert Nathan, Stephen King and H. P. Lovecraft, one of which has been translated into Japanese. He is a published playwright and several of his plays for children have received awards and have been performed widely in America. He resides with his wife, Janet, a professional sculptor, in Teaneck, New Jersey.

Bernadette Lynn Bosky, a Ph.D. candidate and instructor with the Duke University Department of English, has presented papers and published articles on diverse authors, including Charles Williams, Sir Thomas Browne, Peter Straub and, of course, Stephen King. She lives with her husband, Arthur Hlavaty, in Durham, North Carolina.

Thomas F. Monteleone has published eleven novels and one collection of short stories. He has had two plays produced professionally and has written screenplays for television and feature-length films. His recent novels include *Lyrica* and *The Magnificent Gallery.* He lives in Baltimore with his wife, Linda, and their two sons, Damon and Brandon.

Tim Underwood and **Chuck Miller** are authors, editors, critics and publishers who most often work as a team. Their imprint *Underwood-Miller* appears on more than sixty volumes by and about authors of modern science fiction, fantasy and horror, including a previous book about Stephen King's writing, *Fear Itself* (also available in a Plume edition). They have received a design award from The American Society of Illustrators and their series of Waldenbooks collector's editions, "Brandywyne Books," recently won an Innovative Publishing Award. As editors and publishers, Tim Underwood and Chuck Miller have received Howard, Balrog and Hugo nominations. They specialize in popular culture and are currently working together on a book about contemporary American heros.